SIMON & SCHUSTER CHILDREN'S PUBLISHING
ADVANCE READER'S COPY

TITLE: Devious Prey

AUTHOR: Scott Reintgen

IMPRINT: Margaret K. McElderry Books

ON-SALE DATE: 3/31/26

ISBN: 978-1-6659-7893-4

FORMAT: Hardcover

PRICE: $19.99/$27.99 CAN

AGES: 14 up

PAGES: 304

Do not quote for publication until verified with finished books. This advance uncorrected reader's proof is the property of Simon & Schuster. It is being loaned for promotional purposes and review by the recipient and may not be used for any other purpose or transferred to any third party. Simon & Schuster reserves the right to cancel the loan and recall possession of the proof at any time. Any duplication, sale, or distribution to the public is a violation of law.

Please send any review or mention of this book to
ChildrensPublicity@simonandschuster.com.

Aladdin • Atheneum Books for Young Readers
Beach Lane Books • Beyond Words • Boynton Bookworks
Caitlyn Dlouhy Books • Denene Millner Books
Libros para niños • Little Simon • Margaret K. McElderry Books
MTV Books • Paula Wiseman Books • Salaam Reads
Sarah Barley Books • Simon & Schuster Books for Young Readers
Simon Pulse • Simon Spotlight

ALSO BY SCOTT REINTGEN

A Door in the Dark
A Whisper in the Walls
A Burning in the Bones

DEVIOUS PREY

SCOTT REINTGEN

Margaret K. McElderry Books
New York   Amsterdam/Antwerp   London
Toronto   Sydney/Melbourne   New Delhi

MARGARET K. McELDERRY BOOKS
An imprint of Simon & Schuster Children's Publishing Division
1230 Avenue of the Americas, New York, New York 10020
For more than 100 years, Simon & Schuster has championed authors and the stories they create. By respecting the copyright of an author's intellectual property, you enable Simon & Schuster and the author to continue publishing exceptional books for years to come. We thank you for supporting the author's copyright by purchasing an authorized edition of this book.
No amount of this book may be reproduced or stored in any format, nor may it be uploaded to any website, database, language-learning model, or other repository, retrieval, or artificial intelligence system without express permission. All rights reserved. Inquiries may be directed to Simon & Schuster, 1230 Avenue of the Americas, New York, NY 10020 or permissions@simonandschuster.com.
This book is a work of fiction. Any references to historical events, real people, or real places are used fictitiously. Other names, characters, places, and events are products of the author's imagination, and any resemblance to actual events or places or persons, living or dead, is entirely coincidental.
Text © 2026 by Scott Reintgen
Jacket illustration © 2026 by Justin Metz
Jacket photography by Ake Ngiamsanguan/iStock (forest with clouds); Boonchuay1970/iStock (single cloud); sandsun/iStock (beach); and AnnaVolotkovska/iStock (metal background)
Stained edges photography by IvancoVlad/iStock
Jacket design by Greg Stadnyk
All rights reserved, including the right of reproduction in whole or in part in any form.
MARGARET K. McELDERRY BOOKS is a trademark of Simon & Schuster, LLC.
For information about special discounts for bulk purchases, please contact Simon & Schuster Special Sales at 1-866-506-1949 or business@simonandschuster.com.
Simon & Schuster strongly believes in freedom of expression and stands against censorship in all its forms. For more information, visit BooksBelong.com.
The Simon & Schuster Speakers Bureau can bring authors to your live event. For more information or to book an event, contact the Simon & Schuster Speakers Bureau at 1-866-248-3049 or visit our website at www.simonspeakers.com.
Interior design by Irene Metaxatos
The text for this book was set in ITC Veljovic Std.
Manufactured in China
First Edition
10 9 8 7 6 5 4 3 2 1
CIP data for this book is available from the Library of Congress.
ISBN 9781665978934
ISBN 9781665978958 (ebook)

⌒⌒

This one is for Keith Dupuis. I am the writer I am today because I sat down at Cup a Joe for a writing group meeting and read the opening chapter of *The Last Sun*. I knew exactly how much work I had ahead of me if I wanted to be as good of a writer as you are. Thank you for bringing out the best in me.

⌒⌒

DEVIOUS PREY

1

Pearl Trask watched the deckhands unlash the great, knotted ropes connecting the *Grand Gesture* to its bridge tower. The craft shifted restlessly—hundreds of feet in the air—as the bindings fell away. Sails unfolded from the main balloon like paper-faded dragon wings. She might have admired the clever engineering and moving parts if she wasn't so focused on not throwing up.

"Don't forget to breathe."

This came from Aunt Hath. The older woman's knee was pressed firmly against Pearl's to keep it from shaking. Their carefully chosen tickets on the back row of the observation deck offered a full glimpse of the ship and its passengers. Pearl had researched this trade route for weeks. She'd analyzed the seating charts and ticket availability. She'd even studied the records of each of the potential ship captains who flew this route. The *Grand Gesture* had been an obvious choice for their task. Even Aunt Hath—who'd been smuggling far longer than Pearl—had found no flaws in the plan. A continental freighter with just fifteen confirmed passengers? A captain who didn't closely check his paperwork? It had seemed like the *perfect* setup for a smuggling run.

Until this very moment.

"Quit looking at them," Aunt Hath whispered.

Pearl hadn't been looking, but the words drew her eyes to the front of the ship. There were eight soldiers standing in rigid formation. Right before takeoff, they'd boarded the ship. Each one had a pistol tucked into their belt and a silver-tipped spear clutched in hand. Her heart had briefly stopped beating in her chest. They were going to be arrested. The first smuggling run her aunt had allowed her to plan would end in ruin.

But then she'd noticed the boy. That almost felt like the wrong word for him. He was unlike any boy she'd ever seen. He walked with the kind of perfect posture one could only learn in the audience of kings. His unbuttoned jacket was the color of a faded rose. Definitely a city style. None of the farm boys she knew would be caught dead in such a bright color. His hair had been buzzed and it brought out the great roundness of his eyes. As she watched him walk, she'd wondered if he was the son of a famous politician or a famous dignitary. Those guesses faded, though, when she heard the rhythmic clink of chains. A far less romantic answer: he was a prisoner.

The leader of the guards stalked on board behind him, wolflike and watchful. Pearl experienced another jolting shock: he was nearly as young as his prisoner. He had long blond hair and shadowed eyes and broad shoulders. He couldn't have been a day over twenty. She wondered why they'd put someone so young in charge of a military detail—but then, squinting, she found the answer to the question. His right hand was missing. As she watched, it would flicker in and out of her vision. Half-there and half-not. When she could see the hand, it was gloved in a pitch-black material that looked like it had been spun from the deepest shadows in the world. She could feel the *absence* pulsing out from him.

A null glove, she thought. *He's one of the wardens.*

She'd never seen one in person. Only read about them in books. Wardens were known as the only people in Ten Tides who could pacify magic. Watching that gloved hand flicker in and out of existence sent a shiver down her spine. His presence on the ship answered another question: the captive must be a wizard. Pearl quietly reassessed the boy in chains. It was interesting that they had him physically bound even though his magic was severed. He must have been a flight risk—or else someone they considered *very* dangerous. She wondered what crime he'd committed.

One of the guards detached from the detail. She could feel her stomach tightening as the man began navigating up and down the row, speaking with passengers as he went.

"Steady," her aunt whispered. "Steady up now, girl."

It was the same affirmation her aunt used to offer before they butchered pigs on the farm. Set all that fear aside. Steady those hands. Make your work quick and clean—or else you're a cruel god with a squealing mess to deal with. Pearl found it helped to imagine she was back there. Her feet set down in the familiar mud. All those whisper-pink creatures moving around her to form a singular mass of bodies. A great sea of snorting flesh. That image of home was enough to settle her breathing as the guard reached them. He smiled politely.

"We're escorting a prisoner north," he explained. "There will be one unscheduled stop before the ship continues to its destination. We've been assured the delays will be minimal. The captain can make up a lot of the lost time in the air. If you would, please note the locations of the soldiers we've posted at the front of the ship."

The guard pointed. Pearl's eyes followed obediently. Sweat prickled along her scalp.

"No passengers past that point," he said. "Thank you for your compliance."

The guard melted back into the waiting ranks. Pearl darted a nervous glance at her aunt, who hissed for her to keep her mouth shut. The ship had been gliding on all the while, navigating the subtle shifts in the wind as it crossed the city proper. Now that they were beyond the tallest buildings, aimed like an arrow for the eastern seaboard, Pearl realized there was no escape—no escape and a thousand ways that all of this could go wrong.

The secondary engines fired in the cabins below. The prow of the *Grand Gesture* knifed out over the water for the first time. The other civilian passengers flocked to the railings. Pearl knew why. One of the famous "port" islands was docked north of the city for trading. Their ship offered a rare, bird's-eye view of one of the most impressive pieces of magic their world had ever known. A woman named Heatherly had created three such islands near the turn of the century. She'd pulled massive chunks of land from their continent, reshaped them out over the ocean, and enchanted them so that they could be guided by magic up and down the eastern seaboard of Ten Tides. Two were still in operation. Pearl had been looking forward to seeing the famous market island, but right now she did not trust herself to stand up without losing her breakfast.

Below them, another loud rumble from the engine room. Pearl took advantage of all the noise. "What if they check the hold?" she whispered.

"I suspect they'll find crates. Nothing suspicious about crates."

She sucked her teeth, frustrated by that response. How could her aunt be so calm? In her mind, she pictured the five crates they'd loaded into the ship's hold that morning. If any of the guards noticed that something was amiss, she would end up like the boy. A prisoner on her way to some terrible fate. Her mother weeping at the trial. Her father more disgraced than he already was. The people of their town whispering that they'd suspected all along . . .

Pearl slammed her eyes shut. She fought off that imagined nightmare by visiting the pig pens again. She could see them wiggling all around. Snorting in that delightful way. She inhaled that other world, her home, and heard a sharp squeal from somewhere in the herd.

"Stop," she commanded herself. "Calm down."

The focused meditation worked. Her breathing settled. Her mind cleared. She could do this. Everything would be fine. Beneath her, the ship seemed to lurch uncertainly—but the logical part of her mind was back in control. There was no reason to be afraid. Everything would be fine.

2

Marken Burke thought everything was going rather terribly.

"Oh, don't look so sad, Burke." Kell smiled ironically from his perch at the prow of the ship. "This isn't your last flight. No, I daresay your feet will leave the ground again soon."

The other soldiers laughed. Nervously, though. Marken had picked up on the tension between them. They clearly respected the chain of command, but their leader was unsettling, even to them. No surprise there. Wardens were unnatural creatures. Their very existence required a sacrifice that few people could understand. It didn't help that Kell was so young. The youngest warden that Marken had ever met. Surely it grated to take orders from someone with so little experience. The question was how could Marken use that knowledge against him?

Ever since being captured, he'd studied them. One thing

he'd learned was that Warden Kell saw the two of them as point and counterpoint. A grand metaphor for good and evil. He'd been appointed to lead the manhunt for Marken ever since the incident in West Lily. After everything that had happened with Lynch . . .

. . . No. No, no, no. That was not a door he could afford to open at the moment. He needed to remain focused. Marken settled his mind. There were still variables to play with. His magic might be cut off by the null thread that was wrapped around him, but his senses remained sharp. He could feel a probing curiosity from someone near the back of the ship. That sensation was tinted with . . . hints of secrecy? That was interesting. From another passenger, he sensed a grumbling distaste for authority figures. Maybe even outright hatred? He'd have a far easier time navigating all the nuances with the fullness of his magic at his fingertips.

Almost unthinking, he reached for a spell . . .

He saw a brief glimpse of *home*. The only real home he'd ever known. His valley full of lightflowers. And then an invisible thread *tightened* around his abdomen and chest. His vision of that other place vanished as a breathless, bone-crushing sensation consumed him. It was the most terrible feeling. A helplessness. An unpleasant claustrophobia. There was a small voice in these moments that whispered to him that it would be easier, so much easier, if he just lunged for the nearest railing and leapt from the ship. He could have the final say on his own life then. He could be in control.

No, another voice whispered. *This isn't over. You're not dead, Marken Burke. Not yet.*

His eyes flicked back to land. The buildings that were growing more and more distant. He knew he had support out there. The Guild had kept him hidden for nearly a year after the incident. He'd been a marked man, smuggled from basement to basement, never knowing when he'd be rushed out in the middle of the night. Wizards always protected their own. Surely, they wouldn't let one as famous as him be subjected to a public execution. There would be a plan, the gears of which were turning even now, to break him free. It would not do for him to arrive in Pasca.

It would not do at all.

For now, Marken quietly studied the guards. He drank in their voices. He savored every detail of how they shifted their weight or tossed their spear from one hand to the other. Everything that a person was or wasn't could be used against them. And so, he sat there learning how he might destroy each and every one of them.

"Greetings, sir. It is my pleasure to serve as the chef aboard the *Grand Gesture*. Do any of you care to . . ."

The voice came from just over his right shoulder. A young girl. He didn't have to look back to know it was one of the deckhands. It would be the same one who scrubbed the decks between flights. At least, that's how he'd always seen the work divvied up. A chef by day and a deck swab by night. Kell's eyes swung to where the girl was standing.

"Get my crew anything they want," he said. "Nothing for our guest."

He offered that lifeless smile, but Marken preferred it this way. Food was as good as wine for distraction. A guard holding a sandwich would give away details that a guard holding a spear might not. *Eat,* he thought, *and I will learn how to beat you*. Marken looked out at the distant horizon as the guards figured out their rotations. Nearly an hour passed. Some of them on duty while others ate their meals, grumbling that they'd find much better food when they ported. Service seemed slow. It appeared that the girl had been ordered to serve the guards before the actual paying passengers. Marken was still staring out to sea when his senses spiked.

Magic.

It was the second time he'd felt a slash of it in the air. Someone on board was performing a spell. Could this be his savior? He shifted his body, every muscle drawn taut for the coming ambush, until realizing that they were sailing over the ocean. Any ship that crossed over open seas had to, by law, employ a windmaster. That was who he was sensing. A person with the most meager, workmanlike magic that existed. Most of them weren't even official Guild members. He suspected that Kell had handpicked the man too. A pity. He'd find no sympathy there.

There was movement off the starboard side of the ship. Flyers were swinging in great loops around the dirigible, spreading their canvas wings to catch the updrafts. Earlier, he'd watched the ship pass over one of Heatherly's famous moving islands. They must have flown far enough north to reach the first of the coastal cantinas. Marken guessed that—seeing the dirigible pass above—the flyers had taken up their wings in the hopes of striking a few deals. It was normal for these journeys, but what if this was where his help would come from? Some of the guards seemed to have the same thought. He watched their protective formation tighten. Grips setting and resetting on spears. Their sudden focus on the flyers offered him just enough of a distraction to glance back at the other passengers. It was a terribly small group. A dozen? Maybe more? He was quietly compiling numbers and organizing them into groups in his head when his eyes landed on the girl.

You.

The one with the secret. He could feel it pulsing inside of her even now. Like a flame she couldn't fully hide from the world. At least not from someone who'd used magic for as long as he had. She looked to be the same age as him. Maybe a year or two younger. Her hair was beaten gold by sunlight, her forearms tanned dark by the same. She had notably deep-set eyes that made it seem as if she were looking out from the shadows of her own face. He sensed her secret, but layered over that were hundreds of questions. His lips nearly curled into a smile. Most of the questions seemed to be about him. *Tell me, friend, what do you want to know?!*

Their eyes met. The girl jumped a little in her seat. She blushed instantly. Before she could look away, Marken threw her a wink. No one else saw the exchange. Not even the warden, who was whispering an order to one of the guards. He doubted it would do him much good on such a short journey, but if this was truly his last flight, why not wink at her? Why not take in the sunlight that was cutting through the western clouds to warm his skin? He turned back the way he'd been facing, and for a moment, he shut his eyes to the world and did exactly that.

The great ship continued its steady progress up the coastline. The guards shifted and rotated. The crew attended to the ropes and sails. It might have been like any other flight if his arms and legs weren't chained together. When he finally opened his eyes, he saw a different hope emerging on the horizon. Clouds were gathering. Gray streaks bending to black. Marken noted their formations, their quiet threat. Below, the waves were beginning to toss with excitement. A storm was coming.

For the first time that day, Marken Burke allowed himself a smile.

3

Just as Pearl's stomach finally settled, a new set of knots began to form.

Why had the prisoner been looking at her? And was that *really* a wink? Maybe it had been a random twitch. She was letting her imagination get the better of her, surely. After all, she'd never been the sort of girl who received winks. Only the loneliest boys in her village had ever really paid any attention to her. Certainly, no one who looked like *him* had ever given her more than a second glance. The truth was that she didn't *want* his attention, or the attention of the warden. Even thinking about that null glove and it's flickering existence sent a shiver down her spine.

A welcome distraction came from above. One of the flyers finally dove down through the clouds, arrowing toward the ship. He fell straight toward the largest pack of passengers. At the last possible second, he thrust out a pair of brightly constructed wings, coming to a hovering stop and lighting delicately on the railing of the ship.

"Fried turtles!" he crowed. "Two marks for a sack! Fried turtles! Best in Ten Tides!"

He unbuttoned his jacket to reveal a bare stomach, carved and tan, along with several greasy pouches that hung from a makeshift utility belt. A few passengers fished through their pockets for coins. The treats were a delicacy in this area, and his prices far more reasonable than the onboard offerings. "Easy! I've plenty for all! Come on, then. Exact change, please!"

A few exchanges were made before one of the guards worked his way through the knot of waiting passengers. He raised his spear, shouting something she couldn't hear. The flyer let out a bright laugh before back-diving off the railing. His wings flung outward, dreamlike in how they caught the wind. Pearl watched him ride the thermals higher, his laughter tinkling faintly back to them through the clouds.

"Greetings, madam."

The proximity of the voice made her jump. She hadn't noticed the deckhand arrive. The girl was fairly short with her hair trimmed high and tight. Her skin was a delicate chestnut color.

"My name's Agnes. It's my pleasure to serve as one of the chefs aboard the *Grand Gesture*. Are you interested in dining with us?" The girl waved a notepad in the air. "It's seven extra marks."

Aunt Hath leaned across her. "Seven?! Gods. Pick our pockets, why don't you."

The deckhand blinked. "I don't set the prices, ma'am."

"We could have had a sack full of turtles for just two marks!" Aunt Hath pointed out.

The deckhand's eye swung to the now-empty railing. "Looks like that option is no longer available . . ."

Aunt Hath scowled. "Oh? Wow. You know, you're pretty cheeky for a—"

"What are you serving?" Pearl cut in. Aunt Hath had the sort of temper that ran hot and fast. She'd raised her voice without noticing, and right now, they didn't need to catch the attention of any of the nearby soldiers. Especially over a few marks. This smuggling run would cover that minor cost a hundred times over. "We'd love to know what we'd be getting for our coin."

"I'm happy you asked," the deckhand replied, clearly biting her own tongue. "Main course is a flame-seared duck topped with garlic promenade and dribbled bits of basilisk tongue. It does have several pinches of flare pepper, so if you're allergic, our alternative option is an open-faced sandwich with Parnuskan cheese and spiced tomatoes, accented just so by stocking mustard."

Aunt Hath looked annoyed, but after a sharp look from Pearl, she said, "Fine. We'll split the duck. I've a tab with Captain Lyn."

Pearl felt relieved when the deckhand logged their order and moved on to the next row of passengers. She heard the woman repeat the same information. Aunt Hath pushed to her feet.

"I'm going to check the crates. Act normal, please."

Right. Act normal. She watched her aunt walk down their row. The meditation Pearl had done earlier was still working. Her leg had not started shaking again. The rational side of her mind whispered that Aunt Hath knew what she was doing.

The woman was an experienced smuggler at this point. She'd been taking on these side jobs ever since Pearl's father had his first episode. As their pig farm started bleeding profits—and her father retreated more and more—it had been Aunt Hath's extra earnings that kept them from going bankrupt. Pearl felt duty bound to learn this part of their trade—or else they'd always be relying on someone else to save them.

She took another deep breath and focused on the movement of the ship. They were nosing away from the main continent now. Farther out to sea. She'd researched the route, so she knew there were far stronger wind currents out at sea. The captain would harness those in an effort to cut their travel time in half. That was good. The sooner they arrived, the better. She could not resist eyeing the captor and the captive. Both of them were undeniably handsome. Both were also frightening in their own ways. When she started feeling heat in her cheeks, she would look away, preoccupy herself with the sea or the other passengers. As they sailed, the skies grew more and more ominous.

Again, Pearl did not panic.

She had mentally prepared for this. Coastal routes were constantly besieged by storms. That was why there was a windmaster on board. Even the strongest storm could not touch them. As those dark clouds loomed closer, she searched for their ship's hired man—and eventually spotted him just a few rows ahead. Every now and again, he'd lean back in his chair and gesticulate strangely with one hand. She could just barely see the way the air in front of him *fractured*—the light angling in the wrong direction for a brief moment—and then his hand would slump back to his side.

Pearl knew he was making minor adjustments to the

protective layering around their ship. When she'd done her research, she'd admittedly imagined the windmaster looking more dramatic. More like the warden, she supposed. A handsome man standing confidently at the prow of the ship. Perhaps even wielding a staff dramatically as he called out spells in a booming voice.

She had not imagined *this* man. He was old and frumpish, sitting with terrible posture, and she even spotted a dark stain along his collar. It looked as if some chocolate had dribbled down and melted in the glare of the sun. At one point, he openly picked his nose and then reached down and wiped it beneath the seat.

"Disgusting," she muttered.

Finally, Aunt Hath emerged from the hold. This inspection was planned as well. They'd learned that it was customary for customers to check freight during a flight, just to make sure nothing had shifted during takeoff. She watched as her aunt eased back into her seat.

"And?" Pearl asked.

"All is well. The guards already inspected the hold and found nothing suspicious. One of the deckhands said we're not far from the drop point for the prisoner. They'll have no reason to check the hold again. We're in the clear, kid."

Good. That was good. Pearl's eyes swung back to the prisoner. She had a thousand questions about him that she'd never get to ask. Maybe they'd read about him one day, and she'd finally learn what fate befell him. She was about to ask her aunt's thoughts when she noticed the windmaster slumping even further down in his seat.

"Look at that," she whispered. "His magic is so boring he's falling asleep."

Aunt Hath snorted. "Well, the best wizards don't take these kinds of jobs. Three marks says he didn't even graduate from his university."

Pearl didn't take the bet. She'd researched the surrounding universities and learned a little about magic in Ten Tides. Once, wizards had been viewed as rogues or outlaws. A tool that was as dangerous as it was useful. When the Guild—a self-governing group of the most powerful and well-trained wizards—officially formed, they'd quietly transitioned from rogues to respectability. Within a decade, they would be viewed as a pillar of Ten Tides governance. The very best would be commissioned by the government and tasked with traveling through the provinces, solving all kinds of problems with an ever-expanding arsenal of magic. Pearl guessed that the prisoner fit in that category. He wouldn't require such a large escort if he was not deadly. A far higher percentage of hopeful wizarding students ended up like the windmaster. Performing basic grunt work. A dependable job that made a fine wage, but the duties that befell them, at the end of the day, were not all that different from magicless work. At least, she doubted the windmaster had gone to school dreaming of manipulating the same wind currents every day for the rest of his life.

Before she could comment on the subject, the windmaster's arms flailed out unexpectedly. She saw his hands reaching for the back of the nearest seat and failing to find purchase. Pearl frowned. He wasn't snoozing, as she'd assumed. In fact, his face was bright red. His chest heaving.

Something's wrong.

Pearl bolted to her feet. There was no time to think. She raced down the aisle. No one else seemed to have noticed the man's struggling. She'd reached the end of their row before the elderly woman seated closest to him finally raised the alarm.

"Oh. Oh, dear. Help! Someone! Do—do we have a doctor on board?"

Everyone turned to stare. Pearl reached them and found the windmaster already on his back, hands grasping at the collar of his shirt. Most of her medical expertise was with animals. She tried to think back through everything she'd read, hoping desperately those methods applied to people, too.

First, a comforting voice.

"I'm here. Hey. I'm here. You're going to be all right. Everything is all right."

As she spoke, she pulled the small skinning knife from her belt. The man was still tugging at his collar for some reason. She pushed his hands aside and slit the harder fabric there. Maybe he was choking? It loosened instantly, but he continued to panic. One of his hands seized her wrist. His grip was so tight that she gasped.

"It's okay," she gritted out. "Hey. I'm still here. I'm not going to leave you."

Having something to hold seemed to anchor him. His eyes had been darting wildly about, but now that bloodshot stare fixed on her with magnetic focus. The rest of his face was drained of color. She was terrified, but she tried to keep her voice calm.

"Can you speak? Can you tell me what's hurting?"

His mouth twitched. The only sounds that came out were slurred. Unintelligible. Pearl was speaking to him in short, affirming sentences when someone else finally thundered down the row to help her. She looked up. It was the captain of the ship—Arnol Lyn.

"Doctor, what can I do?" he asked. "Tell me what you need."

Pearl stared back at him. "I'm not a doctor!"

The captain looked bewildered. "But—but you're tending to him!"

"Because no one else would!"

The windmaster's eyes shocked a little wider. His body spasmed. Once. Twice. She knew their panicked conversation wasn't helping. She took a deep breath and then locked eyes with the struggling man again. "Hey. I need you to tell me what hurts. Are you choking?"

The smallest shake of his head.

"All right. Not choking. Is it your head? Your chest?" His eyes went wide and she knew. Of course. The way he was grasping at his own collar. The shortness of breath. The inability to move. He must have been having some kind of heart attack. Her eyes swung back to the captain.

"Where's your med kit?"

"They're getting it now."

A quick glimpse showed that every passenger on board had stopped to watch the scene. She saw, too, that there was commotion near the prow of the ship. The prisoner was begging to be freed. He was loudly claiming that he could save the man, but the guards weren't having any of that. One responded by bringing the butt of his spear slamming into the boy's stomach. The warden watched it all with hooded eyes. Pearl was considering begging them to let the wizard try to help when another solution dawned on her.

"Aunt Hath! Your medicine!"

Her mother and aunt both suffered from the same heart issues. Hathaway Trask could work like a horse nine days out of ten, but if she ever forgot to take her pills, she'd get lightheaded. Sometimes she'd even be confused about where she was. Pearl doubted the pills were a perfect solution for the windmaster, but if they could provide any relief, they'd be better than nothing. Aunt Hath tossed them. Pearl fumbled the catch and the capsule went rattling down the aisle. Captain Lyn pinned them with his boot and then slammed the bottle into her palm.

"What are those?" he asked.

"A temporary solution," she grunted. Carefully, she tilted the bottle and two pills tumbled into the windmaster's gaping mouth. "All right, I'm going to ask you to do something for me. I need you to think about how your throat works. Imagine swallowing. Remember the way you've always swallowed. Put all of your mental energy into that motion. Do you understand?"

She waited for his eyes to find hers. There was the smallest of nods.

"All right. Now!"

His mouth shuddered obscenely. Pearl watched his throat convulse. She wiped the sweat from her forehead and smiled down at him. "Good! You did such a good job. Okay, I think you're having a heart attack, but those pills will help. They're going to . . ." She tried to think of something that would sound even close to accurate. "They'll break up the clots in your vessels. They'll loosen that tightness in your chest. You'll start feeling better soon. I promise. Until then I just need you to stay calm, okay? For me?"

More arguing at the front of the ship. Louder now. The

prisoner—in spite of being struck once—was offering to help again. The young warden shouted for him to keep his mouth shut. Other passengers were turning, though, clearly uncomfortable with the lack of action. The guards wore the seals of the official Ten Tides government. "Sworn to protect" would normally mean helping a man who was about to die. She saw the looks on the faces of the passengers echo into concern in the expressions of the guards. One of the stockier guards warned everyone to stay back. A small powder keg was forming on the deck. It might explode at any moment. Pearl was so distracted by all the noise that she nearly missed the windmaster's sudden convulsion.

"No. Wait, no, no, no . . ."

He shook more violently than before. His fists tightened and his eyes bulged wide. Every vein stood out starkly against his drained skin. Pearl reached for his hand, clutching it tightly, but saw she was too late. His body went rigid. There was a gasp behind her. Captain Lyn stared down in shock. Pearl couldn't believe it either.

"He's . . . he's dead."

4

Down in the cargo hold, she lifted her head.

The air had grown fickle and charged. Some barrier had just fallen away. The creature was trapped, cut off from the immediate physical world, but she could still reach the world that existed beyond that one. Her own sentience probed outward. She felt dead things gathered in meaningless piles. Beyond those, she felt *them*. Insensates. All moving around, consumed by their own brief universes. One consciousness prickled against her touch and she retreated, watchful. When she was content that she'd not been discovered, the creature took mental flight again. This time, she called out to sky, to sea, to earth. She screamed in a voice that only the most ancient forces in the world might hear. A language that was more like blood and stone.

Come for me! Break these bindings! EMBRACE ME AGAIN!

In that lightless prison, a response.
Dark beckoned to dark.
It was coming for her.
Yeeeeesssssssss.

5

Marken felt the change a split second before the others did.

The windmaster was dead. He couldn't even see the man, but he knew it was true because all of the man's protective spells died with him. A slash of cold air rushed over the now-exposed deck. His magic might have been simple and repetitive, but that didn't mean it wasn't useful. He'd clearly been keeping the ship at a far more agreeable temperature for them. Now cold descended upon them. Great gusts of wind harassed the passengers. He saw a stray scarf go flying overboard. The sudden chaos had Marken smiling.

Finally, his chance had arrived.

"Unbind me," he commanded. He was no silvertongue. He could not bend others to his will with a magic-laced word, but even the warden had to see exactly how much danger they were all in right now. All Marken needed to do was guide his captor to the reasonable choice. "Look, if you want to save all these people, remove my chains. Dispel your null thread. I can guide the ship back to land before this gets worse. I can ward us against these storms. It would take little more than a snap of my fingers, Kell, and you know it. All you have to do is free me."

Free me, he thought. *And I'll never allow myself to be bound again.*

Great drops of rain were streaking the young warden's face. He considered the storm for a long moment, and then spat on the deck between them. "Free you so that you can commandeer the ship for yourself? I'm sure you'd bring us crashing back down in a place of your choosing. Somewhere you could make another escape. No, I think not, Burke. Take your seat before I come over there and help you back into it."

It was the darkest tone he'd heard from the warden so far. One that he knew better than to test. Defeated, Marken took his seat. No point in earning himself a shattered kneecap. Besides, the wind and the rain and the thunder promised all of this was about to get far worse than it already was. The other passengers were being herded like sheep down into the hold. Warden Kell sent a few of his soldiers to determine the best option for their prisoner. Rain soaked through their clothing as they waited. All Marken could do was silently watch as the captain and his crew slashed around the deck like ghosts, their faces blurred by the rain.

Captain Lyn had not stopped shouting since the windmaster died. Marken saw that two of the braver crew members were being fitted with the ship's mandatory flying gear. They held their wooden wings tight to their sides as the first officer adjusted latches and buckles around their bodies. A little compression engine was hooked up against their lower backs.

The *Grand Gesture* was being dragged farther and farther away from the coastline, but Marken thought that a talented flyer might be able to reach land. From there, the coastal watch boats could be alerted to what had happened. The nearest airship tower would have searchlights they could activate to track them. Rescue ships would be arranged for when the storm abated. He couldn't decide what to root for. He supposed a crash was his best-case scenario. A situation where his magic—and thus his freedom—was the one thing that might keep the group alive. Lightning stroked the western sky. He frowned at the terrible rumble that followed.

Perhaps just a small crash would be ideal.

The two deckhands were led to the railing. Close enough that Marken could hear the words Captain Lyn was screaming at them. "And if you forget those coordinates, Dawley, I will come back as a ghost and haunt you until the very end of your days. Do you hear me, boy?!"

One of the flyers nodded fervently.

"And do I strike you as a kind ghost, Dawley? Do you want the likes of me stalking you for the rest of your mortal days?"

"No, sir."

"Then fly," Lyn replied. "Do your duty to this ship."

Both crew members were helped up onto the railing. After a count of three, they leapt, aided by a shove from the officers behind them. Marken craned his neck to watch their descent. Two smoldering lights announced that both engines had kicked to life. The flyer on the right pushed his wings out. They caught the wind, spiraling him in a tight circle, before leveling out. The second flyer—Dawley—wasn't so lucky. His wings spread, but the right one buckled and snapped. A snatch of wind tore the wing from his shoulders and spun him helplessly into the sea.

All of them saw the splash.

"May your soul find rest, Dawley," Captain Lyn said before turning back to everyone else on the deck. "Helene! Get us turning. Agnes, get downstairs and start covering the exterior windows! Get moving, get moving. Every single one of you! There's not a second to waste!"

There was an answering rally cry from the crew. A few seconds had passed and Dawley was forgotten. His memory belonged only to the sea now. Marken couldn't help wondering if this was the fate that awaited him in Pasca. A quick trial, a brief sentencing, an execution. Would the people of Ten Tides forget him just as easily? Would any memory of his service to them—all the countless ways he'd helped the wider population—carry on after his death? Feeling the sudden weight of oblivion on his shoulders, he turned to the warden one last time.

"We are all in danger," he whispered. "Unbind me. Please."

The warden spat on the deck again. He called for the nearest guard.

"Take him downstairs."

Marken was led by the guard who liked to rock back on his heels. They called him Withers. He was tall and lean. Earlier he'd heard Withers say he had two boys back home. One was a scoundrel and had been caught picking on the other children. The guard thought that better than being the one who got picked on. As they descended, Marken noted the way the man's grip on his collar tightened, as if afraid to lose him in the dark passage. Everything a man was could be used against him. Everything. Too bad there wasn't anywhere for him to go at the moment.

"Open the door," Withers called. "I've got Burke."

The remaining guards were here. All the other passengers had been put elsewhere. As Marken looked around, he noted that their only company in the hold was the windmaster's corpse.

"How charming," he said. "Is he dinner? If things don't go as planned?"

"Shut your mouth."

Right. No sense of humor in this bunch. A cannibalism joke didn't stand a chance. He assessed the room, more out of habit than actual curiosity. There were crates stacked all around them. The hold was far from full, but several larger crates filled the shadows on his right. He frowned. There was a peculiar sensation. Prickling at the very edges of his senses. As if someone had gone through great pains to hide something. He looked away from the spot. Whatever it was, he didn't want the guards to find it. Knowledge was power.

"So," he said. "How is everyone enjoying that famous Ten Tides coastline?!"

"I thought I told you to shut up."

It was the same guard who'd shouldered him a few moments before. Short, stocky, bearded. He'd heard the others call the man Levi. If memory served, the man had no family. Earlier, he'd grown bored of the conversation about children back home, but he'd been quick to chime in when they started discussing favorite brothels. Marken had also determined that

Levi was the one guard assigned specifically to work with the warden. The others were likely a small unit that had been reassigned from other roles in the province where he'd been captured. Forced to take on a temporary escort role. Levi, on the other hand, showed a familiarity with Kell that the others lacked.

Such assignments were common. To become a warden—and to gain the ability to wield null threads—required terrible sacrifice. The forced amputation of a limb. The few who survived those surgeries and gained access to the waiting anti-magic that came with them were left with a potential physical liability. Sure, they trained in one-handed combat, but government protocol was to assign them an expert duelist for added protection. All of that told Marken that Levi was the most dangerous one in the group. A natural-born killer. Marken also recognized something he despised in the man. A person who, when he had power over someone, was eager to abuse it. He'd seen that so many times before. He'd been on the receiving end of those relationships. The sort of small-minded man who made himself bigger by hurting others. These facts did not stop him from probing now to see what fractures existed between Levi and the others.

"Look," Marken began. "I know you're all loyal, government men—through and through. But that storm out there? It's not going to quit for hours. We're being dragged out to sea. All you have to do is say the word, and I could put a stop to all of that . . ."

The expected blow came. Marken took it as well as he could, turning his jaw in the right direction to lessen the force of Levi's strike. It still stung like hell.

"Right," he said, licking blood from a split lip. "Well, don't say I didn't offer."

The room fell to silence. The normal chatter amongst soldiers was drowned out by the prospect he'd introduced. Could their ship really be dragged out to sea? What would happen if the storm didn't abate? *Good. Let those doubts really sink in. Let them fester.* He wanted the group divided over what to do. In the quiet that followed, he noticed a detail that he'd missed before. The windmaster's corpse had been covered by a storm blanket, but the material wasn't quite long enough. His boots were sticking out and one was partly unlaced. It exposed the skin of his ankles. The light down in the hold was fickle, but the detail he noticed now was impossible to miss.

"Might I take a look at the deceased?"

Levi readied another blow, but Marken quickly pleaded his case.

"Hey. I'm not trying to be a prick. I just want to make sure he doesn't have the rot. If we're trapped down here—breathing the same air—we'll all get sick. Be smart about this."

His words caught the attention of the taller guard—Withers. Rot could stay with a man for years and there were notoriously bad cases amongst soldiers. Some of the worst cases led to death.

"Rot can set in that quickly?" Withers asked. "I thought it took a few weeks."

"A wizard doesn't live the way you do, and I promise they don't die the way you die either. There are different variables at play. His magic will accelerate any festering."

The guards exchanged glances. Marken had learned this trick when he was just ten years old. He could get away with pretending that wizards were more mysterious than they actually were—and there were very few people who knew enough to know when he was lying. He sat there, waiting for them to decide something that had already been decided.

"Go on, then," Withers said. "But if you make one wrong move, we'll gut you."

Doubtful, but Marken nodded as if that were true. "Of course."

He was permitted to waddle forward, and nearly fell because of the unsteady rocking of the ship and the limitations of his chains. It was even harder to kneel, bound as he was, but after gathering the shackles in a pile behind him, he managed to drop to a knee beside the windmaster. The two guards maneuvered closer, hanging over him like a pair of angry spirits, their spears angled for killing blows just in case. He ignored them and assessed the pattern he'd noticed from across the room. Dark colorations ran up both sides of the man's ankle. A strange symptom if this was just a heart attack. Careful not to directly touch the skin, he began working at the man's laces.

"Hey now," Levi said. "None of that."

Marken glanced up. "Really? My hands and feet are bound. I have a null thread wrapped around me and not a speck of magic on hand. Do you really think that I can kill you with a boot?"

The guard stared back at him. It was not the first time he'd witnessed the effect of his own mythos on another person. If all the rumors the city governors had spread about Marken Burke were true, it was possible that he'd killed *several* men with no more than a boot. He allowed himself a private smile, set the shoe aside, and began working the other one away.

Next he removed the windmaster's socks. The bottoms of his feet were a festering black color. A confirmation of Marken's suspicions. Little pustules were already forming on the surface of his skin.

"And?" Withers asked. "Is it the rot?"

Marken shook his head. "Take heart. It isn't the rot."

Both of the guards were watching, though, and they were close enough to see that there was something wrong with the man's feet. "Then what is all of that?"

Marken smiled. "Our dear windmaster was poisoned."

6

Pearl couldn't stop pacing.

The cabins provided a false sense of comfort. Magelights glinted out from the corners. The crew members to whom this cabin belonged were fastidious. All four beds were made. She opened a drawer and found their clothes folded neatly within. She ran a hand over rugged cotton and padded leather until a voice startled her. "I'm not sure you should be going through those."

The passengers had been funneled downstairs into two separate rooms. The crew had offered what comfort they could before returning to the main deck to fight the storm. Pearl looked back now to find the person who'd called her out was the same woman who'd been seated closest to the windmaster. She wore her hair in a thick silver braid and was clutching tightly to a small, golden locket at her neck. Pearl stared back, not really knowing what to say in her defense.

Thankfully, Aunt Hath spoke up. "She's just nervous. We all are."

Not to mention, I just had a man die in my arms, you callous old . . .

This time it was Hath who shot Pearl a warning look. She nodded once and slid back down onto the cabin floor with the others. The truth was that she'd seen plenty of death in her life. She butchered pigs on a farm. Death was everywhere there. No, what was bothering her was the waiting. All the not-knowing. Being trapped in this small, windowless space. The creeping feeling of helplessness. The knowledge that if their ship crashed in the open ocean, she'd have no way to control her own fate. It didn't help her nerves that the guards were currently waiting in the cargo hold with the prisoner. What if they decided to inspect the crates? What if the guards found their secret?

Footsteps occasionally raced overhead. There were muffled shouts from captain and crew. Pearl was toying with a lock of her hair when she heard a different noise. A great groan that was louder than anything so far. All of them looked up. Panicked voices splashed down the hallway. In the chaos, their door was thrown open. A figure stood in the ghostly half-light.

"Everyone, get to—"

A massive crash cleaved Captain Lyn's sentence in two. One moment he was there and the next he was gone. Momentum slammed Pearl into her aunt, and then tossed her rag doll around the room. She hit something or someone hard. Screams sounded from every direction. Pearl was just starting to push up to her feet, untangling her limbs from others, when the ship lurched again.

Gravity swung them hard.

Everything broke.

Pearl heard the great cedar beams all snap in booming succession. She reached for something to hold on to but was thrown again as the ship crashed into something far larger. The room was all thunder, until it wasn't, until everything had fallen to a deadly silence.

Then she heard voices.

"Watch out . . ."

"Hey. Get off me."

"Everyone okay?"

"Pearl?"

It was Aunt Hath. The woman had a gash running down the right side of her forehead. She'd balled up one of the sailors' shirts and was pressing it to the wound. She offered her other hand to Pearl and dragged her back to her feet.

"You all right? Anything broken?"

Pearl's head was still spinning, but she grunted an affirmative. Nothing broken. No major wounds. Somehow, she'd avoided any real damage. Aunt Hath slung an arm around her before leading them through the dark press of waiting bodies. The frame of the doorway had an unnatural bend to it. Aunt Hath tried the handle several times before ordering everyone to take a step back. The woman strode forward and kicked the door as hard as she could.

Her second effort sent the wood spinning free of its hinges. Light cut in from the hallway. Other figures were stumbling past. Aunt Hath hooked an arm around her again and led the group out with the other survivors. She saw that the entire front half of the ship had ripped clean away. The front cabins were gone.

Just completely gone. All the stairwells had been smashed to pieces. Their own hallway ended in a gaping mouth of wooden shards. Other passengers were gathered along the ledge, staring fearfully down at the water. For a moment, Pearl feared the worst: that they'd crashed in the middle of the ocean and their only hope was that this shattered ship could remain afloat.

But then, over the heads of the others, she saw the island. A sandy shoreline dotted by trees. It was just a few hundred yards away, framed by the light of either dawn or dusk. Pearl couldn't say for sure. She'd lost track of time down in the cabin. But the sight of land offered unexpected hope. All was not lost. The captain had somehow crashed them somewhere survivable.

"What's the wait?" Aunt Hath called, when the hallway remained crowded. "If that crash stirred up the engines, this whole thing could blow. Get moving!"

Pearl realized fires were indeed burning. She could feel heat creeping out from somewhere behind them. The first line of people leapt. Pearl tucked in tight behind her aunt to wait for their turn. She steadied herself on the ledge and jumped. Her legs hit hard in unexpectedly shallow water. Stumbling forward, she soaked the upper half of her body before finding her balance.

"Grab what you can!" Aunt Hath was shouting. "Just in case! We'll need supplies!"

Debris was floating everywhere. Candles and clothing and half-drowned packs. All bobbing in the surf. Pearl grabbed anything she saw, piled it in her arms, and started forward through the waist-deep water. It didn't take long for her to notice the dead. There was just enough light to make out one corpse floating on her left. A shard of wood had punched right through his chest.

She saw it was Captain Lyn.

Aunt Hath tried to shield her, but as they waded forward, that became impossible. There were bodies everywhere. Ahead on the beach, the dark silhouette of other survivors gathering.

"Over here! Follow the sound of my voice!" someone was shouting. Pearl thought it was one of the deckhands. "Come to shore first! Let us check you before you get back in the water. Everyone understand? I don't want anyone swimming back out until they're looked at."

A few deckhands were kneeling over someone who was writhing in pain. This time, she did not make the mistake of pretending she knew anything about being a doctor. Her hands were shaking anyway. What could she offer them? Except for her own fear? Pearl turned back to the wreckage and spied another procession making their approach. The prisoner had survived.

The boy hissed curses as the guards dragged him up onto the beach. The warden appeared to have survived the crash too, though not without some damage. The right half of his face had an already-forming bruise. The original escort had consisted of eight soldiers. Now she saw only four.

"Our cargo," Aunt Hath whispered, tugging her away. "We need to check our cargo."

Distant screams spilled into the night. Great towers of flame were working their way out from the engine room. There was no telling how many people were trapped inside the ship, or else still struggling to get to shore. After a moment of hesitation, Pearl nodded to her aunt. The two of them waded back into the water. Past bodies and debris. Aunt Hath led her around the gaping mouth from which they'd first leapt. Another nasty gash ran along the starboard side of the ship, ending in a huge, lightless pit. Nearly all the crates had fallen out of that hole and into the water. Aunt Hath sifted through the bobbing boxes until finding one of theirs.

"This one has the harnesses. Here, take it."

Pearl heard a cry for help. Coming from inside the ship. She shivered at the sound, but her aunt kept sorting through the cargo. One by one, they gathered up the crates they'd been using to smuggle their goods north. Pearl accepted her role numbly. Every new scream grated against her conscience. Other shadows moved from the shore and started wading through the wreckage. She found that she was thankful for the half dark around them. She didn't want anyone else to know she was the one who'd ignored those pleading voices.

"Get moving, Pearl," Aunt Hath snapped.

Together, they herded the crates back to shore. Pearl had helped pack each one. There would be a top layer of dried meat and pig flanks. Rather useful, she realized, on an abandoned island where food might be scarce. Underneath that top layer, however, would be all the harnesses and equipment that were meant to be delivered with the creature they'd been smuggling. All specifically designed for training the beast. She also knew those boxes would raise a lot of questions if anyone else saw what was inside.

The water made moving the crates easier. It was only when they reached the beach that they needed to work together, taking one side each and heaving them up out of the sand. They angled themselves away from the other survivors. It was getting fractionally lighter out—dawn, not dusk, she realized—but there was so much focus on rescuing survivors that Pearl thought they could complete their task without being noticed.

"Come on," she said to her aunt. "Up past the trees."

A few minutes later, they were done. All four crates, nestled in a hiding spot just beyond the first tree line. Aunt Hath's chest was heaving, but she still spoke the words that were pulsing through Pearl's mind as well. "Five crates. We brought five crates on board. We need to look for the last one. There's a chance she's still trapped out there . . ."

Pearl nodded. After catching their breath, they went back out into the water. Patiently searching the wreckage. Dawn's slow progress began to reveal the extent of the damage. There were floating bodies everywhere. One man with a snapped neck. Others impaled or drowned or worse. The search parties continued their work even as the fires grew to dangerous heights. It took Pearl and her aunt nearly an hour to locate the final crate. The entire upper half of the box had been ripped away. She saw shards of that oddly tinted glass marking the jagged edges. When they'd gone to oversee the creature's transfer, she'd been as in awe of the crate as she had been of the creature herself. It was lined with enchanted glass that kept the creature sealed. It was something, they'd been promised, that was impossible for her to escape. Unless the crate was thrown overboard in the middle of a crash landing onto a desolate island. Apparently, there'd been enough blunt force to free her from her prison. Aunt Hath was quiet, squinting at the shattered crate.

"Where do you think she went?"

Pearl's eyes swung back to the island.

Where else was there to go?

7

The very air swam with possibility.

She looked back, watching the insensates move like sluggish worms in the water. She'd already shifted her body, melding with the ocean spray, feeling the full embrace of a new form. The sky burned. As she watched, she wanted nothing more than to return to the ship. She wanted to touch those bright, red colors and become them, too. Instinct kept her away. Something told her she wasn't safe. Not yet. Her captors were there in the water, searching for her even now.

That thought made the dragoness hiss. Her great lips retracted, revealing rows of teeth. For now she turned, loping through the shallows and up onto the beach. It was in her nature to change. As she dragged her watery claws across the packed dunes, she drew the knowledge of that new substance into her existence, shifting in an instant of pulsating energy.

Now a creature of sand and stone, she began to run. Down the shoreline she went, enjoying how the wind tried to snatch away bits of her hide, scattering the shards back to where they'd come from.

Long before the sun edged over the horizon, the dragoness was gone.

8

His bindings fell to the sand.
God's body, that feels good.

No more metal digging into his skin. No more half strides or jerky movements. It was a small taste of freedom—ordered by Kell only so that Marken could help ferry the dead to shore—but it felt like a fine beginning. He nodded his thanks to the guards and knew he had just one more prison to escape: the null thread.

As he helped retrieve corpses, he thought through possible strategies. Killing the warden would do the trick. Marken, for all his gifts in magical combat, had never really honed any sort of physical ability. Dueling was out of the question. Even one-handed, the warden would tear him to pieces in any sort of fair fight. But maybe the fight didn't have to be fair? He could always try to kill the warden while he slept. A big enough rock swung at just the right angle? Levi would make that nearly impossible, though. The other guard would be watching him like a hawk.

The best route seemed to be in swaying the minds of the other survivors. If he could rally them to his side, Kell would risk outright rebellion by keeping him magically bound. All of that would depend on where they'd landed and how long it took for rescue boats to arrive.

Desperation was a wonderful motivator.

Marken spent the first hour plotting and scheming, but eventually his dreams of escape were drowned out by the pure exhaustion of their task. He understood now why people used the term "deadweight" as an insult. The bodies—waterlogged as they were—required at least three people working all together to lug them out of the water and up the slight incline of the beach.

He considered quitting. Several times. He was not built for manual labor. Recruited by the Guild at a young age, trained in the arts of magic, he had never done anything this strenuous in his entire life. But as he eyed the other surviving passengers, he knew he'd gain no sympathy if he gave up now. And so, he pressed on instead. Laboring away as the midday sun punished all of them.

Useful items were slowly piled in one spot on the beach. The bodies were taken in the opposite direction to a mass graveyard that was being dug near a stretch of knuckling dunes. When the final body was set down, Marken saw it was the ship's captain. A few of the deckhands gathered around him, paying respects to the man who their entire world had likely revolved around. Ship captains were essentially patrons. If he was not a father figure to them, he was—at the very least—the person who'd kept them fed and whole. In total, there were eighteen corpses. He could see the guards murmuring to one another. Only four of them had survived, and that included Kell in the count. He wondered if they were smart enough to see that their commander's decision had been the root cause of this tragedy. Or was it something he would have to patiently nudge them into thinking?

Everyone looked around awkwardly now that the work was done. For most of his life, this was the part where Marken would raise his voice and take the lead. He'd commanded so many missions. Led small armies into incredibly dangerous territory. It was strange now to bite his tongue and wait for someone else to do the job. And of course Warden Kell was the one to step forward.

"We ought to check pockets," he announced. "Look for knives, coins, compasses. Anything useful really. There's no telling how long we'll be here. Best to salvage now."

It was so utilitarian. Marken watched as the warden's lack of experience finally caused the wrong ripple. He made the mistake of assuming his words, simply because they were spoken first and loudly, were some sort of law—and then he walked in the direction of the captain's corpse.

That's an even bigger mistake, my friend.

One of the deckhands intercepted him. A lowered shoulder that rocked the warden back several steps, but Kell was well-trained. Military, through and through. His pistol was drawn and locked on his target in less than a breath. The woman who'd hit him blinked rapidly at the weapon, but she didn't back down. Marken saw the reason for her confidence. All the other deckhands were edging closer to the fight. He hadn't realized it until now, but they outnumbered the guards at least two to one.

Come on, Marken thought. *Make the wrong move, Warden.*

Those fancy pistols were good for one blast. A guaranteed kill shot at their current range, but that would only be enough to take out the first deckhand. Everything else would fall into hand-to-hand combat. He thought it would be an even fight. Maybe the guards would win, but at what cost? After an uncomfortable stretch, Kell lowered his weapon.

"Fine. Take him, but if we don't loot what we can now, we'll just have to dig them up later." He signaled his guards. "Leave the crew members to them. The rest of these bodies need to be searched before they're buried. Get on with it."

Not a bad recovery. What could the deckhands really say to that compromise? It wasn't like they had jurisdiction over the bodies of the passengers. The rest of the survivors seemed to see the logic of Kell's words too. A few came forward to help. Others asked to be excused, lacking the stomach to be any nearer to the corpses than they had to be. Marken saw another opening. There was a journal and pen set out in the nearest pile of possessions. He knelt down and claimed them before one of the guards could stop him.

"I'll record names," he announced. "So that we can honor the dead."

The sentiment earned a few appreciative nods. Kell glared at him. *Too late, Warden. I've already been hired for the job.* He kept his smile to himself as passengers came by to offer up identifications. The deckhands were the most eager to help. Marken knew there was bad luck associated with being buried in an unmarked grave—and who believed more in good or ill fortune than sailors? He quietly began his task as scribe. *Yes, come forward, let's build some trust with one another.*

"Her name was Lana."

"The first officer. Known him for years."

"Old Ronnie."

Marken noted each name and wrote small, identifying comments underneath. The bodies were quietly rearranged before being lowered into their section of the larger grave. Marken tried to offer sympathies to everyone he could. After an hour or so, he realized he hadn't seen the girl from the ship—or the woman who'd been seated with her. They hadn't been there when he was pulling bodies out of the water either. Did that mean they were casualties? He supposed he'd have to walk the rows one more time before the bodies were covered. For now he continued his work as scribe.

"She sat next to me. Not sure. I think she said her name was Mel."

"Evelyn Richards. We worked together."

Some slumped to their knees, clasping a bloated hand as they wept. There were just three bodies that couldn't be identified. The afternoon sun was still bright overhead. Night felt a long way off. Marken made a show of taking more notes, but really, he was eyeing the current positioning of the soldiers. Kell was all the way across the clearing. The two guards who'd been assigned to keep an eye on Marken were distracted, helping to lower a corpse into its destined grave. He backpedaled away from them, not moving fast enough to draw the eye, but putting as much distance as he could between them and himself. Was now the right time? He weighed his choices and realized he might not get a better chance than this. His offer would mean more too, as they all were face-to-face with what had already been lost. He cleared his throat.

"Excuse me! Everyone!"

Attention swung to him. Kell's eyes were like a pair of daggers. He could hear hissed whispers between the guards. He ignored them, plunging on with his speech.

"My name is Marken Burke! I'm a wizard. I was actually the second-highest-ranked mage in all of Ten Tides before I was arrested for a crime that I *did not* commit. I was being escorted to a trial, where I planned to prove my innocence!" All the guards started moving at the same time. Kell had murder written on his face. "I could have saved the ship! If they had freed me in time, I could have stopped all of this from happening. Hear me now: I can *still* save us. Ask them to let me use my magic. Free me, and I know I can get us all—"

One of the guards lunged for him. Marken sidestepped the tackle but was taken down by the second guard. Kell and the others closed in around him. *Too late. I've already planted the idea of rescue in their heads.* Marken squinted up from his pinned position and saw murmurs running through the rest of the group. The deckhands in particular looked curious about his offer.

"Marken Burke," Kell announced, turning his attention back to the crowd. "Maybe you've heard that name. He's relatively famous, as far as wizards go. He's powerful, too. I won't deny that. But there's a part of the story that he conveniently left out. He's got another name. We called him the Butcher of West Lily. Any of you heard that name before?"

Marken swallowed. A tidal wave of memories pressed in on

his thoughts. He had to shove them back into the darkest corners of his mind. *Not now. Focus, focus, focus.* He watched the reactions from the crowd, and what he saw wasn't promising. Every face darkened. The tragedy of West Lily was famous. What had happened there already bordered on the apocryphal. It was a story of warning whispered in taverns about what wizards were truly capable of if no one kept an eye on them. If they were unfamiliar with the tale, Kell filled in the gaps for them.

"This man executed another wizard on the outskirts of that town," Kell said, his voice carrying easily over the dunes. "An unsanctioned murder. It was *personal*. We learned that he went there to take revenge for some imagined slight from his time in school. Selfishly, he ignored our standard protocols for decommissioning a wizard."

Imagined slight?! Marken thought, burning with indignation. It was *not* some imagined slight. The warden's words were making him sound so small and petty. Even the phrase "decommissioning a wizard" was his way of polishing up the reality of what was meant. It was the politest way someone could refer to what was, in truth, an execution. The same phrase the government used when they purged every silvertongue from the wizarding community a few decades earlier. It was what they called it when a wizard had done something so terrible that not even the Guild was willing to shield them from the other judicial branches of the Ten Tides government. That was what they were planning to do to him when he arrived in Pasca. If he was found guilty of his crime, they would decommission him.

"You might know this," Kell was saying. "You might not. Killing a person who has channeled magic their entire life is a dangerous thing. All that power, matched with the final desperation to live, can lead to unspeakable harm. There's a reason we have rules for how it's done, where it's done, and who gets to do it." Kell pointed back at him. "This man knew all those rules—and he ignored them. He took another wizard's life right outside a small town. He did that *knowing* how much danger he was putting those people in. But the truly unforgiveable part is that he had one final chance to help them. He could have reduced the blast by using his own power—burning some of his own magic—but did he do that?"

Kell turned and spat on the ground between them.

"No. He shielded himself. His victim, in his desperation to stay alive, reached for the nearest source of energy he could find: West Lily. Some three hundred people, drained in an instant, because of this man's selfish actions."

Marken's heart was pounding in his chest. That wasn't true. That wasn't how it happened. It wasn't that simple. Not even close. But the warden turned back to the others and it was becoming clear that he'd practiced this speech. He was pulling from whatever he'd prepared to say to the execution council in Pasca. Everything he'd said so far sounded so polished that even Marken could have been convinced it was the real version of the story. But only he knew the real version.

Only he knew the truth.

"I was one of the first ones to arrive the next day," Kell said, his voice lowering ever so slightly for effect. "All those people, drained like husks. They'd all collapsed in the middle of whatever they'd been doing a moment before. A man cutting wood in his backyard. A woman writing a letter at a table. Three friends out for lunch, their meal gone cold. Even . . ." And once more, Kell turned to look Marken in the eye. A shiver ran down his spine. "A boy and girl. Playing a game upstairs together. We found the marbles scattered all around them . . ."

"That *wasn't* me!" Marken tried to stop him. "I'm innocent! It was Lynch. He's the one—I would never hurt anyone . . ."

The warden ignored him. The audience he wanted was there on the beach before him. All of them listening so intently. "Innocent. I'm sure he'll keep making that claim. He's innocent. He didn't do it. But in my experience, innocent people don't run. They don't even think to leave, because they know they weren't the ones who committed a crime. Not only do we have evidence that Marken Burke was the one outside West Lily that day, but we also can trace his movements south. We know where he went *after* the massacre. There were eye witness reports of him boarding an airship mere hours after the incident. He made no official report of the incident. Offered no testimony. No, he simply vanished. And he had been on the run, hiding like the *rat* that he is, for nearly a year."

Marken saw a terrifying confidence in the warden. He realized that this moment was serving as a sort of mock trial. The warden, testing out his case—and the crowd acting as a potential glimpse at how a jury might react. Every face in the crowd seemed to offer the same verdict: guilty. The warden was in complete control as he finished the story.

"Thankfully, we found him. We caught him. Right now the only thing that's stopping him from doing to you what he did to the people of West Lily is the null thread I've got wrapped around him. If that fails? We're all dead. Hear me say this: a rescue ship is coming. We're going to be found. And when they do, I will escort this man back to Pasca. Justice will be found there. Justice for the people of West Lily. I have no plans to free him. Not unless it's our last resort out here. Does anyone have a problem with that?"

It was one hell of a speech. Even if it wasn't true. Silence greeted the warden's question. No one so much as breathed an alternative plan. Marken felt numb as his chance to sway the group slipped through his fingers. Kell nodded once. "Good. Let's get on with the work, then."

Everyone went back to what they were doing. Marken slumped in the sand. He felt suddenly tired. More tired than he'd ever felt before. He'd spent nearly a decade now performing every task he'd ever been given. One mistake—if that's what it could really even be called—had led him here. There was no justice here. Only a lie that Kell had shined up so that it looked like the truth.

One of the guards pulled him up out of the sand. Movement drew his attention to the other side of the beach. There was a big, shifting pile of all they'd recovered. The beginnings of a shelter. A few people were there, organizing everything, but the movement he'd seen was *beyond* that area. Near the tree line. He watched two people disappear into the forest. The girl and her aunt. Where were they going? And why would they be leaving the group when there were still bodies to bury?

More important, he realized that neither of them had been present for Kell's speech. That was a small mercy. They might be less inclined to hate him. It could barely be called hope, but it tugged at his heart all the same. Not all was lost. Not yet.

"That was a mistake, Burke." His eyes dragged back to Warden

Kell. That dark tone was back in his voice. "Levi, teach the wizard what happens when he disobeys."

The shorter guard was already quietly rolling up his sleeves in anticipation. He set his feet and punched Marken square in the gut. The other guards held him in place. Another shot to the ribs. A final blow to the jaw. They allowed him to slump then. The one-sided fight ended with him curled up in the sand, a half-broken sort of creature. But not without hope.

He spat blood out onto the sand.

All I need is a moment, Warden. Just one moment, and you'll answer for all of this.

9

Pearl followed her aunt into the woods.

Some controversy had been unfolding over by the burial site. Both of them had silently agreed it was the perfect diversion to attend to their crates. The work that they were going to do was necessary, but she didn't love the fact that it required them to be alone in the forest. Not after learning the dragoness had escaped somewhere onto the island.

Aunt Hath echoed her thoughts. "So, she's out here somewhere?"

Pearl nodded. "We need to tell the others. Warn them."

"Warn them? God's body. Think about that, girl. For all we know, the creature ran inland and we'll never see it again. That's the nature of any wild animal. They're unpredictable. But people?" Aunt Hath gestured back in the direction of the beach. "People are very predictable. Tell them that we're responsible for that thing getting loose, and we'll have a target on our backs."

She knew her aunt was right. She'd seen that sort of thing play out before. Once a person got a bad taste in their mouth about someone, it stuck. That was how people viewed her father. A failed contract here. A missing shipment there. It soured business fast. And the truth was, they had no idea how long they'd be out here. Rescue ships could arrive later that afternoon—or they might not come for weeks. Losing social status in a group this small, this isolated, would have consequences. Better to keep quiet about the dragoness for now.

Still, Pearl couldn't resist correcting her aunt. "She won't run inland. Their species builds territory through association. The beach is where she was finally freed. Until she finds a reason to nest elsewhere, she's going to think of that place as her home. She'll keep returning there."

To the beach. The same beach where the other survivors were currently building a makeshift shelter. The same beach on which many of them were taking their first rest since the crash. Aunt Hath picked up on the concern in Pearl's voice. "You said dragons sleep during the day."

Pearl shook her head in frustration. "That's not what I said, Aunt Hath. I said their species commonly sleeps during the day once their patterns of behavior are established. I also said that this dragoness is still adapting to her environment. To this island. Her patterns can't be predicted. She hasn't even chosen her purpose yet."

Aunt Hath grunted. "Her purpose. What purpose could she have besides surviving?"

Once more, this was information she'd tried to relay to her aunt before the journey. "The male dragons are like bulls.

Their only real purpose in the world is to reproduce. They're not smart enough to do anything but breed. The female dragons are different. Fast learners. Quick to adapt to new environments. They analyze their surroundings and then they decide on a primary purpose for their existence. It can be guarding a certain location or hunting a specific predator or pulling ships across a harbor. Anything really. The people who buy them try to manipulate that purpose by creating a certain environment. Nursing them toward specific goals or desires. A lot of the research is unproven, though. People only started domesticating them a decade ago."

"That doesn't sound so bad," Aunt Hath said. "Maybe she'll decide to be our guardian."

Pearl rolled her eyes. "Maybe. Or maybe she'll decide to enslave us. Or that the entire island needs to be burned to the ground. My point is that we don't know what purpose she'll choose. All we really know is that she'll eventually circle back to the beach."

"Eventually," her aunt pointed out. "That gives us time. Come on."

The crates were waiting where they'd left them. Pearl slipped the knife from her belt and went to work on the ropes binding the first one while her aunt popped the top off the second. They were both good at this part—the random shuffling of legal and illegal goods. It took almost no time at all to pack one crate full of the dried pork and the wrapped flanks of meat. In the other crates, they stowed all the harnesses and equipment they'd intended to deliver with the dragoness.

"Do you think we could use these?" Pearl asked. "To capture her?"

Aunt Hath shook her head. "Our contact said they're for transferring her from one crate to another. Not active capture. You'd need her pinned and knocked out for any of this to be useful."

After a brief discussion, they agreed to hide the three remaining crates even deeper in the forest. There was some kind of wasp bush, it's lower branches thick and protective, that hid them completely. Pearl shifted the branches as well as she could and then stepped back. Only someone who was *really* looking would see them now. Aunt Hath gave a final inspection and nodded her approval.

"All right. Let's take the food back. Make a few friends."

Together, they lifted the crate with all their food supplies and started making their way back to camp. Her aunt's idea was to earn favor through this initial haul. Make whatever alliances they could to help with the goal of securing their own safety. Pearl just hoped no one would find their brief disappearance oddly timed. They were about halfway back when her aunt broke the silence.

"This island is strange."

"How's that?"

"Listen."

Pearl did. Beyond the subtle ruffle of their clothing and the muted steps they were taking through the forest, she heard . . . nothing. It was quiet. Strangely so.

"No birds," Pearl noted.

"No bugs, either," her aunt added. "Or at least none of the usual ones. I haven't seen a single squirrel or deer. Even for an island, that's strange. Creatures can make a home just about anywhere—and this place is plenty big. There should be things living out here."

The words shivered down Pearl's spine. She felt they had enough things to be afraid of without adding one more to the list. Any concern that they might be noticed—or marked as suspicious for their sudden departure—faded as they came back through the tree line. Most of the crowd's attention was still focused on the grave site. Anyone who wasn't helping with the bodies was busy sorting through items, deciding what was useful and what wasn't. Someone had gotten a fire started. That was good. It meant everyone would eat well, and they'd eat soon. It would not be the kind of meal anyone who'd crashed on a desolate island would expect to enjoy. Pearl knew that could lift their spirits. It would help them survive.

Pearl enjoyed seeing everyone's expressions when they popped the top off the crate. The realization that they would not starve—at least not yet—swept through the group like a fine breeze. Aunt Hath took on the same role she always did when they were meeting someone to discuss a new opportunity. Swaggering and loud and confident. Quick with a joke, but even quicker to remember a person's name and every detail of their life. The girl who'd started the fire was the same one who'd taken their order aboard the *Grand Gesture*—Agnes. Whatever friction had existed then vanished as the two of them picked out the best flank and discussed the best way to cook it over the open flame.

They'd spent most of the day burying the dead. The food and the fire both served as reminders that they were still standing aboveground. Every single one of them could be counted amongst the living. They were here. Still here. Pearl helped her aunt sort through what to cook and what to put away. She was busy with the task when her eyes found the prisoner.

He was seated at the very edge of the group. Just as handsome in the light of dusk as he had been when he first boarded the ship. Now, though, he looked far rougher. A great bruise was blooming around one eye. His rose-colored jacket had several streaks of dirt along one shoulder. Something about him looked so pitiable that she considered crossing the clearing just to tell him everything would be all right.

But then she saw the warden. He slid into place behind the wizard like a shadow. He was one of the few survivors who hadn't come forward to comment on the food. Instead, he watched everything with hooded, distrustful eyes. As if the food were somehow a sin. She thought he looked less handsome than he had on the ship. Somehow their island surroundings had drawn out the wild of him. His features were more wolflike in the fading light.

The scent of smoked pork slowly stirred into the air. Combined with the warmth of the fire, it was almost enough to convince herself she wasn't stranded on some barren island. She could almost forget that there was a creature out there capable of hunting all of them if it set its mind to that task. The thought drew her eyes to the forest. Was it her imagination, or were those branches twitching with movement? She squinted at the thickening shadows between trees for any sign that the dragoness might be there, watching them, but found nothing.

Pearl's conscience made one plea. There was still time to warn them. If she told everyone about the dragoness, they'd set up a guard rotation. Surely, they were all a little more likely to survive if they knew there was a potential threat out there. But as she watched, Aunt Hath was exchanging stories with a woman who was apparently Agnes's sister. She learned that

Agnes was one of the navigators aboard the *Grand Gesture*, and had only recently convinced the captain to hire her sister as well. Aunt Hath noted that was bad timing, all things considered, and they both had a laugh about it. Pearl watched and watched and could not bring herself to shatter the goodwill she saw being built.

And so, she kept quiet.

She warmed her hands in the pleasant heat of the fire, trying her best to ignore the way her secret was starting to burn a hole inside her chest.

10

As the sun finished setting, the survivors gathered with torches around the grave site. A pair of skin drums had been salvaged from the wreckage and one of the deckhands had enough rhythm to lead a few dirges. The songs were ancient. Most people knew the words, but only hummed along. The resulting sound stirred an unspeakable sadness in Marken. He had been to too many funerals in his life. And each one threatened to transport him back to the first. He had been so young. Just five years old, watching his parents be lowered into the ground. The sudden fear of that memory always left him feeling anchorless. Calm on the outside, but a wild and thrashing child within. He quietly set those thoughts back where they belonged: locked away in some dark corner of his mind.

This was the first funeral he'd ever attended where the dead outnumbered the living. Ten Tides tradition called for the guests at a memorial service to ring themselves around the grave. The idea was that the departing spirit would, regardless of the direction they went, see someone who cared for them in this life. But no matter how their group spread out, there weren't enough of them to fully enclose the mass grave. An ill omen. If one believed in such things.

When no one from the guards or deckhands took the lead, an elderly woman named Gemma guided the procession. She knew all the words and transitions common in a normal service. Marken took note of that. She must have buried someone recently. The older woman held tight to a golden locket that dangled at her neck as she spoke. Perhaps a picture of the one she'd lost sat within?

The naming process required the most time. One by one, each of the known deceased had their names spoken. A small stone was placed over the position they'd been buried. If anyone had a personal word or a prayer to add, they did so quickly and quietly. Some of the dead were commended into the afterlife by people who'd known them for only an hour or two. A few were offered into the afterlife with no name at all. More bad luck. It went on in that slow, deliberate way until the sky was completely dark. A sea of stars winked down at them.

"It is no small thing to lose those that we love," Gemma concluded. "May they know peace. May we remember them long after they're gone. To the God's body we return them."

The drums fell silent. The circle broke. A few people stayed to whisper some final word, but most fled back to the comfort of the fire and the growing scent of spitted meat. The warden escorted Marken back and placed him strategically away from the others. It was a sign of the warden's confidence that he didn't even bother having his guards put Marken back in chains.

In true Ten Tides fashion, the survivors followed a quiet funeral with a lot of noise. Someone had found a few bowls and plates from the ship's meager kitchen. There were three fires going. One for roasting the pig flanks. Another with a salvaged cook pot that held some kind of simmering broth. A small part of him wondered if he should suggest rationing the food—they didn't know when or if they'd be rescued—but then he remembered that his opinion wasn't particularly desirable at the moment, and so he kept his mouth shut.

Someone took up the skin drums again. A much happier beat led to much bawdier territory. An older deckhand named Wally flaunted his talent for free verse with a particularly good song about a princess and a pig. Drinks were being passed around. The crew always kept dozens of flagons of water stored on the ship, but the wine being passed around had apparently come from the captain's own cabin. For a time he simply watched the others. Makeshift friendships. Prisoners of circumstance. Some of the deckhands were obviously close—friends, if not lovers—but most of the others had boarded that ship expecting a quick flight to some other place where, undoubtedly, someone they cared about or worked with would have been waiting for them.

Instead they were here.

A disaster for all of them, but for Marken Burke, it was a final chance. He simply hadn't figured out how to take advantage of the new world he'd been presented. *Be patient,* he thought. *Just be patient and wait for them to need you.* A little mercy came knocking on his door sooner than expected. The girl with the secret separated from the woman she was with. She hesitated for the briefest of moments, and then began walking from her fire to his.

In her hand, a pathetic half rack of ribs. No more than a few bites—and yet when she held it up in the air, he'd never wanted anything more. Her eyes flicked over to the warden.

"Is your prisoner allowed to eat?"

Kell let out a sigh. "I suppose if he's to make it to trial, we need to feed him. Go on."

Marken knew if the girl hadn't offered it directly, he would not have been permitted to eat tonight. Kell didn't want to seem like a monster right in front of her, though. There was a reason the government normally tortured people in basement rooms away from the general public. Marken accepted the food. His fingers gently brushed against the girl's hand as he took it.

"Thank you, Miss . . ."

"Trask. My name is Pearl Trask."

"Marken," he said. "It's kind of you and your mother to share with the rest of us."

She blushed. "My aunt. She's my aunt. And it's the least we could do . . ."

"That's enough," Kell interrupted. "Don't push your luck."

It was hard to tell if the warden was speaking to him or the girl. Either way, his words had her retreating, both cheeks as bright as the nearby fires.

"She was just being kind."

"Kinder than you deserve," Kell replied.

Marken was annoyed enough to push back. He knew he should bite his tongue and keep his head down, but instead, he locked eyes with the warden. "What would you know of kindness? Born as you were? All you've ever been taught is cruelty. Do you think I missed the fact that she offered me—the supposed criminal—a bite of food? And yet she didn't offer you any. I wonder why. Do you think it's because you frighten her? Maybe you frighten all of them?"

He saw the way those barbs cut through Kell's normal armor. A tremor of anger tightening his jaw and bringing out the starkness of the veins in his face. It had been a calculated guess. Wardens *were* born out of a certain cruelty. Most of them were desperate. Lacking any alternative for survival, they volunteered for the government's controversial surgery. Their nondominant hand would be amputated. In the fever dreams that followed, the ones who became wardens were the ones who could master those ghost sensations and force their now-missing limb to reach out and seize one of the unseen null threads that existed in the air all around them.

Subjects were given three days. Those who could succeed were trained as wardens, a military promotion that came with substantial pay and prestige. An entirely new life. Those who failed? Well, the Ten Tides government had always been quite good at cleaning up its messes. Wardens were a relatively new discovery. For so long, the only way to police wizards had been by using other wizards. They'd relied on the Guild to keep a certain level of respectability within its membership. To punish those who stepped too far out of line. The discovery of wardens had been viewed as a vital new tool for overseeing the magical population. But they were still new enough that the public saw them as unnatural. The path required for gaining their powers—and the cruelty involved—remained a topic of discussion in public discourse. Marken could see all of that controversy playing out in Kell's expression now.

Eventually, the warden settled on a cold stare. "The girl pities you," he finally said. "Pity is a far cry from respect. But if you really think she's so fond of you, why not get some flowers for her? I know a place where you can find the most beautiful lightflowers in the world. Row upon row of them . . ."

Whatever reply had been on Marken's tongue died. The words forced him back into a brooding silence, all his venom bled dry. The fact that this abomination knew so much about him, knew things that no one else in the world had ever learned, stuck in his throat like a swallowed bone. The lightflowers were the source of his magic. His own personal anchor—and the warden knew quite well that his null thread was currently keeping Marken from visiting that place. The only true home he'd ever known. Marken seethed just thinking about it. His gambit to rile up the warden had clearly backfired.

All around him, the funeral celebration went on. Several of the deckhands got particularly drunk. Everyone else seemed to have reach the point where the wine was reminding them that they were marooned on an unknown island, uncertain if rescue was imminent or not coming at all. There was still laughter and merriment, but he noticed the way it was being checked by darker conversations. More wood was gathered for the fires. A second flank was being roasted.

Again, Marken resisted the urge to warn them about rations and survival and all the normal things he'd tell a group if *he* was in command. He found himself watching a pair of deckhands down by the ocean. The two of them were skipping rocks over the waves. It was a bright night, the water lit so fiercely by the moon that it looked dusted with snow. The two of them messed around for a while, laughing together, until one turned and stumbled back to fetch his drink. The other followed him before going unnaturally still.

He was the biggest of the deckhands. All muscle with broad shoulders. Someone who was built for pulling cargo out of a hold, or else for delivering a punch to someone who was bothering his friends at a bar. Marken didn't understand why he'd stopped walking until a literal wall of sand and stone appeared behind him. As if the earth were rising up to devour him.

He realized it was a creature only when he saw two eyes glowing over the man's shoulder. Like a picture brought suddenly into focus, he saw the beast. A massive, sinuous body. Great sandy scales and stone-sharp joints. The man hadn't stopped walking out of fear. No, it was the creature who'd stopped him. One of its claws was dug into the back of the man's neck. Marken saw blood flowing down and darkening his cloak. For an unbearable moment, both predator and prey stared up at the beach, seemingly right at Marken.

And then screams. Everyone turned. The deckhand was the one shouting, but he still couldn't move. The creature's lips peeled back in a threatening hiss. They all saw the teeth, made larger by moonlight. Marken pushed to his feet on pure instinct. He had faced bigger creatures than this one. He'd fought toe-to-toe with a dozen swordsmen at point-blank range. But right now he didn't have the one thing that had always protected him in a fight. His magic was out of reach.

Somehow, he ripped his gaze away from those glinting teeth to look back at the others on the beach. Kell was watching in quiet horror. The other guards were reaching for spears, but all the pistols had been set out on a blanket by the fire. The chambers were unloaded. Everything was drying and the bullets were gathered in useless piles. He thought he remembered seeing a crossbow—and sure enough, there it was. Hanging uselessly from a branch some twenty paces away from the group. He bottled his voice into a whisper.

"Kell. Release me. *Now*."

A current of shock ran through the group. Marken turned in time to see the creature begin to shift. The air around it shook and fractured. It kept one dark claw fixed in the deckhand's neck as its entire body shrank and twisted. Marken gasped out a curse when he realized what it was becoming. The eyes were still that unworldly blue color, but sand became skin, stone became bone. Wide-hipped and broad-shouldered, the woman who stared out at them was a frightening echo of humanity. Only movement betrayed just how alien she was in her new form.

And then, even more impossible, she spoke. If a mountain could talk—if the cavernous dark suddenly took on a voice—they might have sounded like this. Ancient and cold and impenetrable.

"Hello," she said. "I have come."

11

Pearl was pinching the skin at her wrist. Hoping that physical pain might wake her from the nightmare she was in. Surely, that's what this was. She'd actually fallen asleep beside the fire, her belly full of meat, her eyes tired from the smoke. This was a dream. The bloodstained sand and the dying deckhand could not possibly be real. Only when the creature spoke for the first time—in *their* language—did Pearl realize it couldn't be a dream. Even as a girl, she'd never had much of an imagination. She couldn't possibly have made *this*. The woman standing before her was so alien and impossible that Pearl's mind accepted the fact that she *had* to be real.

The deckhand's screams had stopped. His shoulders slumped and Pearl felt confident that he was dead. When no one replied to that first pronouncement, the dragoness bristled impatiently.

"Insensates," she said, and it was clear *they* were the insensates. "I have learned you. I am unmoved."

Pearl's stomach lurched. Unmoved? Not good. She could feel the weight of this moment pulsing overhead. Dark and ominous. The dragoness was on the verge of decision. She was preparing to choose the purpose that would drive her actions from that point on. No one else in the crew knew about this except for Aunt Hath. When Pearl glanced over, she saw her aunt was watching the scene unfold with blinking fascination. Her eyes ringed red. She was drunk. Properly drunk. Pearl looked back at the creature and knew it was up to her. If she did not step forward and do something, they might all die.

"Stop," she blurted out. "Wait."

The creature's neck twitched in response. Her body went briefly rigid before relaxing. The creature's eyes found Pearl in the crowd. There was a rather intense warning in that glare. Apparently she did *not* like being commanded to do something.

Right. Don't try that again. Let's use a different approach.

"There's more to learn," Pearl said tentatively. "About us. You can't possibly know us yet."

Her feet seemed to be moving on their own. She sensed that she needed to separate herself from the others. Establish that she was the person the dragoness should be speaking with. And so, ignoring Aunt Hath's slurred whispers, Pearl started walking in the direction of a nightmare. One she knew she was responsible for unleashing. The creature's eyes blinked wrong-ways before settling once more on Pearl. Its head tilted ever so slightly.

"I know you."

She'd never heard three more terrifying words. To the rest

of the group, it would sound like the dragoness was responding to the words Pearl had spoken. But as she took her place across from the creature, she felt certain the words were actually a nod of recognition. The dragoness somehow knew that Pearl had been one of her captors. A second strike against her.

"You don't," Pearl answered. "You couldn't possibly know all there is to know about us. People are not surface creatures. We have depth. You're being hasty, my lady. There's no way you could know us in such a short amount of time."

The dragoness raised a knife-sharp eyebrow. "Lady?"

And then she smiled. Everyone recoiled from that smile. Somehow her human mouth contained the dark multitudes of her creature form. Rows of teeth appeared in ominous succession. Pearl could hear whispers behind her. A hissed exchange, though she couldn't make out what was being said. She found herself desperately hoping they were going to free the wizard in time to save her from whatever might happen next.

"Give us more time," Pearl suggested. "I can show you. We can show you. What we are. What you might not be able to see just by looking at the surface."

"You are insensates."

Pearl frowned. "You keep calling us that. What does it mean?"

Her hands were actually shaking now. Her body seemed to have figured out what her mind hadn't pieced together at the start of the conversation. Those three brave strides she'd taken had unintentionally made her the next target. The captured deckhand appeared to be dead. If the dragoness discarded him to attack someone else, that someone would almost certainly be Pearl.

The dragoness answered, "You move only one way. You are

the hand that takes. You pluck and you pull and you grab and you gut. It is your nature. Sun and moon and water and earth. They are all sensate. Relationships. Flowing in and out of one another. A knowledge passes between them—between all of us—so that there is give-and-take. Not so with you. Your kind only knows how to take. Even the stones whisper this about you."

Pearl wasn't exactly sure what to say to that. She'd never had to defend herself from an accusation made by a stone. It also wasn't all that far off the mark of what she personally believed about their species. They *did* take. They *did* gut. One just had to look to the continent's western forests, completely decimated for the sake of building ships, to know that. But she'd always felt that any animal at the top of the food chain would do the same. They did what they wanted because they *could*. She didn't say any of that aloud, though. Confirming the creature's words felt like a death sentence. Instead, she tried to sidestep the claim.

"We give. We can be sensate too."

The woman's head tilted. Farther than was strictly natural.

"Explain."

Pearl faltered. How did they give? In what ways did they flow with the natural order? She was desperately searching for an answer when she remembered the gardens around their farm.

"We nurture. The trees. Plants. Food. We grow things."

"So that you can eat them. Insensate."

"Fertilizer," Pearl said, grasping at straws. "Our . . . our bodies. We nourish the earth."

The words hung in the air. Just long enough for Pearl to realize they were a grave error.

"Yes." The creature inside the body nodded. "Interesting."

No, no, no. Pearl fumbled desperately for a lie. Anything that might redirect where this seemed to be heading. "Only if we live a full life! Our bodies . . . they only really feed the earth if we've lived out the entirety of our life. It can't be—"

"I am decided," the woman said, cutting her off. "I am *purposed*."

Pearl's breath caught in her throat. She found herself backing away slowly.

"Let it be as you say. You who have taken . . . will be given. I will make it so. I will feed you to the sun. I will give you to the moon. The ground will dine upon your flesh. The ocean will suck the marrow from your bones. What you can give *will* be given—I vow this."

And she snapped the deckhand's neck. It was so terrifyingly effortless. He slumped like a rag doll to the earth, and Pearl's eyes widened as the woman snaked around him with inhuman speed. She planted one foot in the sand and lunged across the space separating them. As she leapt, her form began to change in midair. From that vulnerable human body and into her true hunting form. Pearl saw a set of stone-sharp claws reaching for her unprotected throat.

An explosion split the night in two.

The blast knocked the dragoness sideways a split second before Pearl could be slashed to pieces, but the force of the magic rebounded into her as well. She was punched in the gut, the chest, the leg, the neck. All at once. All with *intense* force. The magic threw her backward through the air and she went spinning head over feet in the sand. Her world was silent. Completely muted. Pearl looked up in time to see the wizard striding forward. He set his boots in the sand, raised both hands, and unleashed another spell at the fleeing dragoness.

Purple light shot out from both palms. The spell was powerful but aimed too high. She watched it soar out over the ocean before hitting a wave. There were two massive splashes, and Pearl knew the dragoness had escaped. Her ears popped and the volume of the world came rushing back to her. An awareness of pain came with it. Her entire body felt as if it had been dragged up and down the beach.

"The crossbow!" someone was shouting. "Get the crossbow! And reload those pistols!"

The wizard turned. His eyes locked on hers—and Pearl saw his attacker a split second before he did. Not the dragoness. No, a great plank of wood slammed into the side of his head. The wizard's eyes rolled and he fell helplessly to the sand. The warden stood over him, his chest heaving. He tossed the plank aside and pinned the person who'd just saved them all. Pearl felt helpless. What was he doing? What was he thinking? Did he not understand the danger they were all in?

Thankfully, she wasn't the only one with that thought.

"Are you out of your mind?" It was Aunt Hath. Sobered enough by what had happened to form sentences. "You've knocked him out! He's the only protection we've got! What if it returns?"

The warden glared back at her. "I've explained who this man is. I've explained how dangerous he can be. I freed him long enough to scare the creature away, but you saw what was about to happen. He was turning around with a spell already in hand. The next spell he was summoning? That would have been for *us*. No chance I'm letting him get the upper hand."

Still half-drunk, Aunt Hath started moving in his direction. Her face was red and angry. The warden straightened to his full height and looked down at her with a dark expression.

"It would be a mistake to come any closer."

Pearl finally found her voice. "Aunt Hath. Please, I need your help."

It was partially true. She could barely sit up she was in so much pain. Her aunt cursed once before giving up the fight and retreating to help. With her added strength, Pearl managed to limp back to the fires, where everyone else was gathered. A mad scramble was happening all around them. Some of the guards were frantically reloading pistols, but they weren't sure if the weapons had dried long enough to actually be functional. One of the deckhands had the crossbow loaded. Everyone else was herded tight together like frightened livestock. She heard panic in their voices.

"What the hell was that thing?"

"It *killed* Dante. It just . . . God's body, it killed him!"

"That branch just moved! Look! Right there!"

Suddenly, the group was shoving to get away from the tree line. Pearl and her aunt were almost trampled in the sudden rush. Another voice claimed the dragoness had circled around them somehow. One of the guards panicked and fired a shot. People ducked and shoved and shouted. It didn't help that the warden had finally reached the rest of the group, and he was dragging the unconscious wizard with him. The rest of the survivors finally seemed to realize what had happened.

"What's wrong with him?" This came from one of the deckhands.

"The warden knocked out our best defense," Aunt Hath spat.

Now anger bled into the panic. There was pushing and shoving and finger-pointing. Apparently, most of the group had missed the secondary fight down by the beach. They'd all been assuming that the wizard was setting up some kind of magical protection for them. The news that he was out cold didn't go over well. Especially not with the deckhands. Their voices were raised and the same one who'd gotten in the warden's face earlier—Agnes—was in his face again.

"Who cares what he did back home?! We need him. Did you see that thing?"

And then she shoved him. One of the guards turned and aimed his pistol, not at the distant forest, but back at the group. Right at Agnes. Pearl could feel everything spinning out of control. Her mind went to the farm. The cold mud under her feet. The squirming pigs and the calm they always offered her. The squeals. She breathed in the peacefulness of that other place—and then she raised her own voice.

"Everyone! BE QUIET!"

Surprisingly, they obeyed. Every argument fell away. No one spoke, but Pearl hadn't exactly planned out what she'd do if she did manage to get their attention. She could feel heat in both cheeks, but she didn't care if she was blushing. All of them were clearly waiting for her to say something that would bring order to the group.

Fine. If that's what you want.

"Look," she said. "What's done is done. The wizard is out. We can talk about what to do with him tomorrow, but God's body, we can't have people firing random shots into the night. Right now we need weapons. We need them in as many hands as we can get them into. It doesn't make sense for the guards to each have a spear *and* a pistol, does it? We need the whole group armed."

She was very careful not to let anything she was saying take on the shape of a command. She felt the warden would pick up on that. Taking authority from him would only cause him to retreat more. Still, it felt obvious that their best strategy for survival was to redistribute the weaponry. She just needed to soften his stance toward the others.

"We never introduced ourselves," she said. "What's your name?"

Their eyes met. She found she could not hold his stare. The sharp jaw and the long hair and the piercing eyes. It was almost embarrassing how handsome he was. But more than that, at this range, she could see the darkness lurking beneath those features. This was not a pleasant person. Knowing what she knew about how wardens came to exist, she thought that was reasonable.

"My name is Warden Kell."

Pearl nodded. "Warden Kell. I'm Pearl Trask. If we can't have the wizard to protect us, we need some other way to defend ourselves out here. Please, can you help?"

She saw the way his jaw tightened. It was clear he didn't want to lose an ounce of whatever imagined power he had out here. There had also been a scene earlier, by the graveyard. She and her aunt had missed that exchange, but it had clearly been something between the guards and deckhands. Which would win out now? Pride and bad blood? Or fear of a far more dangerous threat?

"Fine," he said. "If we agree to keep this man bound, I agree to distribute spears. My guards keep the pistols—but that way, we can all work together to protect the camp."

For a brief moment, Pearl thought the deckhands were going to be foolish enough to reject the offer. Agnes's chest was still pumping up and down with adrenaline. Thankfully, the fiery girl's sister stepped forward. Pearl had listened as her aunt spoke with the woman earlier. She'd seemed like the calmer of the two—and she displayed that same, almost cold, approach now.

"We accept," she said. "Divvy them up."

The other deckhands backed off immediately. Pearl watched with great interest. So, Helene was their new leader? All the guards exchanged glances, but after another nod from Kell, they began the tentative process of distributing their weapons in the way that made the most sense. There were a few people, like old Gemma, who didn't care to hold a weapon. Most of the others accepted gladly, even if they'd never used a spear in their life. When those ran out, anyone without a spear or a pistol was given a knife to tuck into their belts. Pearl found herself in that camp, and couldn't help thinking that a knife wouldn't do a whole lot if the dragoness returned.

Those without weapons went to work organizing the camp's supplies. People would eventually have to sleep. Some were still so drunk that they could not serve the group in any capacity. Creating a space that was both comfortable and defensible wasn't easy. Pearl found that people kept asking for her opinion about every minor detail. This was annoying at first, being asked about where something was stored or which way the beds should face. Eventually, though, she realized it was a good sign that people *wanted* her opinion. It meant she had some measure of influence now.

She turned to mention this to Aunt Hath—and realized she'd lost track of the woman. Panicked, she turned around, searching the camp. Normally, her aunt couldn't go more than a few minutes without giving her opinion. How had Pearl not noticed that absence? She finally spied the woman seated by one of the campfires. Her eyes appeared lost in the flames and her mouth was hanging open ever so slightly. Almost as if she'd fallen asleep with her eyes open. Strange.

Pearl knelt beside her. "Aunt Hath? Are you all right?"

The woman jolted. "Oh. Oh gods, sorry. I must have drifted off there. Sorry, Tilly."

Pearl stared. "Tilly?"

It was her mother's name. Aunt Hath shook herself more forcefully.

"I meant Pearl. You know that. Sorry. I'm just tired."

As if to prove nothing was wrong, her aunt used her spear to push back to her feet. She joined in on a discussion about the guard rotation for the night. Pearl returned to her own tasks, but watched her aunt closely, worried about what she'd just seen. Confusing her for her mother? Maybe it was the blow to the head or one too many drinks. But then she remembered the missing medicine. She'd have to make a point to search for it in the wreckage.

All the planning and organizing felt like a temporary salve. Pearl found her eyes drawn, over and over, to the unconscious form of Marken Burke. The boy who'd scared the dragoness off. An obvious and uncomfortable question kept nagging at the edges of her thoughts.

Can we really fight the dragoness without him?

12

Marken was trying to remember what happened on the beach.

When Kell had dispelled the null thread, it had felt like a cloud lifting to let the sunlight in again. He'd reached for his magic, the energy of his thoughts channeling through the ground of the island and reaching across time and space to the part of the world that he'd anchored himself to all those years ago. The dark barrier that had kept him in exile for the past few weeks was gone. His mind fractured in that pleasant, familiar way. One foot remained on the beach, but the other set down in the quiet mountain valley he'd come to think of as home. He always smelled the lightflowers first. Like smoked honey. After blinking a few times, his eyes adjusting to the light in that other part of the world, he saw the flowers running in their endless rows. Hundreds and hundreds of them.

Their petals were snow white and their stems a dark green that verged on black.

Back when he was just eight years old, the Guild had officially commissioned him. He was to make the famous passage: from boy to man, from apprentice to practitioner. His headmaster told him he would be the second youngest to ever begin that journey. They'd discovered his gift at a young age. Just five years old. His reaction to his parents' passing had nearly set an entire city block on fire. From there, he'd gone right into training. He shivered as he remembered those years. The breathless excitement of learning magic, of discovering that he was actually quite good at learning and applying new knowledge. But that had come hand in hand with being the youngest boy in a place where everyone was competing with everyone. The way he'd been treated. The abuse that he'd suffered . . .

. . . Marken mentally set those memories aside. Back where they belonged. The truth he liked to remember was that he'd gone through rigorous training on every magical subject known to man, and he'd mastered them all. Only when a student demonstrated a full understanding of their power—and all the responsibilities that came with it—were they commissioned. A pilgrimage in which the wizard traveled alone, searching for some part of the world that would serve as the anchor for their magic for the rest of their life.

Some never came back. Turned off by the difficulty of their training, or lured away by the possibility of some other life. Others took less than a few days to find their binding point. His professors had always hinted at the fact that this was a sign of impatience or, worse, immaturity. Most wizards of substance and renown took over a year to find the right location.

Even as a boy, he'd been drawn to privacy. He had secrets that he'd rather the rest of the world not know about him. And so, when he'd set out on his journey across Ten Tides, he'd done so hoping to find a place not easily discovered. It had taken him over a year to find the valley.

The actual mechanics of practiced magic were quite simple. For magic to be born, something had to die. It was a trade. Death for living power. Wizards were the only people in their world who could control *both* processes. The killing and the creating. The first step required them to form an anchor point to a living ecosystem. Most wizards searched for something that would provide longevity and versatility. The current high mage of Ten Tides was bound to an ant colony. Another friend of Marken's had anchored to the world's largest winterspur tree. Whenever she cast a spell, it withered just a single leaf along those branches. A flawless display of control and power.

Finding an anchor point was simple. The exchange—death for life—was also straightforward. The two factors that separated great wizards from the forgettable ones were how *much* power they could draw and what they could creatively *do* with the power they'd summoned. Some wizards lacked imagination. Others lacked the ability to amplify the power they were drawing from their source. Marken just happened to be exceptionally skilled in both categories.

But in school, he'd learned that every potential anchor point came with inherent risks. Choose a location or species that was too exposed and another wizard in training might anchor to it without knowing. A shared binding point would weaken the magic of both wizards. Another risk came from the simple unpredictability of nature. Nothing lived forever. If a bad flood swept away the high mage's ant colony? His power would go with it. He'd met countless wizards who'd lost their anchor points and been forced into early retirement. Hearing those stories, a young and impressionable Marken Burke had quietly promised himself that he would find an anchor point that no one else could possibly find.

The valley had been the answer. There was only one pass that led to the area—and that pass was normally covered by ice year-round. He stumbled across it during a rare hot spell in the heart of summer. Just enough of the ice had thawed to allow his passage. He navigated that terrain and emerged in an untouched valley. Of all the species and ecosystems there, the lightflowers had been the obvious choice. There were enough of them dotting the hillsides to fuel his spells for years. He also suspected the other flowers would reseed the ground beneath any flowers he drained for his spells. Over time, the gaps would fill back in. His supply would be never-ending.

There was also a benefit to using such a uniform source. Most of the flowers were roughly the same size and shape and beauty. That would make his magic far easier to control. Extending the blast radius of a spell, for example, would mean burning eight flowers instead of four. The younger Marken had been giddy over the potential of that place.

And the passing years had proven him right. No one ever discovered the valley. He never came close to burning through his supply, in spite of years and years of use. Before the incident in West Lily, he'd even been on a short list of people in consideration for the next high mage appointment. Wasn't that proof that the boy who'd navigated that mountain pass had succeeded?

From *nothing* to *this*?

The only minor flaw: his present circumstances. He had woken up with dried blood on his face. The light of a new day glared down on him, almost mocking, as he tried to piece together the night before. There was the null thread. Kell had dispelled it, and then Marken had reached for his magic. He'd appeared before that field of lightflowers. They weren't exactly how he left them, either. He could see damage. Evidence of Kell's null thread and its efforts to keep him from his magic. An outer row of withered flowers that made him want to rage, but there wasn't time for that. He remembered why Kell had dispelled the thread in the first place.

The creature on the beach. We're under attack.

As the creature-woman's speech grew more erratic and threatening, Marken had reached for his power. He'd drained ten lightflowers. By the time he'd blinked back to the beach and shaped the projectile magic, the creature was already moving. Marken had hissed a curse, adjusted the aim of his spell, and released the waiting magic.

Deep down, he thought he was too late. The girl was going to die. But he was wrong. His spell hit its mark. If the creature had been in her "human" form, he felt certain the blast would have killed her. It was powerful enough to cave in her chest and puncture the organs beneath. Instead, she had shifted in midair, back into the scaled creature he'd first seen rising up on the beach. His spell still hit her hard. A punch of force that knocked everyone back a few steps. Impressively, the creature had spun end over end before springing back to her feet. The quickness with which she'd darted back into the ocean had caught him off guard.

That was when he'd been forced to make a split-second decision. One that might haunt him. Marken had reached for his magic a second time. Draining six lightflowers, drawing all that power across space and time, he'd considered two potential spells. One was a shield. Defensive magic that would put space between him and Warden Kell. It would have kept him from ever being captured again. But the more reckless side of him—the one who'd become known across Ten Tides as one of the best combat mages in existence—had whispered that he could still finish the job. He could take one more shot at the creature. Save the day as he usually did.

She'd been in the shallows still. Her head and shoulders sticking out above the waves. Gritting his teeth, he'd turned, adjusted his magic, and taken aim. The spell had missed by mere inches. When he spun around to face Kell, the entire world had gone dark. He'd known—before the pain even registered in his mind—that he'd made the wrong choice. An unforgivable error.

Now the dried blood and the throbbing pain were evidence of that reality. Kell must have flanked him. Knocking him out was smart, too, because there was almost no chance the warden would have been able to resummon a null thread that quickly. It would have come to a duel—and Marken would have won that with his spellwork restored. Now he sensed the null thread wrapped around him again. Cutting him off from his magic. From home.

If he didn't search for silver linings, he knew he would go mad. He did his best to look around the beach with new eyes. Guards ringed the edges of their camp. The deckhands had all been given spears. That was an interesting development. He couldn't believe Kell had consented to that. It felt obvious that any future rebellions would now be more dangerous, given they'd been armed. And then there was the girl: Pearl Trask. His eyes finally landed on her.

So, you survived? Good. That's good for both of us.

He hadn't been certain that she would. All it would have taken was a stray claw slashing a major artery, or even his own magic rebounding at the wrong angle. There were bruises running down the right side of her face and neck and shoulder. Hopefully that was the worst of it. When she noticed him looking her way, she pushed gingerly to her feet. With the same unexpected boldness she'd shown the night before, she marched in his direction. Until Marken's shadow stepped forward.

Kell intercepted her. The decision earned a knife-sharp glare from Pearl.

"Move out of my way."

Marken blinked in surprise when the warden obeyed her. That was new. Maybe he'd missed more than he realized while he was out. Did she hold some sway over him? Or maybe over the group? Whatever had happened, she'd clearly earned some measure of respect from him. Marken squinted up at her and winced. The back of his skull was still delicate, pulsing with pain.

"Hey," Pearl said. "I just wanted to thank you. For saving me."

Kell loomed over her shoulder like a watchful hawk.

"No problem," Marken replied. "It was the decent thing to do. Although, I have to say, waking up with a headache and a null thread wrapped around me isn't exactly the sort of thank-you that I thought I'd get for saving everyone's lives."

That drew a snort from Kell. Of course. Marken thought the man was as prideful as he was. The warden probably thought they could have fought the creature off on their own. Marken had his doubts. Certainly, it wouldn't have gone very well for Pearl Trask.

"Your situation is . . . complicated," she finally said. "An agreement was made that we would attempt to shield the camp without your magic first. No offense, but it seems like no one here really likes you. I'm not sure what you did. I'm not sure that I care. If the patrols can keep the dragoness away until we get rescued, you'll remain a prisoner. If they fail? We'll free you. That's just the way it has to be."

At least there was an air of apology in her tone. More signs of a shifting tide within the larger group. Yesterday, everyone had unanimously agreed to keep him bound as a prisoner. Now there was at least an agreed-upon scenario that would free him. That felt like progress, even if the step required to free him was a rather dark one for the group to take. He couldn't resist pointing that out.

"So, you're just going to let someone die?"

Pearl bristled. "No. We're doing everything in our power to defend the camp."

"Well, not *everything* in your power. That would involve freeing me."

An attempt at humor. A failed one. Pearl shook her head.

"Anyways. Thanks again."

And then she retreated back to the main camp area. Kell smirked at him. "Very smooth, Burke," he said. "Losing the goodwill of the one person on this entire beach who actually seems to like you. It's as she said. The entire camp agreed: we won't release you unless we have to. If I catch you trying to scheme or plot something else, you'll be punished. Got it?"

Marken nodded. Regretted nodding. Kell started to retreat.

"Wait. What was it? That creature?"

The warden turned. "The girl says it's a dragoness."

"Pearl did? How would she know? Is she some kind of zoologist?"

"She's a pig farmer," Kell said, as if that were an actual answer to the question. The warden shrugged at Marken's incredulous look. "Her aunt said that she studies bestiaries. Cross-anatomical research that helps them with surgeries and treatments for some of their own creatures. I don't know. Anyways, she says it's a dragoness."

Marken was surprised at how naive the warden was. Cross-anatomical research? Between pigs and dragons? It wasn't a very good lie. He sensed that there was another truth buried there. The girl had to be connected to the creature somehow. There was so much evidence of that in what had unfolded the night before. The way the girl had stepped forward when no one else had. Only guilt would force someone to do something that foolish. Why else put herself in danger?

There was also something to the way the creature had spoken to her. *I know you.* Those words felt more important than he'd initially realized. The only problem was that this theory meant the girl and her aunt had been daring enough to bring a literal dragoness on board the ship.

Is that your secret? You were smuggling that thing in the hold?!

His mind traced back through details. The waves of nervousness that had been radiating out from her when he'd first boarded. No wonder. They'd been smuggling something dangerous aboard a ship that looked empty—and then all of a sudden, a full patrol of soldiers had arrived. Not to mention there'd been that moment down in the hold. He'd sensed something amongst the crates. It felt obvious now: the dragoness. All the pieces were fitting together. He decided not to say anything. File it away for later. Maybe he could use it for leverage.

"I've encountered dragonesses before," Marken said. "I knew they could adapt to their environment, but what she did . . . turning into a person?"

Kell nodded. "I don't think that's what happened. You saw her. It was more like she was wearing our skin. Like a costume. Apparently that's what all her transformations are like. The girl said she can take another substance and put it on like armor. When her claws were in the back of the deckhand's neck, she simply drew the knowledge of that exterior into her own form. Pearl said she might be the first dragoness to ever take on a human form, though."

"Well. Always nice to be a part of history."

Kell finally seemed to realize that the two of them had been chatting amicably. He offered an unnecessary scowl before crossing over to speak with Levi and the other guards. Marken slumped back in the sand. His head was throbbing. Tentatively, he reached for his magic. He caught that first hint of lightflowers in the air, smoky and intoxicating, before an invisible hand crushed down on top of him. Confirmed, then. The null thread was back in place. All he could do was wait for his situation to change again.

Right. Just need someone to die a painful death. How cheerful.

There was a shout. He turned to see a small group had organized down at the edge of the surf. Squinting, he was shocked to find people braving the water. *Really? Do you all have some sort of death wish?* The dragoness had literally come to them from the ocean. That had also been her method of escape. Apparently, the deckhands didn't value their lives as much as he valued his. There were several teams moving back and forth in some sort of salvaging effort. The call had come from one of the teams. It wasn't a shout of panic. No, they appeared to be returning with something that was causing a stir of excitement. Another team went out to help them with the bulky load. Only when they'd made it to the beach did he see what it was.

The ship's wherestone.

It was perfectly round. An amalgamation of magically receptive materials that had been shaped into a perfect sphere and installed in the airship's engine room. The wherestone was designed specifically for search and rescue. One of the keys, really, to surviving a crash like theirs. When a ship didn't arrive at its destination, another wherestone in the flight tower would be activated. That sphere would be a perfect match to the one they were currently hauling up the beach. Designed specifically to seek out its twin through a complex magic. A rescue ship could follow the progress of the activated wherestone and the hope was that it would lead them to the wreckage in time to help rescue any survivors.

As the deckhands set the stone down, Marken saw the reason for all the excitement and the raised voices. They were all arguing with each other. A debate that had started before they'd even gotten the item out of the water. All of them were disagreeing about exactly how screwed they were, because the wherestone was broken.

13

Pearl stared down at the wherestone.

It was still holding together in the shape of a sphere, but she could see great fissures running through the entire object. She probably could have chipped away fragments of it with no more than a fingernail. "What do you think? Is it functional?"

The deckhands all seemed to disagree on the answer. Some believed that it would still work just fine, because most of the pieces were still correctly positioned. Others pointed out that the usual glow that ran through the veins of the stones was gone. A third group explained, over and over, that none of the deckhands actually had the faintest clue how wherestones worked. Captains were apparently tasked with installing the spheres before a ship could be approved for flight. Routine checks were made on the devices, but always by members of the Guild. Often, these were performed by the windmasters themselves—who took on the extra duties of magical assessment to double their take on flights. No one bothered pointing out that both of the people who could have provided some insight on the matter had already died.

Eventually, Helene called for silence. "The damage happened during the crash, which means the wherestone was intact right up to the point when we landed. Look. The ship's right there. It's not like we got pulled leagues away by a current or something. Even if the sphere is broken, the last readout they took would be for this place. They're coming. They'll find us."

Nods all around. Pearl thought that made sense, until a new voice chimed in.

"Not how it works."

Everyone turned. Marken Burke was seated exactly where she'd left him. He looked terribly annoyed that he had to be the bearer of bad news. "Passive magic versus active magic," he illuminated. "A passive spell would work the way you're describing. Regular readings. Ongoing information. It might provide a sort of map of all the ships and their movements in real time. That would be rather clever, honestly. If you survive this place, that might be worth sharing with the head of transportation . . ."

Helene looked more annoyed than complimented by the dismantling of her original theory. Pearl was starting to notice this about Marken. He was undeniably handsome, but his humor—if it could even be called humor—had a knack for stirring the wrong reactions from people. His personality felt like one that developed only when a person had so much power that they didn't actually need to care if anyone liked them or not.

"Get to the point," Helene suggested.

"My point is that they don't activate the matching wherestone *until* the ship is officially noted as missing. The *Grand Gesture* wouldn't receive that status until two hours after its original scheduled time of arrival. So if that wherestone we have cracked *before* they activated the second one, then they have no idea where we are—because the stones only work because they're identical. That's the entire basis for the magic. One stone seeking out its exact counterpart in the world. If it was shattered, they have no way of knowing where we landed."

One of the deckhands muttered that this seemed like a rather large flaw in the whole search-and-rescue system. Pearl agreed. Ever stubborn Agnes was shaking her head, though.

"We sent Beck back to shore, remember? He's the best flyer on our ship. If he made land, he would have gone straight to the docking station to alert them. They'd have activated it then . . ."

"Certainly," Marken said. "That's certainly possible. We might have gotten lucky. Let's hope your friend made it to shore. But until those rescue boats arrive, might I suggest that we try to figure out where we've landed? I'm assuming there were maps on board the *Grand Gesture*?"

One of the older deckhands nodded. "We have them set aside for kindling."

"Maybe hold off on burning them," Marken suggested, and Pearl could tell he was warming up to this role. For the first time, she realized that he had likely led groups of people like this. On missions all around Ten Tides. She could certainly picture it. The natural charisma and easy assurance. As if he knew precisely what he was doing. "I would try to trace our flight path, calculate our current coordinates, and then figure out exactly how far we are from the mainland. Once you know that, it might be worth seeing what parts we can salvage from the original airship. If you can manage to build a small boat that's properly seaworthy, I could power the vessel home."

His words were greeted with stunned silence. He made it sound so easy.

"Well. I suppose I'd need my magic," he added, as if this were an afterthought he hadn't previously considered. "But with a decent sail and solid rigging? It would be pretty straightforward spellwork. Only slightly more complicated than what the windmaster normally does."

The deckhands exchanged glances. A nod from Helene set them to work on both of those tasks. In all of the sudden busyness, Pearl didn't realize it was just her and the wizard now.

"Couldn't you just fix it? The wherestone?"

He shook his head. "No. Those stones are more like . . . works of art. Every wherestone has seven identical matches. One stored in the basement of each of the seven primary flight docks around Ten Tides. If a ship is lost, they activate the other wherestone—which has a very complicated geolocational spell stored inside it. The spellwork is really clever. I studied the designs when I was in school." He paused, lost in thought. "It's actually how we used to hunt wolves."

Pearl could not help feeling fascinated by him. Whenever he spoke, it felt as if he lived in an entirely different world from the one that she occupied, even though they both called the place that they lived Ten Tides. "Wolves, huh?"

He nodded. "They trapped one wolf and applied a reading to similarly shaped creatures across the western plains. Within an hour, they knew how many packs there were, where they were overpopulated, all of that. Fascinating theory, really. I met the man who conducted the original experiment. He became a good friend. Before—"

A darkness clouded his features. He looked lost in the memory of whatever had brought him to this island in chains. Pearl tried to offer him the mercy of another subject.

"What about the dragoness? Could you track her?"

He lifted one eyebrow. "Do you have another one hidden away somewhere?"

Her breathing hitched. His words were so dangerously close to the truth of what had actually brought the dragoness to this island. They pressed right up against the guilt that had been churning in her gut ever since the first dragoness attack. *This is our fault. We put everyone in danger.* It was a truth that would earn her and her aunt serious animosity. Did he actually suspect something? Or was this more of the grating sense of humor? The other survivors hadn't even thought to question her aunt's explanation about why she knew so much about their huntress.

"Fresh out of dragons," she replied. Her eyes found the warden. He looked to be out of earshot. She lowered her voice to a whisper. "You know, I could probably get him to free you if you vowed not to kill him."

Marken leaned in conspiratorially. "Ahh. But you see, that vow would go against the vow I've already made to kill that man the first chance that I get."

She sighed. "Is everything a joke to you?"

"That one's not a joke."

She saw it written in his expression. He fully intended

to kill the warden once he was free. Well, that complicated things. She was trying her best to empathize with his position. He'd likely been practicing magic for as long as she'd been tending pigs. An accomplished wizard who'd only ever known a life of power—and now that power was being kept from him. She understood why he might hate the warden, but according to everyone else on this beach, Marken was guilty of some terrible crime. Which meant the warden was simply doing his job.

"You should be grateful. He could have killed you already."

Marken shook his head. "No, the warden has a distinct moral code. A private execution is beneath his standards. He needs the law to find me guilty. Feels more righteous that way."

"And are you? Guilty, I mean?"

He flinched back as if struck. Pearl watched him carefully, though. His expression shifted a half dozen times before he finally settled on a face that looked like some kind of wounded house cat.

"No. I am not guilty of what they claim."

That didn't mean he wasn't guilty of *something*. His answer fell into a sort of gray middle ground. She considered pressing him to tell her the entire story, but there was another shout. Her eyes swung to the noise. Someone was being brought back from the area of the forest they'd all chosen to be the unofficial bathroom. She thought she saw blood. And then she finally saw who was being helped along.

"Aunt Hath."

Pearl was running. It looked like another knock to the head. Blood was trickling down from a small gash. Two of the deckhands were bent low in their efforts to set the older woman down by the nearest fire. Pearl dropped down beside her aunt. "What happened? Was it the dragoness?"

Her aunt waved her off. "Of course not. I was going to the bathroom. Just tripped on a root. Got a little banged up. Stop your fretting, girl. It's nothing to get worked up about."

Nothing? Add up all the nothings that had happened so far and Pearl felt she had good reason to be concerned. The missing medicine. The slip-up calling Pearl by the wrong name. And now this? Pearl had to physically bite her tongue to keep from chiding the woman. Hathaway Trask—like all the Trasks before her—did not abide weakness. Her father had always been the same way. Prove him wrong, beat him at something, and his claws only got sharper. And so, instead of fretting, she fetched the cleanest rag she could find and tended to her aunt's wound. It wasn't bad, thankfully. The woman was patched up and chewing on dried jerky in no time.

It felt like a settled matter until one of the deckhands pulled her aside. A woman named Pen. One of the two older deckhands who'd survived. "Hey, your business is your business, but you should know that your aunt didn't trip. I was coming back from the bathroom. She passed me. When I turned to say something, that's when it happened. She dropped like a sack of roots. Passed out. I thought you should know. Make sure she drinks plenty of water. Try not to let her back up on her feet, yeah?"

Pearl sighed. "Right. I'll do my best. Thank you."

There was already so much to worry about. The broken wherestone. The secret they'd been keeping about the dragoness. And now Aunt Hath. It would only get worse if she couldn't find the little medicine bottle. She felt a wave of guilt about that. She'd been the one who asked her aunt to part with it in the first place. Which meant it was her fault the medicine was missing. And her responsibility to find it. She decided to put in a special request with the deckhands. Helene and Agnes and the others were lost in their own conversation, though.

"There's nothing here. I mean, nothing remotely close."

They'd marked the map with small lines. She saw the original planned route, the progress they'd made up the coast, and then their best guess as to their location when the windmaster had died. The storm had started pulling them out to sea at that point, which was displayed on the map using even smaller dotted lines. Helene—one of the ship's navigators—had drawn three possible routes from that point on. All of them depended on fractional differences in the wind and rough estimates of the time they'd spent in the air. One problem was that no one knew *exactly* how long that treacherous part of the journey had lasted. Too much chaos had been happening for anyone to perfectly account for the passage of time.

"So, we're lost?"

Helene looked up at her. "Not exactly. We have a pretty good sense of where we are. No, the real problem is there's no island out here. There's nothing marked on the map for fifty leagues in either direction. It doesn't make any sense. These waters have all been charted. Years ago. Any dry land *should* be on this map."

Pearl frowned. "Maybe . . . it's new?"

"That's what we were just discussing. Either it's a recent geological change or we somehow got pulled farther than a normal airship could fly even if it *meant* to go this far. I don't really see how that's possible, though. We were fighting that storm with everything we had. Everything."

She liked the first theory. A new island. As her eyes traced the nearest tree line, she thought there was a sort of "youthfulness" to everything. None of the trees seemed wide enough or tall enough to indicate long lifespans, but maybe there were other reasons for that. Exposed islands weren't known for producing quality vegetation. She didn't really know enough to say one way or another. She was still lost in thought when Helene stood and signaled for Pearl to join her.

Really? One act of bravery and everyone thinks I'm some kind of spokesperson.

"Between you and me," Helene whispered, "we're interested in . . . alternative options. That wizard could be the most dangerous person in Ten Tides—but if he can help us survive out here? I'd rather hold hands with a murderer than die for no reason, yeah?"

A murderer, Pearl thought with a shiver. *Is that what he is?* She hadn't even considered that it could be something so terrible. Now she almost felt naive for assuming his easy smile and odd personality somehow absolved him from being potentially dangerous. Maybe it would be worth it to have a conversation with the warden. It might help her make a decision, one way or the other, if she knew exactly what the accusations were.

"Would you be with us?" Helene went on. "If we made some changes around here."

"I'd have to speak with my aunt," Pearl answered. "See what she thinks."

Helene nodded. "Fair enough. Just wanted to plant the seed. See what you were open to."

Pearl wasn't sure how to say what she wanted to say without incriminating herself in some imagined court of law. "I . . . am very interested in not dying out here."

That drew a grin from Helene. The woman slapped a friendly hand down on Pearl's shoulder before returning to her crew. Pearl barely remembered to ask them to keep an eye out for her aunt's pills. The rest of the camp seemed to be making preparations for the coming night. A pig flank was being prepped by one of the fires. Talk around camp ranged from idle conversation to wild theories. Most of what she heard centered on the broken wherestone and what it might mean for their potential rescue. Pearl saw that her aunt had fallen asleep. She tucked in beside the woman—who was like a second mother to her—and was just comfortable enough to start drifting off herself. Naturally, that was when the screaming began.

14

Marken watched the chaos with great interest.

I told you. I told you this would happen. Now I just need you to blame the right person . . .

One of the deckhands had been wading out in the water near the wreckage, searching for salvageable materials, when he'd suddenly vanished under the water. Another deckhand saw the splash. When his friend didn't surface, a warning cry had gone out, and that was followed by a wave of panic. Now they all saw the ring of scarlet blooming out from where the man had disappeared. The water there was far too shallow for sharks. Everyone knew the dragoness was responsible.

"Enough is enough," Agnes said, raising her voice so that everyone on the beach could hear her. "How many of us need to die before we start using our best weapon out here?"

The words were thrown like knives in the warden's direction. He stared back, unmoved, as his guards maneuvered through the crowd. All of them had pistols, but much like it had been at the grave site, the numbers weren't on their side. And this time the deckhands were armed with spears.

"Your man was outside of our line of defense," Kell replied calmly. "It wasn't a failure with our rotations or our guards. If you swim out in the surf, you're taking on an obvious risk. Our agreement was that the wizard remains bound until our defenses prove too weak. Notice the dragoness hasn't returned to our camp. She hasn't attacked anyone who's armed. The plan is working. I will not release him. Not yet."

Marken saw the way the warden's calm infuriated Agnes. Of the two sisters, she was the one who ran hot and impulsive. There was enough fire in her now to set off a chain reaction that would get quite a number of people killed.

"Who says you get to make the call?" Agnes asked darkly.

The other three guards all raised their pistols. There was a new wave of murmured panic in the crowd. Everyone was standing in relatively close proximity. If shots were fired, people *would* die. Kell raised his hand in the air, though.

"Pistols down. Now." Those shadowed eyes homed in on Agnes. She was younger than most of the deckhands, but slightly older than the warden. That didn't stop him from speaking to her as if she were an annoying child. "We've been on this island for a little longer than one day. If they activated the wherestone correctly, the rescue ships would only be halfway to us by now. If you kill us, and a boat appears on that horizon, you'll be rescued. And then you'll be escorted straight to a prison cell in Pasca. My official rank, as a warden, is the equivalent of a lieutenant general. Can anyone here tell me the punishment for murdering someone with a rank that high in the Ten Tides government?"

His question was met with silence.

"The undercity cells," he answered. "That's where we send you. Average lifespan in that section of the prison is less than a year. The people on those floors are the absolute scum of the earth. Some of the most dangerous people you could ever have the misfortune of meeting. So, be my guest. Pick this fight. Maybe you'd actually win, but you better be prepared to face the consequences that will come if you do."

Agnes looked more than ready to take him up on the offer. "You'd be dead, though. Hard to point a finger at us when you're a corpse, Warden."

Kell smirked. Marken knew this level of argumentation was easy for him. Wardens were trained for combat *and* court. He could strike with his words as well as he could with his spear.

"Of course. I'm sure you'll have a good explanation for why the government-appointed detail all died. And not from the sorts of injuries one might find in a ship crash, but from wounds consistent with spear thrusts. When the time comes for interrogations—hell, throw in a little torture—I'm sure none of your crew members will break. None of them would dare consider cutting a deal to avoid punishment. And let's say they do hold their ground. No one on your crew talks. Well, there's a beach full of other people here who have no loyalty to any of you. What are you going to do keep them quiet? Are you going to kill them all, too?"

Once more, the deckhands exchanged glances. Agnes didn't back down until Helene whispered something that Marken couldn't quite hear. The calmer sister smiled, and her smile felt more dangerous than anything Agnes had threatened so far.

"Fair enough, Warden. One more chance."

Kell held up a finger. Marken thought it was a mistake to keep pushing them. His threat of what might happen to their life back home was a good one, but there was a tipping point with everything and Marken felt the warden was already dangerously close to it. Maybe he didn't understand that this world—this island—would not operate by all the same rules as Ten Tides. At least not for long. It would not take more than a few days for a wilder sort of law to find them. Instinct and survival would become the new morals. Not yet, but soon.

"This 'one more chance' comes with an addendum: if you step outside the camp's protections and you are killed by the creature, it doesn't count. I understand there are basic necessities that require some ranging, but anyone who's taking on those risks isn't a part of the deal. No security, not even the wizard's, could keep everyone perfectly safe at all times. Deal?"

Marken expected Helene to push back, but she didn't.

"Deal."

Everyone quietly dispersed. There was a rotation of the guards. Marken thought the contract and its promises had come too easily there at the end. One of their crewmates had *just* died. Surely there was more anger boiling beneath the surface, but if there was, Helene hid it well. Agnes didn't. She stormed off, but given the presence of the dragoness, she could march only so far without putting herself in danger. It made the whole display a little less dramatic as she circled the far fire again and again. Some of their crew busied themselves once more with the maps. Others stood solemnly by the water, hoping to see some sign that their friend might yet survive.

He never surfaced.

Eventually, even the ring of blood washed away.

Like he'd never existed at all.

15

Pearl dreamed.

She found herself standing in their main pen back home. It had rained. She could tell by the way the heels of her boots sank and suctioned with each step. All the pigs were gathered in the far corner of the yard. Her father called it the coward's corner. It was where they all retreated to when something in their main shelter had spooked them. Once, she'd found a wingfox in the rafters. It had already killed one of the pigs and was hoping the others would return. Her father had hired a local conservationist to rehome the creature—but when it came back the second time, he'd gone out with a crossbow and a grim shake of his head.

In the dream, Pearl crossed the muddy yard and found the reason the pigs were scared this time. It wasn't a wingfox or a horned owl. No, two of their own had died. One by the entrance and the other near the feeding stall. Both of them older pigs—a boar and a sow. She set her hand on the first one's side and felt nothing. All the life had drained from the creature. She felt that small sorrow that always welled up in her when any living thing died. It had gotten smaller and smaller over the years, as her role on the farm had expanded and she'd taken over most of the work with the pigs. Butchering was a requirement. There was no room for feeling sorry. Guilt was like molasses: it only slowed things down. And yet she found the butchering was easier than these sorts of deaths. At least she knew the meat would go to a market. From the market to someone's table. She might have an unpleasant role in the cycle, but it had always helped Pearl to know the final result was someone out there, fed and happy and whole.

When the pigs died this way, though, they had to be buried. There was too much concern about what had killed them. What if it was a disease? And what if their farm was the one responsible for spreading whatever it was to other counties? No, there was too much risk. In the dream, Pearl crossed the yard and fetched the shovel. The pigs squirmed and squealed, as unsettled by her presence as they were grateful for it. They didn't like the bodies. The slow-forming smell of rot in the air. But they had also learned, over years of repetition, that her arrival meant they were safe and would soon go back to their normal routine.

Pearl wondered how long it took them to forget the ones who died. An hour? A week? Did they snort the names of the fallen to one another before meals? Were pigs smart enough for that sort of honor system? Maybe they ate their food and were simply grateful they weren't the ones who'd died. In the dream, the shovel felt nearly almost real in her hand . . .

She woke on the beach.

Night had come and gone without incident. The warden was sipping his coffee—salvaged from the hold—with an almost arrogant satisfaction. So long as the security held, he would not need to free Marken Burke. There wasn't much for the deckhands to complain about if everyone was waking up with all their limbs intact. The result was a slow morning. Pearl felt the weight of immediate danger lifting from their shoulders, but the stress of whether or not they'd be rescued hadn't come down fully to replace it. Which meant they were gifted an in-between morning with a sunrise and warm mugs of coffee being passed around and shared.

Pearl started learning about her fellow survivors. In a way, it made the guilt she felt worse. Learning their stories was a reminder that the ones who'd already been killed by the dragoness would have had stories too. A family or a home or a favorite food. Gemma, the elderly woman who'd been seated near the windmaster, was a widow. She'd buried her husband earlier that year and had promised him, before he passed, that she would go on an adventure. This flight had been her first brave step on an imagined journey of self-discovery. *This wasn't what she'd been imagining.*

Another paying passenger who'd survived was Warner. He was a balding tax accountant who'd been traveling north on behalf of his company to assess new properties for an expanding business. He liked to joke that this island wasn't what they'd had in mind when they'd sent him to seek out investment opportunities. It was funny the first time she heard the joke. Less funny, though, with every new iteration.

The two other paying passengers who'd survived were a couple—Naomi and Prior. Not married. Pearl had learned that Prior was wealthy, and he had offered to whisk away his relatively new girlfriend to the Feckle Islands for the weekend. Pearl remembered having to label the islands back when she was still attending school. They were up off the northern horn of the continent. Ever since the crash, Prior had complained about the state of their camp, about the delay in rescue, and just about anything else he could sink the teeth of his displeasure into. Naomi, on the other hand, had been making herself useful as the primary organizer of the food rations. The fact that they weren't married or even deeply in love, and yet were supposed to function as a pair, seemed to be a strain on both of them. Naomi obviously disliked the fact that he wasn't useful around camp while he was openly annoyed by anyone who acted as if their rescue wasn't imminent.

Pearl and her aunt were the only other surviving passengers who didn't identify as a crew member or one of the guards. They formed an odd third contingent: six survivors who didn't really have all that much in common, beyond the fact that they were seen by the other two parties as potential free agents to bolster their own numbers. If she had to choose a side, she preferred the deckhands. They were a rough bunch, but reliable and honest. Learning their names had proven nearly impossible. Pearl knew Helene and Agnes. One always cool and confident. The other more like something shot out of a cannon. She'd also learned the name of the older woman, Pen, who'd been kind enough to keep an eye on her aunt. The woman's closest confidante was the other old deckhand, a man who'd introduced himself as Wally. Everyone kept assuming the two were a romantic pair. Wally's response was "Once upon a time." But Pen would snort and reply, "Never again." It was the same answer, Pearl supposed, just spoken from different directions. The other six surviving deckhands were hard for her to differentiate. A rotation of lithe bodies and floppy hair and mischievous grins that she'd given up on memorizing.

Marken Burke's guards were another matter. There weren't nearly as many to keep track of, but she found herself not *wanting* to learn more about them. There was Withers, tall and polite. And then Levi, short and cruel. The third guard, as far as she'd seen, hadn't spoken to anyone. All of them had the scent of killers. There was something about the sideways glances they gave everyone around camp. Almost as if the others on the beach were all as guilty as Marken Burke, and pulling the trigger was all it would take to make them guilty of that imagined something.

The afternoon brought warmth and conspiracy to the beach.

There was a rumor that the wherestone might have been tampered with. Another rumor—this one she heard from Gemma—was that the windmaster had been poisoned. There were suggestions that everything was a grand conspiracy by some underground organization to free Marken Burke. That seemed so unlikely to her. The warden had boarded the ship mere minutes before it had taken off. How would anyone have even known he'd be aboard the *Grand Gesture*? Her eyes eventually swung over to Marken. He was asleep—or pretending to be.

Could all of this really be about him?

She was still staring when a noise rang out over the beach. Loud and piercing. A screech that seemed to echo across the entire island, from every direction at once. The conversations on the beach all fell silent. It seemed to be coming from deep in the forest. There was an inhuman quality to it. Marken Burke was on his feet. Everyone, including the current rotation of guards, had started backpedaling toward the center of camp. There were no signs that the dragoness was nearby.

"Was that her?" someone asked.

Marken shook his head. "That sounded . . . industrial."

"She could have a form that's metal or stone," Pearl reminded him, her voice just loud enough for most of the group to hear. "The form she had when she first attacked me was some kind of sand-and-stone mixture, but she might have found something in the wreckage. The tip of a spear or a shield. That would be enough for her to learn a skin like that."

"But what could she do to make *that* sound?" he asked, and Pearl didn't have a good answer to the question. "Even if I clanged pots together, it wouldn't echo across the entire beach. We're right by the ocean. Plenty of noise out here, and we all heard that sound clear as day."

"Maybe her lungs transform?" This idea came from the warden. She saw an eagerness in his expression. As if he didn't like the fact that Marken Burke kept asserting himself in these conversations. Allowing his captive any real sense of authority would not serve the warden's agenda. Especially if the horizon remained empty for another day or two. "When she takes on a new form, is her entire body altered? Maybe that was her roaring—but the sound she produces changes depending on the internal construction. The shape and the material . . ."

Pearl nodded. "Interesting. That's possible."

"If guesses could float," Marken quipped, "we'd have enough to build a raft and sail home."

That earned scowls from both Kell and Pearl. The rest of the survivors had fallen into whispers. They kept waiting to hear the sound again, but never did. Night wasn't far off. There were conversations about the dragoness and their delayed rescue, but the strange and unidentified noise now occupied their thoughts too. Some of the deckhands believed it was proof this island wasn't abandoned.

"We need to send out a search party," Helene said. "We could send two of the pistols with them and keep the other two pistols here. Maybe a few spears in capable hands. They can go north along the beach the first day. South the next. We all heard that noise. For all we know, there's a port town on the other half of the island and we just haven't been smart enough to walk around the corner and find our rescuers."

Kell declined the offer. "I'm sure the dragoness would like it if we split up. You can expose yourselves if you'd like, but I'm not wasting our guns on that. Not yet. We're still within the reasonable time frame for a rescue procedure to take place. All we have to do is wait. The wherestone just needs more time to find us."

Pearl saw a flicker of annoyance in Helene's expression. It was smoothed out before the warden could look up and see it. The woman nodded calmly back at him.

"Fine, but if we go beyond that 'reasonable time frame,' we'll need to send out expeditions to see what other resources are out here. The longer we wait, the more restless everyone will get."

"Restless" seemed like a calmer word than what Pearl was imagining could happen if all the survivors were forced into a more desperate, animalistic mode. They'd already witnessed a little of that after the dragoness's first attack. Everyone shoving and pushing and shouting. A random shot fired into the forest. Restlessness could turn into rioting fast.

Dreading all that they'd have to navigate in the coming days, she retreated to the only safe person she had on that beach. Aunt Hath had been quiet most of the morning. Pearl asked how she felt, and received a grumbling response to stop pecking her like a mother hen. For all her bluster, though, Aunt Hath paused each time she stood up. As if her head was spinning and she was too dizzy to walk unless she took a long pause to get her bearings. The woman was also the first one to fall asleep again that night. Her body was forcing rest on her, and for good reason. Pearl confirmed which shift they'd be taking on the guard rotations before tucking in next to her aunt and following suit.

A presence woke her. Nothing dangerous, but she sensed someone set their blanket right beside hers on the beach. Everyone had been sleeping in roughly the same area. A place where the sand was not too soft or too hard, but there was enough room there that they weren't sleeping on top of each other. There was a clear sense of space between the separate groups. It was surprising for someone to be this close to her. In the nearly dead light of the fire, she saw it was Helene. The woman fussed with a blanket for a few seconds, curled up, and went to sleep.

Pearl frowned. The two of them were so close that she could feel one of Helene's boots touching her own. The proximity had to be deliberate. For several minutes, nothing happened.

Then finally, a voice. "Girl."

Barely a whisper. Barely intelligible.

"Don't move. Don't turn around. Don't speak."

Aunt Hath didn't stir. The wind around camp continued to blow. The waves continued to crash. Helene whispered her next sentence perfectly beneath those other sounds.

"We are going to free the wizard. Tomorrow night."

Pearl had to remind herself to keep breathing normally. Helene had told her not to respond in any way. It felt obvious she wanted to communicate this missive without the guards noticing.

"During the third watch," Helene said. "If it happens at night, in the dark, no one can truly say who was responsible. There aren't any real witnesses, then. Third watch is when the fires are lowest. Two of his guards will be asleep. If you're with us, tie your hair up tomorrow. If you're not with us . . . make sure you stay the hell out of the way."

Pearl heard a rustle and guessed that Helene had turned the other way. It would look as if she'd simply shifted restlessly in sleep. Her aunt still had not stirred. Pearl would have to tell her everything in the morning. Her mind was running through all the potential consequences of each decision. Moves and countermoves. Worst-case scenarios. She wondered if the deckhands could even triumph in a fight. If they failed—and she supported the attempt—would she be guilty of treason? And what if the warden's prediction came true? What if the rescue ships arrived the next day only to find their government-appointed detail had been murdered and buried? There were no easy answers to those questions. Instead, she was left with the gut feeling that whatever choice she made would be the wrong one. Both groups were courting their own dooms—and she wished that she didn't have to join either.

16

For the second night in a row, no one died.

A minor miracle that Warden Kell was all too happy to claim as his own divine handiwork. He walked around camp like a deity who'd granted his worshippers rain during a drought. The man was so confident, in fact, that he missed the smaller details that Marken had trained his entire life to notice. Something was being passed around from deckhand to deckhand. Some private word or instruction. He saw the way it moved from one corner of the camp to another. Just a whisper and a subtle nod before it found the next person. He also noted the way that same message, whatever it was, skipped over the areas where Kell's guards patrolled. Whatever was being spoken wasn't some generic camp message about food or the patrol rotations. Some game was beginning.

How curious.

The second clue was in the subtle shift in behavior around camp. Helene and Agnes set up a game of pegs. A few of the other deckhands participated. Yesterday, they'd been obsessively talking about logistical concerns—building a boat, exploring the island, rationing food—but today they were playing games and wasting time? All that urgency had bled dry that quickly? If the warden noted the subtle shifts in behavior, he didn't comment on them to Marken or to any of his guards. In fact, when the patrols rotated, Kell closed his eyes and napped by the fire.

Marken's final clue came from Pearl Trask. She and her aunt waited for the peak busyness of breakfast and first conversations to slip off into the woods together. Too long for it to just be a bathroom break. Less than a minute after their return, he saw eye contact between Pearl and Helene. Then, for the first time since they'd crashed, the girl pulled her hair up into a ponytail. It brought out the starkness of her features. A sort of sharp beauty, he supposed. He hadn't really even thought of that until now. When she was done putting her hair up, she nodded once to Helene, and then sat down by the fire to look out at the sunlit ocean. That exchange had his mind humming with possibilities. What else could the two of them have come to an agreement about? If not something to do with him?

All I have to do now is wait. Be patient.

It felt as if the island heard him, though, and now moved to offer the group alternatives to whatever plan was brewing. An hour later, that same metallic shrill from the day before sounded. Everyone reacted the same way. An initial tightening—the same way any prey reacts when, for a brief moment, they realize their concentration had lapsed and their hunter might be on the verge of leaping—and then there was the gradual realization that the noise was *out there* somewhere. He thought of the dragoness. Could that really be her? Roaring in some altered form? But then he looked up. The sun was tracing a path overhead. Unless he was mistaken, the noise had sounded at *exactly* the same time as it had the day before. Creatures, however predictable, did not function that way. No, the only things he'd ever encountered that repeated—day after day with such precision—were man-made. Humans liked their systems and their consistency. And that led him to a new set of rather uncomfortable questions. What if this island *was* populated? Could there really be a fishing town on some other unexplored part of the island? If there was, why had no one come for them? The ship crash had been loud enough to wake a god.

Imagining civilization so close at hand had Marken's entire chest constricting. The null thread felt tighter than ever. Claustrophobic almost. He needed to escape it *before* they were rescued. Otherwise, he would be right back where he was at the start of this journey. Nothing gained. Everything to lose. It was the older deckhand—the man named Wally—who spoke the words that might ruin him out loud to the others.

"That's got to be machinery," he said. "It made that noise at the same time yesterday. Like it's running on a cycle. There's *something* out there that's man-made."

Marken considered making up a lie. He could pretend what they were hearing was some inexplicable magic that only he would know about, but what would his excuse be for not mentioning it the day before? He needed to dredge up some explanation—and fast. The warden was having a whispered conversation with his man Levi. The deckhands were stirring excitedly too.

"Machinery means people," Helene said. "Maybe it's one of those drilling rigs. You know the ones they've got in all the northern harbors now. If there's a little fishing village or something over there, we might be saved."

All eyes swung to Warden Kell. The man in charge of the guns. Marken waited, breathless, for what his response would be. *Say no. Please, tell them no. Be your usual, stubborn . . .*

"Go," he said, before adding a small clarification. "If you want to go, I won't stop you—but no guns. They stay with us. My men and I have been charged to escort a prisoner safely home. We will stay with the ship and the wherestone. I wish you the best of luck if you decide to go on this little . . ." And here he paused to put an unnecessary amount of derision into his tone. "*Jaunt* of yours. I won't stand in your way, but our guns stay on this beach."

A sense of relief flooded through Marken. It was the one time that the warden's stubborn logic was working in his favor. Helene wasn't as reckless as her sister. She wouldn't take a trek around the island, exposing herself and her crew, without proper defense. And all of them knew that a few spears wouldn't make anyone feel safe. They'd need pistols—or Marken's magic.

"Fair enough," she said. "We keep waiting, then."

She turned away from the conversation, as if it were a settled matter, and returned to playing her game of pegs. Kell looked rather pleased with the result. Once more his pride was blinding him to the smaller details. The way fists were tightening amongst the deckhands. The cold impassivity that now stretched over Helene's face. The almost violent way that Agnes moved her pegs as they resumed the game. Marken hid a smile.

You're a dead man, Kell. You just don't know it yet.

17

Night.

Pearl found herself waiting restlessly for promised violence. Helene's plan involved a lot of risks, and yet Aunt Hath had been adamant they were making the right decision in joining them. Pearl leaned in that direction mostly out of guilt. The two casualties directly caused by the dragoness so far had been members of the ship's crew. She felt as if she owed them her help in some twisted way. Certainly more than she owed the warden anything. Her aunt's position was far more practical: she believed that freeing the wizard was their best chance at survival. If the warden would not see reason, then what other choice did they have? Pearl considered pointing out that murdering a government official should have been a last resort, but the truth was her opinion didn't matter at this point. The deckhands were set on a mutiny and her aunt was determined to join them.

Unsurprisingly, her aunt had already fallen asleep. Not a trace of nervousness in that woman. And why be nervous? What was a little midnight mutiny amongst friends? Pearl knew that Hathaway Trask had proven her nerves of steel a hundred times over. When their family farm had started to fail, Pearl's father had transformed into a broken thing. Nothing like the man who'd raised her on lessons of determination and how to put one foot after the other no matter what happened. Instead, she'd started finding him drunk in the barn most days. Polishing up tools that didn't need cleaning or reading useless books of poetry out loud in a slightly slurred voice. There was plenty of work to be done. On a farm as big as theirs, there was always work to be done. He just didn't see the point in doing it anymore. They'd fallen too far in debt.

It was Aunt Hath who'd forged a new partnership with one of the northern townships. All the restaurants there wanted cheap pork—and their farm had a surplus. They wouldn't see profits in the first year, Hath had noted, but if they proved themselves to be good partners? The collective would double their order the next year and they'd have more than enough to cover operational costs. What other choice did they really have? When Pearl asked how they were going to afford an entire year without profit, Aunt Hath had the answer to that, too.

"I owe your father," she said. "He saw me through tough times. Everything that happened with Ben; he didn't bat an eye. Now he's the one who needs steadying. That's all."

Pearl hadn't understood that her aunt's plan was to take on smuggling work. Illegal activity that put her at great personal risk, all for the sake of helping their family. The shipments north had connected her with some less-than-savory folks who needed a way to move their merchandise through the province's checkpoints without getting flagged by authorities. It began with a crate here or there. Always labeled with the same branding mark as their farm. The authorities never noticed. Before long, there were enough of those extra payments to keep them as happy and fed as when the farm had been fully operational.

The "steadying" that Aunt Hath had mentioned, however, had the opposite effect on Pearl's father. He began retreating even more into himself. Perhaps it was shame that his sister could save them when he couldn't. Or maybe he'd simply strayed too far to find his way back to the man—the father—he'd once been. Pearl knew they couldn't keep forcing Aunt Hath to take on risk they weren't willing to take on themselves. She asked to be a partner in her aunt's side business.

It was one of their worst fights.

A shouting match out by the slaughterhouse. Their raised voices scattering the pigs back over to the coward's corner. In the end, Pearl won. She could be convincing when she needed to be. It turned out to be for the best. The two of them worked well together. Her aunt would never admit that she enjoyed Pearl's company. Nor would she admit that it helped having an extra set of hands to load and unload everything. It didn't take long for them to increase the illegal freight they were taking on each month. Why not? With another person there to work shifts and help out?

One day, as she looked through all the numbers, Pearl realized they were outperforming the farm's most recent profitable years by a significant margin. That realization brought on a tangled sense of pride and pain. Her father's ancestral home—everything he'd worked so hard to sustain and build—was being outpaced by far-less-reputable work. She had to set aside that guilt eventually. The truth was they *needed* the money. It wasn't long before they were approached with a more complicated shipment. A contact of a contact reached out. The man chose a specific tea shop in which to rendezvous. Pearl could still picture the way he held his teacup, pinched between two fingers with perfect elegance, and how he'd taken just two sips before diving straight into business.

"This task will require travel by airship. Are you comfortable with that?"

Aunt Hath had nodded without a second thought. "Of course."

This was one of the many lessons her aunt had taught her. Always agree at the start. Nod along and smile and make them feel like everything they're requesting would be simple, straightforward work for you. If there are ever concerns, discuss them *after* signing. The elegant man had relished her confidence.

"Very good. Given your occupation, I can only assume you're good with animals . . ."

Once the details were set out before them, Aunt Hath had hesitated. This wasn't some illicit, back-market good. What they were being asked to ship was *alive*. That was a first for them. It was Pearl's enthusiasm—an *actual* dragoness, she had whispered under her breath—that eventually won her aunt over. Besides, it wasn't as if they'd be directly handling the creature or tasked with subduing it in some way. All they'd really get was a glimpse of the beast as it was transferred into some kind of specialized containment crate. As ever, the only true risk they'd be taking was that their names would be on the official documents that came with the crates.

The only true risk.

How wrong they'd been. Pearl sighed, turning over and trying to get comfortable beneath her blanket. The other risk, never considered by either of them, was that their airship might crash on a desolate island. That the creature they were transporting—deadly and powerful and unhappy at being detained—would turn on them. *What were the odds of that? A thousand to one?*

Her aunt had stopped snoring. The waves came and went. Guards were circling their camp. It was still the first watch. She knew she needed to sleep. Rest some before the third watch arrived and brought all of that bloodshed with it. She tried counting stars. Gave up on that. Tried lying on her back, then her side, then her other side. Nothing.

Sleep came only when she stopped trying to figure out how to fall asleep. Her mind was tracing back through the pages of one of the books she'd been reading back home. When they'd found out about the dragoness, she'd wanted to do some research. There had been one memorable passage about how there was some evidence that dragons might have their own theology. They were smart enough to invent their own pantheons. Pearl wondered, as she drifted in and out of consciousness, if their dragoness—their own personal huntress—was looking up at the moon right now. Did she think it the unblinking eye of some watchful god? Or maybe a searchlight of some kind, held in the massive hands of some deity who wanted to bless her hunt with its brightness? Pearl stumbled from those strange thoughts and into the world of dreams . . .

. . . and then the night exploded. *Crack, crack, crack.* A rapid and too-close thunder. She rolled on instinct toward her aunt, covering the woman as well as she could with her body, pressing herself low to the sand as she did. From that vantage point, her eyes moved from madness to madness. One of the deckhands stumbled past, hands clutching at his own gut, blood pouring out through the gaps in his fingers. Beyond him, she saw two other deckhands had a guard pinned beneath them. His pistol had fallen out of reach. The older woman she'd come to think of as tender—Pen—brought a rock slamming down on his head. Pearl saw the way his feet twitched and went still.

But where's the warden?

She finally found him in the chaos. There, on the other side of the beach, a different story was unfolding. Three of the deckhands were already down. Two were dead. One was well on the way. It was clear that the guards had fired their pistols and that the rest of the melee would come down to hand-to-hand combat. Three surviving deckhands stood in a defensive formation—Helene and Agnes amongst them—and they were trying to hold Kell and Levi off for long enough that their reinforcements could arrive. In that brief glimpse, she saw exactly how deadly Levi was. Kell's trained man moved with liquid precision, perfect footwork. His spear darted in and out of each blow with such speed that all three of the deckhands were forced back a step. Kell wasn't bad either. Pearl saw the way he attacked at just the right moments. As she watched, the tip of his weapon caught Agnes in the stomach.

"Our spear!" Aunt hath hissed. "Give me the spear, girl!"

Pearl had been so startled that she forgot they were actually *in* this battle. The crucial moment was *here*. It was *now*. If they didn't act, the deckhands might not count the two of them as part of their rebellion. But if they did act, and Kell somehow won, they'd be guilty of treason. Their spear was on the ground to her right. She shoved to her feet and reached for the weapon at the same moment that the fourth guard came stumbling back into camp.

It was Withers. The tall one. She had no idea how he'd been missed by the deckhands. Maybe he'd stumbled off to use the bathroom right before the attack began. Now he saw the weapon in her hands. His eyes flicked to the fighting beyond. One of his own lying dead on the ground. The others in the middle of deadly combat. Moved by terror and instinct, the man raised his pistol. He aimed it at the nearest threat. Right at her.

She knew, logically, she could say something to stop him. Anything. She felt as if she were watching the moment of her death unfold from a distance. Like some strange angel hovering over the waves. No more than a witness. A split second before the shot exploded out, Pearl was shoved hard. She stumbled to her right and screamed, but the noise was swallowed by that larger explosion. She looked up from where she'd fallen. A delicate curl of smoke was in the air. Withers blinked rapidly at the damage he'd done. Maybe he wasn't the hardened killer she'd assumed him to be. His entire face went pale. The pistol dropped from his trembling hand.

Aunt Hath was on the ground.

Her eyes stared up at the stars.

Blood. Blood was everywhere.

"No, no, no . . ."

Pearl scrambled across the beach, collapsing beside her aunt, only to realize that Withers was still there, still a threat. When she looked up, though, she saw him bolting for the woods.

"Hey! *Stop!*"

Her command pulled him up short of the forest. He spun back, clearly torn between the instinctual desire to flee and the forceful plea in her voice. Anger was coursing through her entire body. Tracing a path through every vein and whispering in every thought. She was trying to think of the cruelest thing she could do to this man. What fate would really be justice? What could make right the bleeding mess of her aunt's chest? Before she could make up her mind, one of the deckhands stumbled into the fight. He lunged with a spear. Withers, who was still frozen in place, his eyes locked on Pearl and her dying aunt, took the blow square in the gut. He went down awkwardly. Like a felled tree. Another deckhand came in and finished the job with a downward stab.

Pearl's eyes dragged back to her aunt. She'd worked with animals long enough to know there was no way to save her. Not with that much blood. Not with that much damage. That did not stop her from trying. She pressed her blanket to the wound to stop the blood flow. It seemed to work. Then she realized the bullet had gone through one side and out the other. A circle of scarlet continued to darken the sand. Pearl's fingers came away sticky and colored.

"Pearl." The voice barely sounded like her aunt. "Get home. Whatever . . . takes. Keep yourself safe . . ."

Her vision was blurring. Tears came hot and fast. Her hands were shaking too, which made it harder to keep the blanket held tight over that gaping wound. Without warning, Aunt Hath reached out and seized her by the collar. Her aunt's eyes mooned wide in a final, desperate plea.

"Don't tell them."

The lights in her eyes guttered out. Pearl slumped down into the sand. Distantly, she could hear the deckhands calling to each other. Kell had fled into the woods with Levi—though Levi was wounded. They had control of the beach. Marken Burke's voice sounded then. Bitterly, Pearl realized she hadn't seen him during the fight. Had he known to stay out of harm's way? Or had one of the deckhands managed to hide him before the first shots rang out? These questions would echo back later. For now all her curiosity was bleeding out in the waiting sand beside her. The woman she'd come to love so much—come to think of as a true partner and a second mother—was dead.

18

Marken could feel power *thrumming* through his entire body. He cupped his hands—the same motion a person might use to cradle a baby bird—and then gave a small twist. A brief dome of light appeared around the entire camp. He guided that light, coaxing the edges out, until the magic fractured and vanished. A rare lapse in concentration. Helene stood a few paces away with a small frown on her face.

"Look," he said. "It's a *complicated* spell."

"Four people just died to free you," she reminded him. "Figure it out."

Right. Figure it out, he thought. *Just knock off the rust of being without magic for a few weeks, snap my wizardly fingers, and perform a spell that has seven layers without breaking a sweat. Never mind the fact that I've had a null thread wrapped around my subconscious or that I just watched several people die or that the guy who wants to imprison me is still out there in the forest or that there's a dragoness hunting the group . . .*

When he looked up, he saw Helene was still watching him. For a brief moment, he feared he'd been mumbling his thoughts out loud. That was one of his many bad habits. He tended to mutter under his breath when he got frustrated. It had caused issues before, though normally those issues were easily settled by reminding the offended person that he was more powerful than they were. Marken knew that kind of bravado wouldn't work for him out here.

He needed alliances. For now.

"Of course," he said. "I'm on it."

Marken's mind fractured, setting him down in that other place. The valley he thought of as home. He saw the great rows of lightflowers running in every direction. Once more, he noticed the effect of Kell's null thread on his anchor crop. The outer row was completely withered. Marken bent down and rubbed the blackened petals between his fingers. They dusted in the air. The damaged flowers wrapped in a perfect circle around the field. That made sense. Kell had created a barrier between him and the waiting magic. He could also see a few locations where the dead flowers slashed inward from that outer circle. The damage he saw reminded him of a blight. That word stirred uneasily in his gut. What if that's what this was? Not temporary damage—but a disease. Something that might spread. He shoved the thought away.

Focus, he thought. *You need to impress your new friends.*

On his second attempt, he drew on the life force of seven flowers. One for each layer of the spell he was crafting. As he guided that power—death traded for life—he kept his hand motions precise. The shield flickered into his vision. This time, the magic didn't fracture. He watched it settle like a blanket of moonlight over the camp. Sheer enough that they could see through it, but just substantial enough that the boundaries were visible. Marken walked the edges, inspecting his work, before returning to Helene.

"There you go. One camp shield. As you requested."

The deckhand nodded. "Can we still go in and out?"

"Of course. The magic simply dices you up into a million pieces and then reassembles you on the other side. You just have to hope the magic is powerful enough to put everything back in the right order. I'd hate for you to end up with an organ in the wrong spot . . ."

She stared at him. "That was a joke?"

Marken smiled. "Yes, that was a joke. The shield will allow anyone with relatively human anatomy to pass through. Which . . ." Oh. Interesting. He'd forgotten about the dragoness's human form. "I guess technically she could pass through if she wore that human skin of hers, but I don't think she'd do that. If she's going to attack our camp, she'll approach in her strongest form. But this does mean that Kell and Levi can pass through this shield. It's not going to keep them out. The only defense I've installed against them is a proximity warning that's attached to the exterior layer. Any time someone comes *back* into camp, we'll hear a noise . . ."

"What kind of noise?"

"I . . . I went with wind chimes?"

Helene snorted. "Really? Not a horn? Or anything that usually indicates danger?"

"Oh. Right. I guess it was just the first noise I thought of.

Honestly, I was going to go with a foghorn—but then I imagined that blasting us every time someone came back to camp and it sounded rather annoying to deal with."

"Aesthetic over function," Helene noted. "You'd make a terrible deckhand."

"Oh, I have no doubt you're right about that. Although, is it too soon to point out that you—the lead navigator on an airship—crashed us on an abandoned island that you can't find on a map?"

Helene smiled, all teeth. "Yes. It is too soon to point that out."

He offered his own tentative smile back. There was a small momentum between them that he was trying to nurse. The truth was that he'd worked with people like Helene often. At least a decade or so older than him, but the sort of steady-minded person that cared more about his ability than his age. He'd always enjoyed it when he was assigned to work with soldiers like that. Until this point, he'd really been working the angles with Pearl Trask, hoping for any sympathy at all. But now it seemed Helene and the other deckhands could overlook his supposed crimes and focus on his utility. That was a rather good turn for him. Especially given her current position in the camp.

"So," Helene said, picking the conversation back up. "If someone comes back, the wind chime goes off. What about the dragoness? What happens when she tries it?"

"The dome will activate," he answered. "She'll have to destroy the entire structure to get through to us."

Helene nodded. "And how long would that take?"

"Several minutes. At least. Long enough for us to form up

ranks and make a stand. We could attack or defend, depending on what you want to do. You recovered one of the pistols, right?"

"Two of them," she said. "But we've only got three total shots between them. It looks like the warden was keeping most of the extra ammunition with him."

"Not a bad starting point. I have plenty of combat spells that can do serious damage."

He saw a sort of grim satisfaction in her expression when he used the words "combat spells." She nodded once and told him she needed to attend to other logistics. It took him a moment to figure out that she meant making preparations for burying the newly dead. The smile on his face faded as he saw the way the survivors were attempting to ferry their fallen over to the original grave site. Thankfully, the burial location was inside the radius of the shield he'd created. A happy accident, really. He hadn't been thinking about the corpses at all when he performed the magic. Looking around, he was struck by a second realization: the deckhands weren't the only casualties.

Pearl Trask was tugging the corner of a blanket to cover her aunt's lifeless features. A sort of makeshift shroud. After that task was done, he watched her stagger away, down to the surf to wash the blood that had dried on her hands and wrists. Sympathy drew him across the beach.

"Pearl, I'm so sorry."

She swung around to look at him. Her expression couldn't seem to decide on hatred or misery. It was the first time since meeting her that he thought she looked truly beautiful. Wild and lost and eternal. She reminded him of those statues in museums—made more beautiful by the grief the sculptor had drawn from the marble.

"Sorry?" she said. "Yes. You ought to be sorry. You're why she's dead."

He shocked back a step. A voice rattled through his mind that her response was unfair. It was *not* his fault this woman had died. He didn't stir a rebellion. He wasn't the one who stubbornly refused to free their best defense. And then an even more pointed thought: *I wasn't the one who brought the dragoness aboard the ship in the first place, was I?* It took all the calm he possessed to not blurt these truths out one by one. Instead, he schooled his expression, looked down at his feet, and humbly nodded. "I know. That's why I'm sorry. Truly, I am."

Pearl shouldered past him. He hesitated for a moment, then followed. When she knelt down by the corpse, he knelt down as well, knowing she might snap for him to go away. Instead, he was permitted to help lift Hath's body into the air. Together, they started across the beach. Pearl didn't complain about the weight—and so in spite of the burning pain he felt in both arms, he pressed on and they made it to the waiting graveyard. There was already a discussion happening about the other corpses and where to put them. Gemma—who'd suffered only a minor scrape during the battle—had managed to track down the little book in which he'd written his previous notes about the deceased. She started scribbling what she heard from the others. Before they could begin the work of digging in earnest, he realized he could spare them the effort.

"Wait. Allow me."

Perhaps it was a waste of magic—but at this point, any extra goodwill would go a long way. He withered one flower for each grave, using his spell to scoop away the hardened earth with unnatural ease. When he arrived at the fourth grave, however, Pearl Trask shook her head.

"Stop."

He felt his entire body go rigid. The girl looked ready to shout at him again.

"I'll dig her grave myself."

He wanted to tell her it was no trouble, but he couldn't seem to form the words. Instead, he stood there like a fool until Pearl glanced back up at him.

"Please, just leave me alone for now."

And he did.

19

The survivors didn't hold an official ceremony this time. Instead, when the graves were filled and tamped down, everyone went about the business of saying their private goodbyes—or else they returned to camp, eager to put their hands to use so they could put their minds to rest.

As Pearl whispered goodbye to her aunt, she realized a literal, physical presence was gone from her life. She caught herself leaning slightly to her right. A natural tendency to put all her weight on that half of her body, because normally, when they stood side by side, her aunt had always liked to lean up against her. Pearl had instinctually taught herself to lean back in response. She knew her aunt didn't actually need the support. She'd been as fit and as tough as anyone Pearl had ever met. No, she realized now that her aunt had wanted physical touch. Long separated from her terrible husband—and without any new suitors that Pearl had met—Aunt Hath simply wanted to feel her body pressed briefly to another body. A reminder of her existence and theirs. A sensation that Pearl had taken for granted, not even realizing she was experiencing it until it was gone.

Aunt Hath is . . . gone.

The thought tongued through her mind like lightning. Killing certain ideas. Bringing to life others. Pearl felt the subtle changes happening inside her. Before, she'd been aware of the dangers of this place, but she hadn't felt them in full. There had always been a sense that, as long as Aunt Hath was with her, she'd shield Pearl from the worst that might happen. Just as she'd literally shielded Pearl during the deadly shoot-out the night before.

As she looked around the beach now, she knew no one else here would protect her that way. Sure, she might have some friends and alliances scattered around the camp, but that was not the same as having your own flesh and blood with you. They would not prioritize her safety in a moment of crisis. She was alone. All she had was her voice and her mind and her secrets.

Pearl's insides steeled over. The new version of Pearl looked out almost coldly at their camp. She started by counting up the remaining survivors. Six deckhands were left. Agnes and Helene had both made it, though Agnes had suffered a gut wound during her duel with Kell. It didn't look deadly, but out here? Even a small wound might fester.

Gemma was alive. The elderly woman kept expressing shock over how events had played out—making it obvious she'd not been invited into the plan. Warner had survived as well. The poor businessman didn't look like he was having a good time anymore. None of the usual, overworn jokes. Instead, he'd turned quiet and brooding. Apparently, he'd been left out of the scheme as well.

Curiously, the couple had split. Naomi was with them still. Even now she was handing out rations of food to those who were returning to the fires. Prior, on the other hand, was gone. It tracked that he might have run into the woods with the warden—thinking of him as the only true authority figure worth following out here. Good riddance, as far as Pearl was concerned.

And then there was Marken. The wizard her aunt had believed was the key to their survival. He moved freely about the camp. His magic domed overhead. A glimmering shield that he'd promised would keep the dragoness at bay. Even now she heard the subtle hum of that waiting power. She'd also noted a subtle shift in his attitude. All pleasantries and humility. He seemed to be answering all of Helene's requests, casting spell after spell. She wondered how long that could go on.

Back in Ten Tides, wizards could be ordered by the government to attend to a certain region or crisis—but how they did that was usually up to them. She highly doubted Marken Burke had ever taken such specific orders from anyone in his life. Pearl recalled the way he'd come to her and helped her carry Aunt Hath to the grave site. There was some connection between them. Guilt or loyalty or affection. Maybe all three. That could work in her favor. She'd want to keep him close. If the back-and-forth with Helene began to annoy him, she could become his most trusted ally. It's what her aunt would have told her to do. She felt certain of that.

"Well, what do we do now?"

The question came from old Gemma. She was nervously rubbing that golden locket of hers. The ten other survivors looked around before attention eventually swung to Helene. The deckhand looked rather pleased to be the focal point.

"First, my apologies to anyone who was surprised by last night. We kept that plan to a tight circle, because if the warden caught even the faintest scent of what was happening, he'd have struck first. No hard feelings for anyone who was left out. Our decision came down to one thing: we need *him*." She pointed to Marken Burke. "I don't care what he did back in Ten Tides. As long as he helps us survive this place, his past doesn't matter. See the shield that he cast around camp? We're already twice as safe as we were with all those rotating spears and pistols. Thanks to him."

Pearl bit her tongue. *Twice as safe, unless you're one of the ones who was killed to make us "safe."*

"Maybe the rescue boats come," Helene went on. "Maybe they don't. We're going to organize into two teams. One will be an exploration unit. We need to see what else is on this island. It would help to figure out what's making that awful noise we've been hearing. The other team will stay here and be tasked with building. The idea of making a smaller raft and having the wizard power us home is a viable one. Most of our weapons need to stay with that team. The wizard can be the one who leads the other party out for exploration. If you have a preference, one way or the other, come talk to me. Otherwise, we'll start drawing lots. Daylight is wasting. Let's go."

The selection process was surprisingly smooth. Gemma and

Naomi wanted to remain at camp. Helene ordered Agnes to stay as well, hoping her sister's wound would keep healing, and then she picked three other deckhands to leave behind. Decent strategy, Pearl thought. If Kell and Levi returned, she felt confident none of the ship's ordinary passengers would take up arms against them. None of them could be counted as a reliable number in a fight. Leaving four deckhands—and both pistols—meant they'd have numbers and firepower. Warner raised his hand, like he was a student in a recitation. "I'd like to go. Exploring sounds better than . . . this."

Helene nodded. Her eyes landed on Pearl. "What about you? Staying or going?"

There was a touch of pity in the woman's voice that set Pearl's teeth on edge. Helene felt bad that Aunt Hath had been one of the casualties of their rebellion. As if a little freedom might make up for a loss like that. Pearl considered the decision from a pure survival perspective. Whenever possible, she wanted to be near Marken Burke.

"Going."

Another nod from Helene. "Get prepped and ready. We leave in five."

Everyone started making preparations. It was decided that the exploration party would travel north along the beach. Any suggestions of going *into* the forest were dismissed quickly. No one wanted to risk those tight quarters yet—and Marken agreed that his magic would be more versatile out in the open. Pearl adjusted the straps of her borrowed carrier bag and started after the others.

There were five of them: Marken, Helene, Warner, Pearl, and Wally. She thought the older deckhand was a curious choice, given their goal to range as far and as fast as they could. She'd never seen him move faster than a plodding limp around camp. It took until the first slight bend in the beach for Pearl to figure out Helene had left the best fighters back at camp with her sister. A protective move—and the first whisper of weakness she'd seen. If she was making decisions to prioritize one person's safety? Pearl might be able to take advantage of that if she needed to later.

"So . . ." Marken said, as the camp grew more and more distant behind them. "Everyone having a pretty good time on the island so far?"

That jolted a laugh out of her. She couldn't help it. One part of her wanted to throw a rock at his head, but another part appreciated how he never quite lost his sense of humor. Even after all that had happened to them. He offered her a quick smile that reminded her of the wink back aboard the ship. She'd have to ask him about that. Whether or not she'd been imagining things. Just not in front of the others. Instead, she said the only other thought on her mind.

"You know, you're pretty annoying."

His smile only widened hearing that. "Yes. I've been told. I believe it was Senator Vern who referred to me as 'an insufferable, crass little thing.' I'll confess, that was the moment that I gave up my future in politics. Decided I'd focus on the whole 'magic' bit instead."

Ahead, Pearl saw another slight curve in the beach. She'd been expecting rocky shorelines. Maybe an inlet or two. The waiting beach appeared to be surprisingly uniform, however. A nearly perfect match for the stretch of beach they were leaving behind. Helene picked up the conversation.

"Were you really the second most powerful wizard in Ten Tides?"

Marken sighed. "I mean, if you're speaking in terms of pure talent? Sure. I doubt they would have really elected me as the next high mage, though. Again, politics. I don't shake enough hands. I'm too young. I . . . annoy people."

He was using Pearl's words, trying to make it sound like a joke, but she heard a flicker of insecurity beneath all his playfulness. He seemed like the kind of person who knew a lot of people but didn't have many actual friends. Hearing his response—and considering Helene had been the one to open the door—she decided she was allowed to be curious too.

"What's your anchor point?"

He stared back at her. "My anchor point? God's body. That's a pretty personal question to ask a wizard, you know. Like asking how old someone is or how much money they make."

She would have liked to know those answers, too. Normally she'd have dropped the subject and tried her best to avoid anything awkward. But the bolder version of Pearl wanted to press back.

"What? You don't trust us? This is the alliance that risked their lives to free you."

He considered her words as they continued to walk. She had no doubt some snarky comment was forming on the tip of his tongue, but then he surprised her with honesty instead.

"Lightflowers," he said softly. "I am anchored to a field of lightflowers."

His words cast a lovely image into her mind. It was nearly enough to distract her from the boredom of their current surroundings. A repeat of softly sloping shoreline, gentle waves, and the flanking forest. Pearl found that detail nagging at the edges of her mind. An answer to a question that she didn't know to ask.

"I'm surprised you can access them," Helene was saying. "From all the way out here."

"Distance doesn't matter," Marken answered. "The land and the tides—they're connected. Every molecule in this world has brushed shoulders with the rest. Or if you're religious, it's all the massive body of a fallen god and the arm's connected to the shoulder, which is connected to the neck, and so on and so on. Whatever you believe, we've learned that it's all bound. You could be on the other side of the known worlds and still reach your anchor point. There are only three ways a wizard can be disconnected from their magic: the destruction of their anchor point, a null thread, or—"

"Height," Pearl supplied. "They learned that during the *Razorback* Experiment."

Marken's face lit up. "Well, well, well. Someone's read their obscure history books. Yes, the *Razorback* Experiment. It was one of the first commissioned airships. Not sure if you all ever crossed paths with them?!"

This he directed to Helene. She shook her head, but old Wally chimed in from behind them. "I crewed on that ship for a year. My first paying gig. Good captain. Solid crew."

"Well," Marken said, and once more Pearl saw how he warmed to these sorts of subjects. "When the ship was too old to pass inspections, they used it for testing. Wizards were taken up to heights that those ships would normally never risk. After quite a few attempts, they determined there *is* a height that wizards can travel to that separates them from their magic.

Some prat called it the Primal Height. It was the one place in the worlds where the 'God's body' was inaccessible. If you subscribe to that particular dogma. Obviously different religions had different opinions about what the discovery meant. All we really know is that the experiment proved our power derives from the land—and from the things that live in it."

Helene looked bored by this more academic turn in the conversation. "Why'd you pick flowers? It's kind of feminine, isn't it?"

Marken frowned. It was clear he'd never even thought of that. "The flowers I anchored to are hidden in a valley that's well protected, which means they're unlikely to be destroyed or discovered. They're also relatively uniform in size. That offers predictable measurements for each of my spells. Besides, those societal norms you're thinking of regarding flowers and bright colors and who gets to enjoy which things? Well, magic doesn't particularly care about any of that. Those pretty flowers of mine have created some of the most devastating and powerful spells ever cast in Ten Tides history."

There was defensiveness creeping into his voice. Pearl also noticed the way he seemed to catch himself mid-sentence. The word "devastating" was dangerously close to drawing the group's attention back to the fact that he was currently accused of murder. Marken redirected, almost too abruptly, and Pearl knew he was hoping to distract them from that.

"What would have been a more 'masculine' choice, in your opinion?"

Helene shrugged. "I don't know. Wolves?"

Marken snorted. "Right. Wolves. Okay, let's say I anchored to a pack of wolves. The largest groups have twenty members, but an average pack has eight. So, does each spell I use kill off one of them? If so, then I'll need to plan out a magical career in which I can cast eight total spells. Not exactly an intelligent decision, is it? Besides, most wizards avoid animals. It's annoying enough to deal with all of these mayors and governors who want you to walk them through every spell you're planning to use while you're in their city and exactly what the consequences of each one will be. Trust me, it's far harder to explain all of that when they know you'll also be killing off a litter of cats to get the job done." He shook his head as if this was an argument he'd had a dozen times. "Now, insects? Far more palatable. No one's going to bat an eye if you're draining inchworms to cast your spells, but anything that's small and fuzzy and vaguely pet-shaped? Not worth the trouble. You'd have protestors in the town square demanding your resignation. Just ask Anson Moore how all that goes . . ."

Pearl's stomach had turned uncomfortably with the direction the conversation had taken. She found herself wishing she'd never brought it up in the first place.

"He was . . . killing cats?" Helene asked.

"Not cats," Marken replied. "That was someone else. No, Anson killed horses. He was *really* wealthy. His father was some kind of duke. Anyways, when he finished his training, he returned to his father's main paddock and anchored himself to their herd. He thought it was clever, because they were so well protected from the outside world. But he also made the mistake of assuming he could kill off small parts of the horse. A hair or a hoof or an eye. The same way some wizards drain the life of a single leaf instead of killing the entire tree."

"I'm guessing it didn't work that way?" Helene asked.

"No. He didn't have that much control over his magic. So, every time he cast a spell, he'd end up killing the entire horse. Now, the magic he produced *was* powerful. It had no nuance or creativity whatsoever, but the sheer amount of force he could draw each time was *absurd*. There's a shield-wall that he cast around Pasca's harbor that's still there. No one's ever had to touch the thing up. It's that strong. But when people figured out the horses on his family farm weren't just getting sick, and that he was the one responsible for their deaths, no one wanted to hire him. His father was pissed too. He'd killed off two of his best racing horses."

"That's grim," Helene concluded. Pearl agreed. She was starting to feel truly sick to her stomach. A little lightheaded, too. Helene couldn't stop asking questions, though. "Is it true that you can control people? Make them do what you want with magic?"

The new topic drew a smile from Marken. "If I could do that, do you think I'd be here? When the warden showed up to arrest me, I would have just told him to go away if I had that kind of talent. No, you're thinking of silvertongues. One of the 'deviant magics,' as they're officially labeled by the Ten Tides government."

"Why deviant?" Helene asked.

"Oh, it's just a fancy way of labeling them as *other*. Most wizards—like me—channel and shape magic with our hands. It's all about touch and feel and manipulating the drawn power with distinct hand motions. We're like . . . potters with invisible clay, you could say. And that's how ninety-nine percent of wizards wield magic. The rest of them are considered deviant branches. People who shape magic in some other, unique way.

Eyelocks possess a sort of visual magic. Auralites can magically adapt their hearing. I knew one who could hear the truth being whispered underneath the words people were actually speaking. Always thought that was fascinating. He hated it, though. It's apparently rather difficult to go on a date when you can hear what someone really thinks about you between bites. Anyways. Silvertongues, they're the most famous deviant branch. Wizards who can weave magic into spoken commands. Forcing people to do their bidding, as you put it."

"Famous? Really?" Helene asked skeptically. "I couldn't name one."

"Exactly," Marken replied. "That's why the Ten Tides government designated them as 'deviant' magic in the first place. It made it easier to outlaw silvertongues altogether. That's why you can't name one. Most are executed before they can become properly famous. Every now and again, you'll hear about some duchess or prince who's been secretly employing one of them. Thinking they'll get the upper hand in all their business dealings without anyone finding out. But the inevitable always happens. They start wondering, 'Hey, if this person can control my enemies, then how do I know they won't do the same to *me*?' It always ends with a public apology, an execution, and then a bunch of senators whining about instating new policies . . ."

Pearl had stopped walking. Her stomach was tight as a corkscrew. She could feel sweat prickling along her forehead. She wasn't the only one who'd stopped. Warner had paused farther back down the beach. He was pointing inland.

"Hey . . . is . . . is that . . ."

All of them turned. All of them saw it. Right there, in a gap between the trees, was a massive tower. There was no natural explanation. It could only be something man-made. Constructed of some sort of dark stone that refused to reflect back the light of day to them. They were still quite a distance away from the structure, but she guessed it had to be at least four stories high. It was truly a shock that they hadn't seen it from their own beach. The trees there must have been just tall enough to blot out their view. She wondered, too, how the deckhands hadn't seen it during the crash. Maybe there hadn't been enough light yet? It had been predawn when they'd stumbled onto the beach. Pearl felt her stomach settling. The focus of the group shifting to that distant place helped. Marken, in his usual way, said what they were all thinking.

"Can't really call us an exploration party if we don't go explore that, can we?"

No one smiled, though. The tower was too strange and ominous a thing to joke about, but his words confirmed their new plan. Abandon the beach. Explore the tower. All of them started walking in that direction at the same time. Who had built it? Was there anyone still there? And how had they built something like this so far out to sea? Why build here at all? Surely those questions were echoing in the minds of the others. No one spoke them out loud. Instead, they stumbled over the dunes, hesitated briefly at the edge of the forest, and then plunged into the waiting half shadows.

Almost as if they were being drawn to that place.

20

Marken kept his magic close. There was a certain art to quick casting that he'd learned through years of practice. It relied on the ability to keep his mind partially split. One part of him navigating the forest while the other was reaching for lightflowers, ready to pull magic across time and space to defend them as needed. He hadn't been this excited in a long time. It felt like some of his earliest missions. When he'd been tasked to investigate some random mystery and was allowed to temporarily play the role of detective. As they walked, he thought it might be wise to keep learning about their potential enemies out here. Especially in the tighter quarters of the forest.

"Pearl," he said. "What else can you tell us about the dragoness?"

He saw the usual flicker of surprise on her face. *God's body, did no one ever speak with you before? Were you never asked questions where you came from? Why are you always so surprised when someone says your name?* Those nervous reactions made her more courageous moments—moving to help the windmaster and being the first to face the dragoness—even more mysterious. For the first time, he wondered if that nervous exterior was for their benefit? A facade she wore in public? Could it be that the real version of her was the one they'd seen in those other moments?

"What do you want to know?" Pearl asked. "I only did some pre—some minor research."

Marken held back a smile. *It sounded like you were about to say the word "preliminary." Careful now, Pearl. I know your secret, but I doubt you want the deckhands to figure it out. They'd have a new person to hate.*

"Well, your *minor* research is better than my usual approach of *no* research. I'd personally enjoy hearing more about how the thing managed to become a human."

Pearl nodded. "There wasn't anything like that in what I read. I told the warden it might have been the first time it's ever happened. But what she did matches the normal transformation process. When she touches something with her claws, she can draw the knowledge of that substance into her armor. If she touches water, she can create a water form. Sand would summon a sand skin. It just so happened that her claws were . . . in human flesh at the time."

He saw Pearl dart a nervous glance over to Helene. The man who'd died that night was one of her fellow deckhands, but if the memory of his death upset her, Helene didn't show it.

"It's fascinating," Marken said. "How many skins do you think she's learned by now?"

"Well, there's sand, stone, water, and human so far. I thought she might have some kind of metallic form, because of that noise we were hearing . . ."

"But now we know it's possible the noise was coming from *that*."

Marken nodded to the tower. It was getting larger and closer with each break in the tree line. He guessed they had just a few more minutes left before they reached it. Thankfully, there'd been no sign of the dragoness—or the warden. He'd been quietly scanning gaps in the trees just in case. He half hoped Kell and Levi *would* attempt to spring a trap. He'd prefer a direct fight. Easier to sort things out here and now than to get home and find himself being hunted all over again.

"Exactly," Pearl said. "She might not have a metallic form— but I think we can assume a woodland skin based on all the trees out here. The other thing is that once she has a skin, she has it forever. She can always access that ability and rotate between them as she pleases. For now the stone skin seems the most dangerous to us."

Marken shrugged. "It would make our pistols and spears less effective, but I like the idea of meeting her in stone form. I've got quite a few counterspells for that element."

Pearl looked relieved by that. So did the others. Marken found that he rather enjoyed being seen as useful again. It was far better than the sideways glances people seemed to reserve for people who were accused of murder.

"There are some elements I hope she doesn't find," Pearl was saying. "Like diamond. Or fire. Fire would summon a pretty terrifying form."

Marken nodded. "We'll have to keep an eye on our campfires. The other day, I heard you say that she's territorial. Is that why she's hunting us? We're in her territory?"

"Not really, no. I mean, it doesn't help that we're out on the same beach that she'd like to occupy—but the bigger issue is that she purposed herself to hunt us. Dragonesses are known for that. The females in the species select a purpose, and they primarily focus on that task for the rest of their lives. People have started trying to domesticate them—and the first step is trying to guide that purpose into something helpful. This dragoness just happened to decide it was her sacred duty to feed us to the moon or whatever it was." The girl paused for a moment, chewing on her lip, then looked around at the others. "I'm sorry about that, by the way. On the beach, I tried my best to lead her in some other direction, but I . . . I think I screwed it up. It's like I pushed her even further."

Helene defended the girl before Marken could. "We were all there, Pearl. You did your best. If you hadn't stepped forward, it might have been even worse. You bought enough time for Kell to slip Marken free so he could blast her. Who knows how many people would have died if you hadn't talked to her for a few minutes? The creature seemed pretty set on that course from the start of the conversation."

Marken nodded his own enthusiastic affirmation. Pearl gave her usual shy smile and the group kept walking. Their path had tightened somewhat uncomfortably, running into more and more choke points along the way. Wally was the first one to point out that there were no bird sounds. No wild animals darting out of their path. Not even the usual sounds of crickets or frogs. Pearl said her aunt had noticed the same thing the first night.

"It's a strange island," Helene confirmed. "Even the beaches are odd. No real diversity at all. I've visited plenty of islands over the years. You'll see huge cliffs in some spots. Sandy dunes in others. Big inlets or bays. We walked for half an hour, and there was nothing."

Marken hadn't noticed that, but he felt certain of one thing. "We're about to find some answers."

For the first time, he noticed that Warner was counting under his breath. He frowned before realizing the man was counting their footsteps. Trying to measure out exactly how far inland they'd walked. Perhaps the businessman wasn't a completely useless addition on the trip. Navigating became trickier. Not because of undulations—the land was mostly flat—but because there was no true trail. Often they would walk through what felt like an opening and find themselves in even denser forest than before. They'd also left behind the breeze back on the beach. The forest was swampier—all the heat from the sun but without any of the ocean's relief. Marken was starting to recall how much he actually hated "adventures" when the group broke through a thicket of low-hanging branches. Helene stumbled to a halt. The others fell silent as they took in the view.

It was not just a tower.

There were buildings. A small circle of buildings constructed around the tower's base. Marken stared along with the others. The huddle of dark structures looked old but not ancient. The style suggested something built in the last few decades. He found himself squinting.

"It's abandoned," Pearl said.

Marken glanced over. "You can see that far?"

"We would see movement," she replied. "There's none."

Helene was less certain. "There's plenty of places to hide over there. If it was abandoned, it's possible our two friends found it already. If they did, there's no chance they moved on to some other part of the island. Not with all this natural shelter. Potential supplies. It's very possible they're here. We need to proceed with caution."

Once more there was no question about whether or not they should explore the place. Going forward wasn't their safest option, but which one of them could resist the lure of the waiting mystery? What was this place? Who'd built it and why? There was something faintly familiar about the tower and the buildings, but Marken couldn't put his finger on what exactly felt familiar. Not without getting closer and seeing everything eye to eye.

"Weapons at the ready," he said. "I'll take the lead."

It was a mostly useless command. Their group had no pistols. He wondered if Helene regretted her decision to leave them now. She and Wally had spears—though he wasn't sure that Wally had the agility to do much with his. Pearl and Warner both held knives out before them. At a glance, they didn't look sharp enough to actually cut through flesh.

I suppose it really is up to me to keep you lot safe.

"With me, then."

They started forward. The first building was by far the largest. A primary residence? But as he assessed the other structures, he felt certain they were homes too. Which told him what, exactly? Did the first building simply belong to the wealthiest person who'd lived here? Or the biggest family? As he walked, there were no signs that the other structures were built with other uses in mind. He saw no ironworks or butchers or any of the usual additions you might find in smaller, isolated communities. That suggested they'd built this place with the belief that they'd have regular contact with the outside world. Regular imports, at least. But from where? This island was well beyond any of the normal trade routes. Were they smugglers? He'd raided plenty of underground organizations and he couldn't remember any that used such fine building materials as these. The tower, with its elegant stonework and polished finish, seemed entirely out of place. Even if it was some sort of lookout tower, most smugglers would have thrown together a crow's nest on the tallest tree and called it a day.

"And where'd they get these stones from?" he wondered out loud.

The others were too busy taking in the village to hear him. As he looked around, he felt this was something else. Something more than a smuggler's den. Between each building, he saw abandoned gardens. Nothing was growing. That was a little surprising. Even untended gardens would sometimes go wild with growth. They might not produce the *best* crops, because of a lack of pruning and attention, but there'd be *something* growing. Everything here had shriveled and wasted.

As their group circled the tower, they all saw a . . . lump. That was the best word he could think of for it. A human-shaped lump. It was not Levi or Kell. This figure had been decaying for some time—and there was a curious set of clues arrayed all around it. First he saw the windows of the nearest buildings had been blasted out, leaving dusty, gaping frames. Half of one roof had caved in and even the metalwork framing the doors had bent and warped. The body, he saw, was lying next to what had once been a well. Now it was mostly rubble.

Dead ground ringed the body, fighting away the growth of wild grass in a perfect circle. Even the tower on that side had taken some damage, Marken noted. The stones were bent slightly inward. Not quite enough to bring the entire thing down, but it wouldn't have taken much more to accomplish that task. Marken paused beside the body and looked up. Near the very top of the tower, there were windows. They offered a view in every direction. Even from below, he could see that the window on this side of the tower had shattered.

For him, it was a final clue falling neatly into place.

"I know what happened," he said. "And I know where we are."

Before he could finish his sentence, a gunshot sounded. There was that brief *flinching*. One of his shields flickered to life, summoned in a split second, but the shot was not from any nearby pistol. It sounded far away. Back by the beach. They all heard a second shot, slightly muted by his shield, but there was no doubt now. Something was happening at camp.

An attack was underway.

21

Pearl saw the tortured expression on Helene's face. The woman hesitated, only for a moment, and then started jogging away from the tower.

"Come on," she called back. "We need to help them."

"Helene," Marken said, his voice unnervingly calm. "It's too late for that."

The deckhand's head whipped around. The stare she offered him was the single coldest and most frightening thing Pearl had witnessed since landing. A promise there would be blood if he said anything like that again. Not that Marken was likely to lose a duel between them. Pearl saw Helene's predicament immediately. The realization that this power she'd unleashed to serve her purposes wasn't truly in her control. There had seemed a mutual dependency, but if push came to shove, he was powerful enough to excuse himself from any demand.

"Look," Marken said, trying to keep the peace. "I'm not saying I won't help. I'm just trying to think logically. They had my shield-wall. They had the pistols. If it's Kell and Levi, they probably chased them off. If it's the dragoness, hopefully one well-aimed shot sent her running. By the time we get back there, the fight will already be over. We can't *help*. We can only survey the damage. Good or bad. We can't make a difference by rushing back. I think we need to discuss this—"

"More talking? While my friends die?"

Pearl sympathized with both parties. Marken was being gentle for once, and Helene's fear of losing her sister was palpable. Seeing the normally calm woman with her chest heaving up and down brought out a darker thought: *Good. Now you know how I feel.*

"We can't risk losing the tower," Marken said bluntly. "If Kell or Levi find this place and take control of it, even I would have a hard time wrestling it back from them. This place . . . do you know who Heatherly is? This island is *her* island. It's one of the—"

"Damn your stories," Helene said, spitting on the ground. "I'm going back. Either you're with me or you aren't, wizard. I'll remember this choice. How many enemies do you want out here?"

The tension between them held taut for a few seconds. A cord that Pearl felt she could reach out and pluck like the whisper-tight string of a violin. It was finally broken by Wally. "I'll stay. Go back—the lot of you. I'll stay here and watch the tower. Too tired to walk back anyways."

Marken's face showed exactly what he thought of this plan. Without him saying a word, she knew he believed that Wally had as much chance of defending their tower as a stray cat. But then Warner surprised them by volunteering as well. "How about that? The two of us stationed at the door? We can hold it. If this place is that important, we'll sit right inside there and bar the door until you get back."

Marken glanced around before bowing his head in defeat. "This tower is our way home. Helene, I'll go with you but we need to move fast. This is crucial."

Nods all around—and then their smaller group was on the move. Just the three of them, starting off at a jog back through the woods. Marken's mention of Heatherly was the missing clue that Pearl had needed to arrive at the answer. Heatherly was famous. One of the more powerful wizards of the previous generation. Her most famous magic? The three portable islands. Pearl knew the woman had sold two of those islands to the Ten Tides government. Those two were the same ones everyone saw moving up and down the eastern seaboard of the continent. Over the years, they'd become two of the most profitable mobile markets in existence.

Every few years, someone would write an article in the papers predicting that airships were on the verge of replacing them. Or maybe the new trains that were being built out west. But the truth was that the islands could use the tides to move at a speed the airships still couldn't match. Combined with their size—the sheer scale of goods they could move from location to location—and there really wasn't any one-to-one comparison. The rumor was that Heatherly had retired on her third island and would only occasionally bring it back to dock on Ten Tides soil. A decade ago, however, the third island had gone missing. Heatherly and her extended family had gone missing with it.

Until now.

As Pearl raced after the others, a stitch forming in her side, she understood the intensity Marken had shown. If the wherestone couldn't find them and if constructing another vessel from the wreckage proved impossible—then their new way home was the island itself. She hadn't seen the other islands before. She cursed herself for being too nervous to glance over the railing at the outset of their voyage. But she suspected those other islands would have a tower like the one they'd just left behind. She also suspected that tower either housed the mechanism for how the island was controlled and steered, or it *was* the mechanism. Marken hadn't had the time to inspect it, but his hope had to be the same hope she had now: that whatever incident had caused the island to be "lost" in the first place hadn't damaged it beyond repair. That they would be able to get the mechanisms working again, at least long enough to get them home.

Ahead, she felt the slightest pulse of magic in the air. The forming stitch in her side vanished. The subtle pain in her calves went away too. Marken called back to both of them.

"Pick up the pace. I've just cast boons on both of you. Come on."

She'd never felt anything quite like it. The way her body elevated to match the spell he'd put over her. Even as she picked up her pace, there was no physical consequence. She even felt more sure-footed than normal, darting over and around stray roots with ease. The three of them made it back to the beach in less than half the time it had taken to journey out to the tower in the first place.

"This way."

Helene led them south. Pearl saw the way she tucked into

the tree line to hide her approach. Marken and Pearl followed suit, trying to keep moving at speed, but hoping any potential enemies would not see them until it was too late. Her stomach was turning once again. The prospect of waiting violence stirring uncomfortably. Her mind flickered briefly back to the pig pens as she searched for that familiar, calming assurance. She breathed in the sweat and the mud and the distant scent of a wood fire. It settled her nerves as they turned the corner and their camp came into view.

"Where are they?" Helene asked. "I don't see anyone."

The camp was empty. Abandoned much like the buildings they'd just left behind. There were signs of a struggle, though. The main "structure" at the heart of camp had been knocked over. Items were scattered around.

"My shield's gone," Marken noted.

She could feel him holding magic, ready and waiting, in the palm of his hand. Unshaped but crackling with a waiting heat. If the dome was gone, that meant the dragoness was the likeliest attacker. Although it seemed possible that someone who could use null magic might be able to dispel active magic? She wasn't sure. No one had discussed that possibility. She moved into Marken's shadow, eyes flicking from the tree line to the water with an equal amount of fear. Helene was the one who spotted the next clue.

"Blood. There's blood here . . ."

Now that they saw it, Pearl wasn't sure how they'd missed it in the first place. A terrible trail pointing into the forest. Evidence, too, of a body being dragged. She swallowed at the sight of it, and then pointed out the one positive she could think to point out.

"It looks like just . . . one body. Right?"

The dragoness had left tracks on either side, and it was clear she'd been dragging the body with her teeth as she backpedaled into the waiting forest. Someone was dead, but the tracks seemed to suggest just one person had been killed. That was better than finding the entire camp dead.

"Then where's everyone else?" Marken asked.

The answer was waiting for them on the southern end of the beach. She saw a few dots of blood, but not anything like the other trail. There were several sets of footprints. All human. Whoever had survived the initial attack had fled that way. Pearl could only assume that the dragoness hadn't pursued them. There were no signs of her tracks. Evidence pointed to an attack, two gunshots being fired, and then at least one mortal blow. The others had run, and instead of hunting them, she'd taken the time to finish off her other quarry.

"I want to pursue her," Marken said, his voice deadly calm. "It's possible she's still feeding. It's only been about ten minutes. This trail—it looks fresh."

Helene looked too terrified to weigh in on the decision. One dead was better than they'd initially feared, but the one who was dead could still be her sister. "I'm going to find my crew."

"We split, then. Pearl?"

It wasn't like before. Helene had given her the decision to stay or go out of some sense of pity. Marken seemed to *want* her to come with him. There was an abandoned spear nearby. She plucked it out of the sand, wiped the blood on the hem of her shirt, and then nodded.

"I'll come with you."

Helene didn't wait for further discussion. She started south at a jog. Pearl and Marken exchanged a weighty glance, then turned to face the darkening woods. The sun wasn't set. Not yet, but it had slid low enough on the horizon to leave everything in a thicker set of shadows than what they'd traversed a few minutes before. After gathering their courage, both started forward.

Into the woods.

22

Marken *liked* this part.

When the adrenaline started burning to life in his chest. When there was an enemy waiting for him in the distance. He might not know how to shake the right hands or speak the most eloquent words, but when it came to a fight? There was no one else in the world he'd bet on over himself. The more powerful wizards lacked his versatility. The most creative mages lacked his punch. He was, in so many respects, the deadliest person in the world.

That power didn't make him a fool, though. He knew the creature he was currently hunting was dangerous in her own right. A proven and capable predator. He followed a winding trail of blood into the darkling woods with his eyes open and his magic ready.

Finally, a proper battle.

He could hear Pearl Trask following after him. He considered suggesting that she go back to Helene, stay safe, but she deserved to make up her own mind at this point. The resolute way she'd claimed her spear and trailed him into the woods spoke volumes. Now the two of them moved like forest ghosts down the trail. There was a grassy hush to each step they took, as both of them did their best to walk where the moss had grown the thickest. His senses prickled as he rounded one of the thicker trees. He shoved a fist into the air and Pearl paused beside him.

There was the victim.

Pen. The woman was lying in the middle of a clearing about thirty paces away, staring lifelessly up at the canopy. Her chest had three great slashes across it. Blood puddled in each one. Marken maneuvered a little closer to the scene and could just make out a streak of blood beyond her. Moving on into another section of the forest. A few splashes and half of a footprint. For some reason, the dragoness had dragged the woman this far and then left. He was weighing the likelihood that Kell or Levi might be nearby when a sudden *gasp* made him jump. The woman was trying to breathe. Still alive. Choking on her own blood. Her hands reached out. Desperate for anyone to come and find her.

Marken kept his eyes pinned to the gap through which the dragoness had vanished and then started forward. He tapped one ear, trying to indicate to Pearl that she should listen out for any movement. The girl stayed pinned to his hip, her spear up and ready. Pen was still coughing obscenely. As they got closer, and she saw them, her eyes shocked wide with the sort of pure, adrenal fear that he'd only ever seen in the near dead.

"It's okay," Pearl whispered. "We're here, Pen. It's going to be okay."

Marken thought that was a bit too much to promise the woman, but he bent down and set to work on her wounds. Pearl kept whispering affirmations. He reached for a simple spell that would close and seal the three main gashes. It wasn't proper medical practice, where you'd cleanse the wound and cast something for infections, but he'd never learned any of those more nuanced castings. Besides, he felt the important thing was to stop the bleeding given how much she'd already lost. Pearl's eyes widened when the wounds puckered tightly back together.

"You can . . . seal someone up? Just like that?"

"I tried to tell you all back on the ship. I could have helped."

He saw the gears turning in her mind. All that might have been avoided if the warden had simply released Marken back on the ship. He decided it was best not to mention that if he *had* been freed, he likely would have commandeered the *Grand Gesture* and forced Captain Lyn to land them at an undisclosed location of his own choosing. All of that felt rather beside the point.

As he started treating Pen's other abrasions, he noticed the woman trying to mouth something. Her lips worked open and shut like a fish. Pearl leaned in. The woman coughed again and Marken winced seeing the little splashes of blood. He wasn't generally squeamish, but the idea of having someone breathe their blood on his skin? That was where he drew the line. Pearl must have had a stronger stomach, because she bent again to listen to what the woman was trying to say.

Her eyes shocked wide.

That was his only warning. Pearl turned and shoved Marken hard in the chest. He went stumbling back a step, and it was just enough to save his life. A claw raked down the length of his right shoulder. He cried out as his skin split and his muscle nearly ripped apart. The force of the attack sent him spinning away, but he knew on instinct it was a glancing blow. The dragoness had meant to crush his spine—and had missed by a fraction. As he fell, he reached for his magic. A brief severance of time and space. The flowers draining at his touch, and then *power*. One extra roll brought him onto his back, staring up at the huntress, his magic at the ready. He blinked at what he saw.

The forest was *moving*.

Leaves and roots and vines shifted in such a way that he couldn't immediately make out where the creature's body ended and where the forest began. When he finally saw her, she was bigger than expected. That first night, he'd hit her with a spell right as she transformed—and then he'd cast another spell as she was fleeing. The encounter had left him with the wrong impression. That she was a little larger than a person. Now he saw that she was over ten feet tall and even longer from nose to tail. Her entire body was armored in green scales to match their surroundings. These interlocked with slabs of bark and twisting roots. Great vines tossed from side to side along her back like a mane. Only the creature's eyes, bright and blue, stood out against the forest backdrop. Her mouth opened in a hiss. That glimpse of teeth was a fine reminder that he was about to die.

She lunged, but he was faster. A shove of magical force had him gliding away from her outstretched claws. He'd picked up this talent through years of tighter combat. Spellcasting was the simple art of using summoned energy to push and pull one's self through the combat zone. Like using a wind no one else knew was there to avoid the enemy's attacks while striking with your own. He smiled grimly as the dragoness skidded by where he'd just been, and then reached for his second spell. This one formed in the air—a crackling sphere—and he concentrated the summoned energy into a blast of pure, blunt force. There was a great *crack* as it struck the creature's side. She let out something that was half hiss and half scream. His third spell came a fraction later. As she tried to escape, he drew like to like. The roots on the ground sprang upward. They snatched at her legs, roping her in place.

His fourth spell demanded adaptation. He hadn't known what form he'd be facing. For wood, fire worked best. The air filled with a sudden, rippling heat. He didn't bother shaping it. Fire preferred chaos. It was meant to spread. He unleashed a blast. A split second too late.

The dragoness transformed. Desperate to break free, she burst into flames. A conflagration so hot that he was forced to avert his eyes, stumbling briefly away. When he turned back, he saw her—an inferno in the shape of some towering lioness. Her claws looked like burnished embers. Only her eyes were unchanged. She released a furious roar that sent flame spitting in his direction. Any other wizard would have panicked. Not Marken Burke.

He'd planned for this. "Got you."

To kill a flame? Deprive it of oxygen. He unleashed his final spell. There was a great rush of wind as he suctioned out one of the core elements to her current existence. The first wave of his spell had the flickering edges of her form rippling inward. Another push of his magic and her entire body looked on the verge of collapsing. He thought he could see the bones underneath. Whatever she was without these precious skins she'd collected.

One. More. Push.

But then he saw Helene. He didn't know where she'd come from or when she'd arrived, but she stood behind the dragoness. She was taking aim with one of the pistols. He tried to shout a warning, to tell her he had this under control, but she fired the weapon not knowing how terrible a mistake she was making. The bullet *exploded* against the fiery exterior of the dragoness. A great splash of force and energy and air that canceled out his trap. He felt the magic slip out of his grasp.

The dragoness sensed it too. She transformed in that moment of freedom—from fire into wood—and before he could cast his next spell, she'd snaked through the nearest gap in the trees. He ran after her, high-stepping roots as he went, but she was clever enough to keep out of his line of sight. He lost her just a few seconds after that.

"Damn it," he shouted. "I had her! She was finished!"

He shook his head. It took effort to not curse Helene for what she'd done. He knew she had no clue how close they'd been to defeating the dragoness just now. When he finally turned back, he saw she'd lowered her weapon. The rest of the survivors were huddled in the shadows beyond. All of them came tentatively forward. The deckhands knelt down next to Pen. Marken saw the woman was no longer coughing or twitching. No, her body had gone perfectly still. Helene performed the task of closing the woman's eyes.

Dead.

He sagged down against the nearest tree. *God's body, I was so close.* The usual post-magic exhaustion was claiming his limbs. Tugging him away from the waking world. It was Pearl who eventually came to keep him drifting too far. She knelt down beside him the same way the deckhands had been kneeling next to Pen.

"Are you okay?"

He nodded. "You saved me. Thanks for that."

"Trap," Pearl said grimly. "That's what she whispered to me."

Marken nodded again. A clever trap at that. The dragoness had dragged the woman through the forest and then left her there, knowing *someone* would eventually pursue. She'd blended back in with the canopy, positioned herself above the victim, and waited. It was possible that the trap had been intended to catch any of the survivors, but he felt certain it's true design was for him. If that was the case, then the dragoness was smart enough to know who her greatest threat was. And patient enough to sacrifice someone as bait. She was far more cunning than most predators. Worse, she'd be more resistant to his magic the next time they faced each other. A standard law of diminishing returns stated that it was more difficult to subject the same form to repetitive magic. She'd have an edge against him. Several edges, really.

"Your shoulder. It's kind of bleeding a lot."

Marken saw how the front of his shirt had begun to heavily stain. To his surprise, Pearl pulled something from her carrier bag and started tending to the wound. She pressed a spare shirt to it, holding tight. He realized it was the closest the two of them had really been to that point. He wasn't someone who was accustomed to physical touch. If anything, he'd grown used to people keeping their distance. As such, he couldn't help the way his entire body involuntarily shuddered as her hand lingered by his collarbone. If Pearl noticed, she didn't say anything. Instead, she sat there in silence, keeping him alive yet again.

"It's getting dark," Helene announced. "Do we head for the tower or the beach?"

"Tower," he and Pearl said at the same time. She offered a quick smile, then surprised him again by reaching for his hand. He shivered, mistaking the gesture for something intimate, but then she carefully set his free hand atop the cloth on his opposite shoulder.

"You're going to want to keep it tight," she said. "Tight enough to stop the flow of blood."

"Thanks," he whispered back.

She pushed to her feet, maneuvering back to the rest of the group to discuss resources and numbers. Thankfully, Agnes had been wise enough to secure the crate with the rest of their food inside. The supply was running lower and lower each day, but for now it was all that was really keeping them fueled. When Marken realized they were all waiting on him, he awkwardly took his feet.

The adrenaline of the fight with the dragoness was fading. Now his mind was forced to shift to an entirely new fear. What had happened back at the tower? Were Warner and Wally still there? Was their way home secure? He also couldn't help glancing over at Pearl every few seconds. He caught her doing the same. Apparently they were both aware of the sudden strangeness looming between them. This unique bond. This pulsing interest. A promise that whispered in his ear: *if we are to survive, we need to survive together.* As the light faded, they started walking to the distant tower.

23

Pearl struggled to prioritize her thoughts.

There was the instinctual fear that came when any creature that large simply dropped from the canopy on top of you. Then there was the understanding that she hadn't been the target of the attack. The dragoness clearly understood Marken was a threat to her and had set up that trap with a specific pecking order in mind. It was an interesting adaptation on her part.

And then there was everything Pearl had witnessed *after* the initial shock of the moment. She'd been knocked away. By the time she'd turned around, Marken had been in full battle mode. His magic was breathlessly quick and surgically precise. She'd noted the way he slid to one side—spellcasting, she'd heard it called—using the actual flow of his summoned magic. There was also the way he'd cast spell after spell without a moment's hesitation. She knew she needed to speak with him again, when everything calmed down, but she felt certain he'd nearly won. Before Helene fired her weapon. The primary lesson was that all his bravado was deserved. He was really that good.

Finally there was what happened after-after to unpack. The numbness of another death, but also the undeniable connection between her and Marken. When she'd first watched him board the ship, she'd thought him too handsome to even consider. Boys like him never fell for girls like her. She was too plain. It had been so easy to dismiss the possibility. But she'd discovered that he was not the boy who'd thrown her a random wink at the start of the journey. No, he was fumbling and soft and unpracticed. Remarkable with magic, sure, but a total novice on every social front. She had felt the way his *entire* body trembled beneath her touch. A reaction to their proximity. A reaction to *her*. And what was a connection like that? If not another potential path to power?

Pearl filed the thought away as the group continued inland. The dark tower was framed by a bruised-purple sky. Night was shoving dusk aside. She saw the lightless, hunched buildings come into view. She could not help wondering if their two sentries had survived. Would they find themselves facing yet another enemy?

Helene was very intentionally attempting to reclaim her leadership of the group. She strode ahead, raising her voice so that it echoed off the buildings. Marken and Pearl exchanged a glance that confirmed there was no chain of command. Not anymore. She'd witnessed his power—and she also knew where she stood in his mind. They would not be subjected to anything they didn't want to be subjected to. She felt certain of that. For now they allowed Helene to proceed with the show.

"Wally? You in there?"

"Aye. We're in here."

The voice calling back sounded tired. They all listened as something was removed, and then with a great creak, the door at the base of the tower swung open. Warner had fallen asleep. Wally blinked back against the dying light and nodded in greeting. Pearl saw the way he kept searching and kept failing to find Pen amongst the survivors. His eyes swung back to Helene.

"She's dead?"

The woman nodded. Pearl saw how it briefly wrecked Wally's expression. He breathed in sharply, like he was trying to gather up all he remembered of his friend, and then somehow went right back to the business at hand.

"We had no sign of the warden. No sign of his friend, either. Not a whisper of excitement. As you can see, my partner drifted off. But we've kept your tower safe, wizard."

Arrangements were discussed then. Marken still looked exhausted to her, but Helene—and all the others—wanted to know more about the tower. It seemed only Pearl and Marken had figured out what it was. "This is one of Heatherly's islands," Marken explained. "I'm sure you all know the famous portable island markets. There were originally three of them. This one was lost a decade ago. The rumor was that Heatherly decided to sail west and never turned back. It appears that theory wasn't one hundred percent accurate."

He gestured to the corpse.

"That looks to be Heatherly. It appears that she either fell or was thrown from the top of the tower. Not sure which. For our purposes, it doesn't matter a whole lot. You can see how she attempted to save herself. One final spell. It's common . . ." And here he cleared his throat, eyes darting around uncertainly. Pearl didn't understand why. "It's common when a wizard dies. Reaching for magic like that. Her final blast leveled the nearest buildings, blew out the windows, and almost knocked the tower down too. My guess is that when she died, they were already pretty far out to sea—and no one else knew how to steer it back on course."

Helene looked skeptical. "Come on. How hard could it be to just turn it around?"

"Oh, I imagine the steering is quite simple—but the island can only be powered by magic."

That caught everyone's attention. Pearl hadn't ever read that detail in any of the historical entries about the three islands. Marken smiled at the looks of surprise in the crowd.

"That's how these towers work," he said. "I know the wizards who were hired to guide the other two islands. The ones that belong to the Ten Tides government. Magic is required to activate the mechanisms—the turbines—that are installed below the island. Heatherly did that so the government couldn't just claim the islands for themselves. They had to work with her people—with the Guild—if they wanted them operable. And it's not work that anyone can do. It requires a very gifted wizard."

Pearl saw a few people rolling their eyes. Agnes was one of them. She spoke on behalf of the group. "I'm guessing this is the part where you tell us how lucky we are to have you?"

"Oh, I'd never have been so bold as to suggest that," Marken said wryly. "But now that *you* said it? Sure. This is the part where I tell you you're lucky you've got me. I *can* guide the island home. The only real question we'll have to figure out is whether or not the island still works. If it's been a decade since it was used, I don't know what state the turbines are in. It's also possible that the outer parts of the island have gathered extra sand and weight on its shorelines. Enough weight that it might not be as easy to sail. Really, I don't know what I don't know. But the simple truth is that if the island is operable, I can get us home. Maybe in a day or two. Depends on the tides."

While he'd been speaking, proper night had fallen. Everyone looked so hopeful, so ready to be anywhere but this cursed island. It was agreed that they'd go up and explore the tower—and all of its various mechanisms—in the morning. Pearl watched Marken circle the camp. Even in his exhausted state, he carefully summoned new barriers. If she wasn't mistaken, it looked like he was casting slightly altered versions of his previous shield-wall. When he returned to the tower, she felt comfortable enough to ask him why.

"Diminishing returns," he said simply. "If I hit you with a stun spell, the first time it would knock you flat on your back. Maybe you'd even pass out. Hit you with that same spell the next day? It's going to hit about half as hard. The third time? Barely a flicker. People—and creatures—build a natural resistance to the same spells. That's why variation and creativity matter so much. It also means that if we face the dragoness again, I'll need to have a different set of spells ready."

Pearl was nodding. "It seemed like you had the upper hand . . ."

He sighed. "Yes. I was a few seconds away from finishing her off."

That alternative reality hovered in the air between them for a few moments, but "almost" didn't do them any good. "If you beat her once, you can beat her again."

"Maybe" was Marken's answer. "I burned some of my best combat spells, thinking if I beat her then I wouldn't have to beat her again. A second fight would lean more in her direction, which is why I have no plans to seek her out. My hope is that she's scared enough by the encounter to stay clear of us. I'd rather focus on getting the island moving and getting us home. We can let the gaming commission of Ten Tides deal with her."

Pearl didn't bother pointing out that the decision might not be theirs to make. The dragoness could come back tomorrow to harass the edges of their camp. Maybe sooner. She also worried about the warden and his guard. Where were they? The darkest thoughts had led her to thinking that they'd return to the tower to find Wally and Warner dead. The fact that both were alive and well felt almost like fool's gold. As she watched the others settled in around their new camp, she realized they'd left most of their possessions back at the beach. A thought struck her.

"What if a ship comes? While we're here?"

Marken considered that. "They'd see the remnants of our camp. If it's a search boat, they'd investigate and they'd find the graveyard. We'd have quite a bit of time to run out and ask for their help, I think. The whole point of this tower is that it offers the 'driver' a view of the surrounding ocean. If a ship comes, we'll know."

Once more, his inability to control his tone worked against him. She could hear how much he didn't want to be found. The subtle hope that a rescue boat *wouldn't* arrive. Instead she sensed a pulsing excitement over the discovery of the tower. The truth was that if he could drive this island home, then he could also choose where to dock them. Marken would control his entry point back into Ten Tides and he'd be far more likely to avoid capture. As long as Kell didn't resurface.

Pearl didn't mention any of her thoughts to him. Instead she went to help Naomi collect wood for the fire. Gemma was there, complaining about tired feet and cold hands. She felt a small, gnawing affection for the group. Even Helene and Agnes had their moments. As the first flames stirred in the pit they'd made, she did her best to quietly kill off those affections before they could properly take root.

Small affections could get a person killed in a place like this. Their enemies were still out there. A huntress who might find new ways to prey on them. A warden who would undoubtedly want revenge on the group who'd mutinied against him. Better to keep her distance from the others and stay close to the person who was most likely to help her survive. She secured some of the jerky, claimed a ration for Marken, and sat back down beside him in the drafty room at the base of the tower. Everything inside creaked and groaned. She found she didn't mind the noises. Marken looked surprised when she set up her blanket beside his, but offered no snarky commentary for once. He took his ration, chewed in silence, and then curled up to go to sleep. She did the same.

As always, when she was nervous, Pearl dreamed of the farm and of her pigs.

24

In the morning, they began their ascent of the tower.

The staircase leading up spiraled tightly within the cylindrical confines of the tower. Marken felt more and more justified over the intensity of his stance the day before. It was pretty clear that if Kell had taken this tower, it would have been difficult to wrestle control back from him. There was a landing about halfway up that led into what looked to be a living space.

He saw evidence of Wally and Warner's exploration from the day before. Footprints leading back and forth through the layers of dust. He could only assume the room had been built as an easy resting place for the driver of the tower. Somewhere to sleep in between travel sessions. In this case, it meant this was Heatherly's room. The poor woman. He couldn't help wondering which of her family members had thrown her from that tower. And why? Maybe the rumor was true and the woman had been sailing them into uncharted territory. When reason and logic failed, they'd killed her—and doomed themselves to drift farther and farther out into open seas in the process.

The space consisted of one rotting bed, a few chairs, and barren cabinets. There was also a small closet full of moth-eaten clothing. Marken saw a set of dangling keys on a hook that had rusted long ago. After a cursory search, the group continued their climb. It was a little crowded. Pearl, he didn't mind, but Helene and the other two deckhands—whose names he couldn't even recall—had insisted on joining them. Another attempt from Helene to maintain some sense of control over the group. Even if that sun had already started setting.

Nearly three more stories brought them to the lookout room. The view was breathless. Sprawling ocean in every direction. His eyes searched for ships, and to his great relief, the horizon was empty. He shivered a little. The temperature in this upper room was far colder than below. A credit to the broken window through which Heatherly had been thrown. Even now he felt gusts of wind nipping at his skin. He'd have to remember to bring up a blanket or an extra coat.

Turning, he saw that their view was nearly perfect. There were a few spots—such as the location where they'd made camp—where the trees had grown wild enough to veil the shore. They had eyes on everything else. Emerald-green seas stretched in every direction. The kind of view most people would charge money to see, but it was only half of what the room was designed to do.

"Look at that thing . . ." Helene said.

There was a stunning black chair at the heart of the space.

As much a throne as any chair he'd ever seen. It appeared to be carved out of the same stone as the exterior of the tower. A sort of piercing black that swallowed the light instead of reflecting it back. Marken knelt down and saw several pipes—or rods?—extending down from the bottom of the chair. For the first time, he saw the seat had been positioned somewhat terrifyingly above an opening in the floor. A lightless maw that he could only assume ran all the way down to the base of the tower. It was relatively narrow. He found it hard to imagine someone actually falling down into it, given how the chair was positioned, but as he looked down, he suspected if someone *did* fall, they'd be falling for a while.

"That's interesting," he muttered. When he looked up, he realized the others were all watching him. *Right,* he thought. *I'm supposed to be the expert on this.* "I'm pretty sure this well runs all the way down to the base of the tower and then *through* the crust of the island too. So, not just to ground level. Imagine this tower is . . . double the size of what we see from the outside. There's all the height built aboveground, and then an almost equal amount built down into the ground. At least a few stories. That way the structure bores through the lower crust of the island and these . . . instruments reach the ocean beneath. Did any of you notice an access room? Down where we slept last night? I'd imagine there'd be some kind of maintenance room that leads underground."

Helene frowned. "Arlo, head down and check."

Ahh, Marken thought. *So that's what your name is.*

Two of the surviving deckhands looked too similar to keep apart. Both appeared to be in their thirties, both were fit, and both had unruly, long hair. He'd been side-eyeing the two of them during the ascent and wondering if he'd be forced to address them as "guy" or "you" or something awkward like that. Arlo's departure spared him. Although, a second later he realized the other "guy" whose name he didn't know was up top with them and searching the rest of the room. There were several closets. Two were open and he could see rows of empty shelves inside. The door to the third one was locked or jammed or both. Helene tried to shoulder it open a few times before giving up. Marken remembered the key ring down below. Maybe those would work on the door?

Pearl had spent the entire time eyeing the surrounding forests.

"I can see the dragoness," she said unexpectedly.

That announcement had everyone rushing to the window. She pointed and they all squinted and sure enough, there she was on the southern beach, loping easily in her stone form. As they all watched, she paused, sniffed the air, and then continued running until she was out of sight. Pearl pointed out the obvious.

"She's visiting our old camp."

"Good," Marken said. "Better that she's there than here. Maybe you can find the warden, too. He's got to be out there somewhere. I think it'd be smart if we have a scout or two up here at all times. We'd have eyes on anyone who makes an approach. At night we could all retreat back inside the tower to sleep. Even the dragoness would have a hard time breaking down that front door."

There were shouts from below. Helene leaned around the corner, listening, and then reported back. "No hatch doors that they can find."

"Not in this building," Marken said, his eyes tracing their surroundings. "Have them check the other buildings? Maybe there's access through one of the basements?"

Helene hesitated for a moment, perhaps realizing she was about to accept and execute a command he'd given, before calling down. He'd have to keep an eye on that. Push her too hard in the wrong direction and she might actually get it in her head to move against him. It would be foolish, but weren't most people fools?

"How does it work?"

This came from Pearl. She'd given up her watch on the surrounding forests and crossed the room to inspect the chair. He sensed the way it hummed with power at her proximity. As if the chair had been hungry for an occupant after all this time. Marken came to stand beside her. There were a series of levers and knobs built into the arms of the chair, as well as a few foot pedals. He didn't know exactly how the controls would operate, but he'd studied Heatherly when he was at school and felt any design she'd created would be intuitive.

"Shall I test it out?" he asked.

Eager to assert her control, Helene nodded. "Do it."

The other two exchanged a glance before quietly backing away to the edges of the room. Marken felt his chest thrumming with excitement. He was about to walk in Heatherly's footsteps. A legend. His eyes flicked over to the shattered glass window. *Well, best not to follow all of her footsteps.* He cautiously settled into the chair. Nothing happened. When he reached for the levers along the arms, though, he felt it. An unreasonable amount of latent magic. An absolute breathless well of power. He couldn't fathom how she'd managed to put so much into the structure, but he did sense how the mechanism would work. Understood, without a second thought, what his role in the system would be. His mind executed that familiar split.

He stood in his valley. Reaching out, he drained a single flower. That's all it took. It was like his magic was a key that unlocked the rest. There was a great rumble beneath their feet. He could feel energy pulsing through the walls, churning to life in the depths of every connected stone. He tightened his grip on the largest of the levers, settled his feet against the pedals, and pushed his magic into that metaphorical keyhole.

A grotesque, metal groan. Unbearable in volume. He saw the other three cover their ears, shrinking away from the noise. His arms, though, were seemingly locked in place. He couldn't cover his own ears, and so he was forced to suffer through a noise that he recognized as the very same noise they'd been hearing from the beach. The ship's mechanisms trying to start or restart. That's what they'd heard. Except now he was being forced to hear it at point-blank range.

Right as the sound felt like it might destroy him—obliterating thought and identity and dream all at the same time—he turned the lever hard. There was a stuttering flex of magic, and then the gears down in the bowels of the island won whatever battle they were fighting. The noise stopped, but the room went mute around him. He saw Pearl and Helene moving. They'd taken their hands down from their ears. The two of them were talking. He heard them at a distance. Like they were standing at the end of a very long tunnel. And then they were pointing.

He saw it too. The island was *turning*. A nearly imperceptible shift, but when one stood at the top of a great tower with the sun at such a specific angle—one could see it. Curious, he pushed down on the pedal on his right. There was another *surge* of the power he'd unlocked. They felt another rumble and thankfully this time it didn't result in that terrible noise. Instead they all watched breathlessly as the island began to *move*. He didn't know what some of the other mechanisms would do, but he'd learned how to turn and power it in less than a few seconds. He grinned up at them before realizing they were shouting something.

His ears finally popped. A sort of half sound rushed back in.

"Stop! Hey, Marken!"

He started to release the controls. It felt a lot like scraping skin from bone. Every part of him—all that magic pumping through his veins—wanted more, more, more. Thankfully, he had enough control to let go. He pushed himself out of the chair. "What? What's going on?!"

"You're bleeding," Pearl said softly, coming closer. "Kind of a lot."

He looked to the wound on his shoulder. The bandage seemed fine, but then he finally saw what she meant. Drops of blood falling down on the fabric. He reached up to touch his earlobe. His fingers came away slick. Glancing right, he found a window with enough reflection to serve as a mirror. Both ears were bleeding.

"Damn," he said, and even his voice was slightly muted. "Okay. I'm okay."

There was shouting down below. Nothing was coming to him at full volume.

"It's your magic," Pearl said. "Come on."

She steadied him on the first few steps. Good thing, too. Two strides brought out a brief vertigo. Maybe it was the blood loss or the fleeing magic or the brightness of the room. Maybe all three. Either way, Pearl kept him on his feet. He was grateful for the breeze in the room too. The way it swept across his sweaty forehead. Helene stood near the top of the stairs. She'd already sent down the other nameless deckhand, but she was waiting on confirmation from him.

"It worked?"

He nodded. "It worked. I think I knocked off the rust, too. It should be easier next time."

That was all she needed to know. She didn't bother asking if he was okay. Like most folks, she saw him as a tool. Confirming the tool was the right one for the task, she went down to check on her crew. Pearl didn't abandon him, though. She hooked an arm through his and led him patiently downstairs. By the time they reached the second landing—Heatherly's room—he'd steadied.

"Are you okay?" Pearl asked.

He grinned back at her. "Oh, I'm more than okay. We're going home."

25

Pearl handed Marken a wet rag—which he distractedly used to paw at his own bleeding ears—as the rest of the group gathered outside the tower. The first complication to their plan was waiting there in the empty, colorless air that surrounded the camp.

"It vanished," Agnes reported. "Your magic disappeared at the same time that awful noise sounded."

She was gesturing to where the protective domes had been cast. Marken offered the rag back to Pearl, who made a face. He seemed to realize the rag was covered with his own blood and tucked it in a back pocket instead. Looking at him, she was worried he might have caused permanent damage to his eardrums, but he seemed to be able to hear what Agnes was saying.

"Okay," he said, a little too loudly. "I know what happened.

My passive magic was dispelled when I placed myself within the tower's established magical order. If the spells were more established, more attached to their subject than to me, they'd likely hold. But since they're so fresh? They're still partially relying on their attachment to me. What I felt when I powered up that tower was . . . all-consuming. There's just no room for me to keep hold of any other magical attachments. They're severed the second I activate the tower. Which means guiding the island home is going to require all of my attention. The rest of you . . ." He shook his head. "You'll be at the mercy of the dragoness any time we want to power the island. We'll just have to think through a plan. I can always detach from the chair, but you saw what happened up there. It'll take at least a few minutes for me to get my bearings and gain enough strength to summon new magic."

Arlo came jogging back to the group. His chest was heaving slightly.

"Hey," he said. "Have any of you seen Arlo?"

Pearl blinked and barely resisted saying: *You are Arlo.* It was the other deckhand, though. The one who'd remained topside with them when Marken activated the tower. Pearl, embarrassingly, couldn't recall his name no matter how hard she stared at him. Helene turned, calling out the missing deckhand's name, and the search began. Arlo had followed orders to look through the basements of the nearby buildings to see if there was a maintenance access to the tower's underground sections. He'd never come back. Everyone searched in pairs and there was serious concern that Kell and Levi might be hiding somewhere underground. Five minutes later, Wally and Warner called everyone over to the largest of the other buildings.

Pearl followed Marken and Helene inside. The others waited like sentries above. This building had more furniture than the other houses she'd seen. More decor on the walls too. Everything was covered in a double-thick layer of dust. She saw footprints leading to a door at the end of the hallway.

"He went downstairs," Wally reported. "There's a tunnel there. He followed it . . ."

Surprisingly, the way was not dark. Older magelights glinted in the basement and in the tunnel. Perhaps activated for the first time in years by their passing. The three of them followed Wally through the damp space. The tunnel was carved neatly, and even though they were underground, she could tell they were moving in the direction of the tower.

"And here is where his trail went cold," Wally said.

Noise had rumbled to life—louder and louder—as they made their approach. The waiting chamber was built in a perfect square. Pearl saw dozens of tools hanging along the walls. One was a diving harness of some kind. At the very heart of the room, a circular pit. She knew it connected to the one above because she could see the same pipes running down as they'd seen topside. Pearl didn't go any closer to check, though. She could hear what was down there.

Ocean. Wild, untamed, lightless. Remarkably, no guard rails had been built around the edge of the pit. Her heartbeat quickened as she stood there thinking about how easy it would be to fall into that void. How easy it would be for the tide to pull a person away from the one place that they could surface. She saw a cable, presumably for the diver's suit to attach to, but everything about the space they stood in was shivering down her spine. She did not want to be here.

Marken spoke: "Well, it seems obvious what happened."

"Does it?" Helene asked, clearly annoyed that she was a step behind him again.

"The sound would have been even louder down here," Marken said softly. "I'm guessing he came down, found this room, and he was standing near the edge of this pit when the turbines started turning. This close to the gears? That noise would have been at full blast for him. Loud enough to knock him out. And if he fell, this close to the edge . . ."

Pearl didn't want to hear any more. Of all the dangers and deaths that they'd faced, this one terrified her most. An ocean could not be reasoned with. It was too powerful and wild for any one person to fight. Imagining what it must have felt like for Arlo to plunge into that deep, waiting cold? Lost with no way to get back? She found herself hoping he'd already been dead when he hit the water. She also didn't want to wait around as they discussed the death. Instead, she turned and marched back through the tunnel. If the others were having some important debate, Marken would catch her up later. She couldn't handle another second so close to those waiting jaws.

Home. She wanted to go home. For the first time, she felt certain she would do whatever it took to get there. Her aunt's death had awakened some dormant instinct in her. This moment, however small it seemed, was a solidification of that earlier promise. *I will survive,* a voice in her mind said. *I will do what I must to go home and never set foot on this island again. Whatever the cost.*

As she passed the other survivors who were standing guard, they saw from her expression what had happened to Arlo. They were wise enough not to ask questions. Outside, a clear sky.

A miserably bright day. She took another ration of food and sat chewing in silence as the others emerged. She kept herself apart. Marken almost approached, then saw the look on her face and thought better of it. She could hear their discussions.

A temporary ward was cast. Helene agreed they'd keep the movements around camp tighter. Not that there were that many people left. By Pearl's count, only ten remained: Naomi, Gemma, Helene, Agnes, Not-Arlo, Warner, Wally, Marken, and Pearl. The thought of calling the curly-haired man lounging off to her right "Not-Arlo" was almost enough to drag a smile onto her face. How did one break the news, after all this time, that they hadn't learned one of their fellow survivors' names? Her aunt would have said that ship had sailed and to just avoid him.

An unspeakable pain bloomed in her then. Something large enough to begin devouring her from the inside out. She realized that even if she survived—made it through all this—she'd be returning home to her sickly mother and her coward of a father. Going home to report a smuggling run gone wrong. There might be consequences. She wasn't sure what exactly they'd be, but she knew she'd likely face them alone. *Some reward,* she thought. *Beat impossible odds and you get to go live your impossible life again. How lovely.*

More plans were being made. Marken was heading up to activate the tower again. Cautions were being taken just in case that terrible noise sounded again. She saw Marken lingering on the first floor of the tower, glancing out to see if she might join him. When she didn't stand, he started the ascent. Helene and a few of the others went with him, presumably to provide guiding coordinates and scouting. The soon-setting sun would be a helpful marker for their route.

Pearl ate another piece of jerky. A small attempt to gain more strength than what was currently leeching out of her with every negative thought. A few minutes later, she felt the same thrum of power as before. As if the entire world was vibrating. Marken's prediction came true, though. That terrible sound lasted for a fraction of a second this time. Like the gears of those great engines below just needed to remember what they were—and then: movement. She could feel those subtle shifts like pulses in her own body. A call came down from the top of the tower.

"It's working! It's working!"

The rest of the group was ordered to retreat back inside the lower room. Pearl obeyed that command. Pure self-preservation. They closed the great door and barred the entrance just in case. She had to fight off the nausea of feeling trapped in yet another small space, but at least this time there was logic in the decision. With Marken engaged in powering the tower—the entire island—he had no way to protect them. They were vulnerable to the dragoness, whether their huntress knew that or not. She settled in with the others and hoped Helene was at least wise enough to be actively scouting up there. The rest of them had no visuals down here. The entire world could be on fire outside their door and they'd be blind to the coming danger.

An hour passed. Visuals or not, they could all hear and feel the island's mechanisms working beneath their feet. The great mechanical churn of a machine so complicated that Pearl could not begin to fathom its creation—or its creator. She'd read about Heatherly a dozen times. Never once had she imagined how complex the magic of this place would be. The little girl in her had always pictured these islands like large floating devices. A massive safety vest that bobbed on the surface of the ocean and floated almost whimsically up and down the coast. The chair she'd seen, and the terrifying maintenance room below, were more evidence of a world she hadn't ever imagined existing. It felt similar to the first few times she'd spoken with Marken. The strange sensation that even if they'd crossed paths a dozen times, he'd lived in some other version of the same world she called home. She was Pearl the pig farmer. A girl who'd only barely crossed county lines. All while Marken traveled the great breadth of their continent, called on by kings and ambassadors to execute their wishes. It was a bitter taste to think about how much she hadn't seen of the maps her father kept in his barn. All those places she might never visit.

The tower's interior gradually darkened. The light from the halfway room struggled to reach them. There were regular reports from up top. Always Helene's voice echoing down. There'd been no sign of a ship—not yet—but Pearl felt certain they were making steady progress back to Ten Tides. Glancing around, she saw hope written on every face. She realized she'd been throwing a pity party for herself, even as their rescue became more and more inevitable.

That word gnawed at her, though. Inevitable. What if it *wasn't* inevitable? So far everything that could go wrong had. It had her mind searching for the possible faults in their plan. The bottom of the tower was secure, but she remembered one weakness. If the dragoness *wanted* to attack them, her entry point was obvious. She could scale the tower. Attack them through the shattered window. Pearl's heart started beating double in her chest. She excused herself and went to warn

Marken and the others. At the last second, she grabbed a few rations. Marken would be famished when he finished powering the island.

Helene was the first one she saw as she rounded the final curve in the tower.

"Pearl. Feeling better?"

Marken's eyes flicked over to her. He'd been in that chair for a long time now. He was sweating a good amount but didn't look the way he'd looked last time. Ghost white and bleeding. No, he appeared to have found his rhythm. He looked rather in control of the island's magic now.

"I'm fine," Pearl said. "Just needed some food. And I wanted to mention the window. We're all sealed in downstairs, but if the dragoness wanted to attack, she could scale this tower. They're natural climbers."

Helene nodded. "Didn't think of that. Thanks. Wally's watching south and west. Ellis has eyes north and east. We've seen no sign of her. No sign of Kell or Levi either, although we did notice a set of docks on the opposite end of the island. They seem empty, but there are a few structures we can see through the gaps in the trees. Maybe designed for shipments. It's possible they made their way there and are hiding out. We figured we'd keep pushing until nightfall. Then we can shut the tower down, let Marken rest, and we'll all bunker downstairs for the night. Start it all up again in the morning. Sound good?"

"Sounds good," Pearl replied.

She mentally noted that Not-Arlo's real name was Ellis. After eyeing the distant forests, she looked back to Marken. He'd seemingly been waiting for her to look. He offered a small nod.

A check-in nod of sorts. She nodded back to say: *I'm here. I'm with you.*

"I'd love to stay up here," she said, turning to Helene. "Scout a little?"

Helene looked pleased to have a request funneling through her again. "Of course."

There was something remarkable and breathless about that final hour of daylight. Watching an entire island be driven like some kind of massive steamer. The setting sun painting the sky with golds and garnets and finally a pink-laced, dying gray. There were still no ships that they'd seen, and no real way to mark how far they'd progressed, other than Helene's navigational guesses. Pearl had the terrible thought that maybe they'd been going the wrong way. What if Helene was a terrible navigator? What if they just kept on sailing, following her poor guidance, into some uncharted abyss? A far more reasonable voice said that they'd cross paths with a shipping lane soon enough.

When proper dark claimed the sky, Marken slumped out of the chair. Wally and Ellis headed downstairs, exhausted by their scouting. Helene waited until Marken told her he'd come down and cast the protective domes. With that promise extracted, she abandoned them too. Pearl joined Marken, handing him a ration, and both looked out at the lightless island below.

"Are you all right?" she asked. "I feel like they're asking you to do too much."

He grinned at that. "I've been asked to do too much my entire life, Pearl. This is nothing."

Her thoughts strayed briefly to before. The strange chasm that existed between her experiences and his. The wizard who'd traveled the world. And then a darker thought: *The wizard who was accused of murder.* "I know . . ." She trailed off, unsure how to proceed. "I know that you don't want us to find a ship. You're hoping to power the island all the way back to Ten Tides. Aren't you?"

His smile faded, but only slightly. "Yes. I am."

"You want control over where we land," she concluded. "That way you won't be captured."

A nod from him. "Yes. God's body, you don't miss much."

She shrugged at the compliment. Tentatively pleased to be seen for who she really was. A person who was actually quite good with details. A person who could research and learn and adapt to her environment, even if her grades in school had always suggested that she wasn't smart.

"I don't miss much either," Marken said, his voice no louder than the flick of a knife. She saw the way his eyes slid to the stairwell. Checking that they were alone. "Like the fact that you're the one who brought the dragoness aboard the ship in the first place."

She threw back a confused look—and knew immediately it was too exaggerated to be believed. Marken snorted. "Don't worry," he said. "I won't tell anyone. Let's just say I didn't believe the whole 'studying their anatomy to perform surgeries on pigs' concept you presented. Honestly, I'm surprised the others bought it. But you have one of my secrets and I have one of yours. If we both keep quiet long enough, we'll get home and we can go our separate ways."

It sounded so final, so transactional. She nodded a confirmation before glancing over and seeing the subtle traces of pain lining his face. Perhaps he'd only been testing her with that comment. Seeing how eager she was to turn what existed between them into an exchange, instead of something more meaningful. She'd never wanted it to be this way, but she didn't really know what other way it could be. What else was there? She hated that she'd even broached the subject. Now something felt spoiled between them, something she wanted to fix.

"Look," she started. "It's not like that. I don't want you to think—"

A hand slapped down over her mouth with enough force to rattle her jaw. Pearl's eyes shocked wide as her peripheral filled with movement. Marken was being seized as well. A familiar, black-gloved hand had him by the throat. A flickering hand that was there and not. She felt Marken reach for his magic—and then felt the terrible blanketing feeling that came down over top of that. Kell used his real hand to cover Marken's mouth, keeping him quiet. He was tall enough to pin the wizard to the wall, his feet not even touching the ground. Pearl tried to push back but the hands that were holding her were deadly in their strength: Levi. It had to be Levi.

Marken tried to reach for his magic again. Pearl felt a slash of desperation and then Kell's null thread answered. This time it cost Marken far more. His eyes rolled back. He slumped to the ground. Pearl felt helpless and trapped. Desperate, she tried to use Levi's hold on her, leaning back into him before kicking at the shattered glass on her left. She was hoping to make some noise. Maybe it would be enough to stomp her feet so that someone else heard them down below, but Levi used his leverage to keep her airborne. She thrashed wildly, kicking the empty air, until she felt a knife at her throat.

"Try that again and I'll slit you, girl."

Her body stilled. Kell was allowing his gloved hand to hover just above Marken's chest. She saw the subtle movements. How he was working the null thread patiently around the wizard. When Marken woke up, he'd be cut off from his magic. As helpless as Pearl felt now. The gauntleted hand over her mouth was keeping her from doing or saying anything. Hot tears streaked down her face. The warden finished his work and glanced up at her without any trace of pity.

"Pearl Trask," he whispered. "The girl who smuggled a dragoness onto an airship and got dozens killed. Don't worry. You'll get your trial too. Maybe we can get the two of you adjoining cells in Pasca, since you're so fond of each other. Levi, give her to me."

There was another creak across the room. Pearl's eyes widened as Prior edged into view. He was peering out from the closet they hadn't been able to get open earlier. The lock that they'd thought was jammed, and it had been hiding these three. She tried to plead with her eyes. Begged him to do something. Anything. Instead the coward whispered, "Please, don't hurt Naomi."

And then he ducked back into the shadows. The closet door closed with a muted click. The warden shook his head in disgust before turning back to the business at hand. The business of what to do with Pearl Trask. Levi pulled her in close again. The knife dug into her neck.

"I'm not kidding. If you make a noise, you die. I'll gut you like a pig."

When she whimpered, he took a fistful of the back of her shirt and shoved her across to Kell. Pearl had a split second where her mouth was not covered. She knew she could say something. Shout a warning. Speak a word. But her thoughts were tangled and panicked. The words caught in the back of her throat. The only sound that came out was a low sort of moan. That noise was swallowed as Kell clamped down his good hand over her mouth. He maneuvered behind her, nearly separating her shoulder as he tightened his grip.

"Take both of the pistols," he whispered to Levi. "Priority targets, yeah? Be savvy about it. Pick your battles and then fall back to me."

Levi moved with silklike quiet to the stairwell. He paused there, listening for noises, and then began the descent. Somehow, he didn't make a sound even then, avoiding all the steps that creaked as he vanished from their sight. Again Pearl was struck with the desperate urge to stomp or scream or do *anything* to warn the others. A glance showed Marken was out cold.

She could hear the others talking. Not their words, but the sounds of their voices. Casual conversations. Likely discussing what they'd do when they were rescued. Unaware that an angel of death was descending upon them. She knew she had only seconds to act. She gathered up her strength, keeping her body calm, and then tried to stomp her feet again. Kell nearly fumbled her, but corrected his grip at the very last second, rearing back so she kicked helplessly, soundlessly in the air.

"Stop," he hissed. "Pearl. Don't make me—"

A shot fired. Loud and echoing within the confines of the tower. It was followed quickly by a second. There were screams. A tangle of voices that Pearl couldn't quite make out. Who was dead? Who was alive? What would happen next? She took a deep breath and knew she needed to stay focused. She could still free herself. All she needed was a moment. Just one moment. There was loud shuffling. A fight had broken out in the halfway room. She could hear spears clacking. Another scream.

Kell finally moved. His hand slid away from her mouth—clearly not worried about her making noise now—and down to her shoulder. He kept a tight fistful of her shirt and began edging closer to the stairs, trying to hear what was happening. He could not possibly have realized the mistake he'd made. Pearl had been careful this whole time. A part of her mind briefly left the dark tower. She retreated from all the crying and the dying. She was back on the farm. Looking around, she found the oldest pig in the herd and whispered an apology to the creature.

Then she was back. Kell's grip still tight on her shirt.

"Let go of me."

Magic wove through the command. The warden frowned—but obeyed. Pearl's mind was racing. What was the best way to do this? She considered their surroundings, considered Levi downstairs, face-to-face with how many of them? After a moment, she made up her mind.

"Walk to the broken window," she commanded.

Like a marionette, he marched across the room. She watched him pause there before all the shattered glass. Wind whipped at his cloak. He knew her secret. Both of her secrets. He knew about the dragoness and now he would know her for a silvertongue. And she had learned enough about the warden in their time together to know he would not cut a deal with her. There would be no middle ground with this man. No mercy for someone as dangerous to the world as Pearl Trask.

There was only one choice.

When Warden Kell looked back for further instructions, she gave them.

"Jump."

He did.

26

Marken's valley was *burning*.

He'd pushed too hard. Shoving back against the barriers of the summoned null thread, and now he was cursed to witness his mistake. Great lashes of force had tongued inward. All of his magic shoving up against a force that, for once, was its equal and its opposite. That friction had somehow resulted in heat. And heat had birthed flame.

My flowers are burning. My magic is burning.

He couldn't do anything to stop it. Not while the barrier still held. All he could do was stalk the edges of those smoking fields like some kind of penitent wolf. Two voices echoed. Like mountain gods bellowing down to him. He could not make out the words they were saying. Nor did he know the voices that were speaking. Finally, one of the voices spoke with an air of finality.

The barrier fell!

He sprinted forward. There were two separate fires. One appeared to be dying out. The other, though, was growing at an alarming rate. *Think, Marken. Think, think, think.*

Drawing magic wouldn't work. He could not draw on his power *and* stay in this place to use it. That wasn't how the mechanism operated. If he drew on the power of his lightflowers, he'd naturally pull that magic *back* to where his physical body was. That was how the exchange had always operated. Death for life. Power from one part of the world transferring to some other place. If he could not use his magic here, then what? He considered taking off his cloak, trying to beat the flames back, but that felt like a waste of precious time. The fire was already too widespread.

An invisible hand gripped his shoulder. Someone trying to wake him up or pull him back, but he couldn't go back. Not yet. He shrugged the feeling away. That booming voice sounded again. The god had returned. They were speaking his name this time. Over and over and over. He did not answer them. He had to save his magic first. He had to do *something*.

Wait. The fire can't spread without the lightflowers.

Of course. The grip on his shoulder had vanished. Enough that he could steady himself and focus on the task at hand. Curiously, another god seemed to be speaking. A new voice that was lower and crueler than the first one. He shivered a little to hear it. He knew that voice.

Levi.

Marken remembered it all suddenly. The tower. Kell and Pearl and Levi. All those thoughts came slamming back into him—and now his goal shifted into a two-headed creature.

He needed to save his flowers and he needed to help Pearl. That must have been the voice he'd heard before. All the shaking too. If he didn't act quickly, he couldn't help her. Marken rushed forward and tried to locate the midpoint of the spreading flames. Next he calculated how many rows of flowers he would need to drain in order to stop the fire. It would kill off an uncomfortable amount of his crop—more than he'd ever drained before—but he knew the rest of his flowers would survive then. *Three rows,* he decided. *I need to drain at least three rows in both directions.*

Marken reached out to the closest flower, and then he began to pull . . .

. . . his eyes blinked open. The details of the room had changed. Kell was gone. Where had he gone? Levi had replaced the warden. The guard had a knife raised and was slowly backing Pearl into the far corner of the room. She had both of her hands up. She was begging for him to show mercy. Saying the words over and over again. "Please, please, please."

Then her eyes flicked over to Marken. A slash of hope cut across her face. Levi turned to look—and Marken hit him with a two-ton anvil of magic. He'd never harnessed that much power for a single spell. It showed. There was nothing to hide the sound of the man's ribs all cracking simultaneously. Nothing to veil the way his entire body bent inward with enough force to rip skin away from bone. The magic hit him so hard that he briefly took on some inhuman shape before colliding with the far glass window. It shattered instantly. They both saw a single, frozen image of him suspended in midair with a look of terror on his face. Then he fell out of sight.

Pearl sank to her knees. "Thank you," she whispered. "Thank

you. I thought you might not wake up. God's body, I thought you might not . . ."

"Where's Kell?" Marken hissed back, already reaching for the next spell. Half of his vision filled with that other place. He saw his plan had worked. The bigger fire was contained, quietly burning itself out. He'd just have to be careful with how much magic he used now. At least until he could take a proper inventory of how many flowers were left. "Where's the warden, Pearl?"

She shook her head. Tried to speak. Shook her head again. Eventually she pointed to the original broken window. "After you passed out, Levi went down. He . . . oh, Marken. He attacked the others. They're dying down there. Kell stayed with me. When he went to the stairs to look, I knew I had one chance. I pushed him. I pushed him out . . ."

Marken's eyes widened in shock. It was such a fortunate turn. Such a rare lapse in concentration for the warden too. He was still considering the angles and the story when a loud groaning sound interrupted his thoughts. Both of them whipped around. It was Prior. The prat from the beach. He had both of his hands raised, but Marken had already drawn on his magic. A knifelike projectile formed in the air between them. Before he could launch the weapon, Pearl blurted out, "Prior didn't fight. He was hiding the whole time. Like a coward."

Marken saw the man had pissed himself. His entire body was shaking violently. They both listened as he mumbled about his innocence. "I didn't know the plan! No one told me! When it happened, I just ran. I thought the deckhands might be killing us all off. A play to get their hands on the food or something. I ran and I didn't realize that there were two sides to all of this until we got here. I promise you. I just . . . I just want to go home. It's none of my business. I just want to go home. Please . . ."

Marken suspected he'd been singing a different tune to the warden, but he also couldn't bring himself to murder this man simply for lacking a spine. Instead he rotated the projectile in the air and sent it flying over Prior's head. The man gave a little jump when the weapon sank into the wood behind him with a threatening *thunk*.

"Go back in that closet and wait for us to come back for you."

Prior didn't need to be told twice. He darted back into the shadows like a frightened rabbit. The door closed. Marken saw Pearl was still staring at the door with clear concern.

"You're sure we can trust him?" she asked.

Marken shook his head. "I don't trust him at all, no, but if he didn't join them during the attack, he's not going to suddenly jump into the fray now. You're sure Kell is dead?"

Pearl nodded. "We can check, but he fell from here with nothing to stop him. Marken, we need to get down there. Levi, he had both pistols. He ambushed them. There might be survivors . . ."

He didn't need convincing. Both of them began the descent. He wanted to compliment Pearl on getting the drop on Kell. God's body, she'd managed to take care of his greatest adversary out here with no more than a shove. It felt like something out of those dramas they performed in the bigger cities. A play. She'd taken out his enemy and then he'd returned just in time to blast Levi and save her. If they could survive the dragoness, they'd have quite a story to tell to the bards back home. Any thoughts of heroics slipped away the moment they reached Heatherly's room. Wally had been killed. Expertly killed. Levi had slit several key arteries and the older man was already gone.

Downstairs, they found worse waiting for them. Both Helene and Agnes had suffered pistol shots. Helene's had been from behind. A point-blank blast that left no mystery to her potential survival. Agnes, on the other hand, was still alive. For now. There was a gaping hole in her gut. Gemma had bravely come back inside and was pressing every spare rag she could find to the girl's wound. The others—Naomi and Ellis and Warner—hovered in the doorway like they were trapped in some sort of purgatory. Afraid to come too far inside and be shot. Afraid to go out and be vulnerable to an attack by the dragoness.

"All clear in here," Marken called. His voice sounded tired, even to him. "Levi and Kell are both dead. You can come back in. Let's close that door for now."

Naomi obeyed. Her eyes searched beyond them. "Any sign of Prior?"

"Alive," Pearl reported. "He's upstairs. He asked them to spare your life, but he was ready to let the rest of us die."

Naomi shook her head in disgust. Her right cheek was painted with blood spatter. Marken knew she'd never be the same. One could not witness something like this and be unchanged. None of them would ever be the same. Ellis had dropped to Agnes's side and was holding her hand. Marken realized they were the last two deckhands left. He knelt down and offered what magic he could, trying to seal the edges of the wound, but the girl's insides were wrecked. She slipped out of consciousness and he doubted they'd see her open her eyes again.

It felt cruel to discuss logistics. There were still warm bodies in the room. But when he brought up the subject, every single one of the survivors spoke up for once, without Helene's commands to drown out their voices. Marken wondered if they were simply desperate for that word—survivor—to continue applying to them.

First they moved the dead. He used his magic to help ferry them out through the main door. It was agreed that they would not bother to dig graves. Not yet. Instead they set the corpses against one of the waiting buildings as respectfully as they could before retreating back inside the protection of the tower. Marken paused only long enough to confirm the other two deaths. Kell was there. Completely shattered. He'd promised to kill the man so many times in his mind. He'd never considered that someone else might do it for him.

I'll have to thank Pearl later.

Around the other side of the tower, he found Levi looking just as dead as the warden. It was finished, then. His eyes traced the shadowed forest. There didn't appear to be movement, but that didn't mean she wasn't there, wasn't watching them. Their final enemy might be anywhere now.

He shivered at that thought before heading inside.

27

No one slept.

Dawn's fingers scraped across the sky. In that morning light, they were forced to reckon with more death. Agnes had passed. They carried her out and set her beside the others. Pearl saw that Marken hadn't bothered with the usual protective wards. Perhaps anticipating the fact that they'd just be dispelled the moment he activated the island's engines again. Their party had moved up in the tower and was occupying Heatherly's room. There was just far less blood there. Less of that sickly scent and a few windows to help waft it all out. Gemma and Ellis had recovered the two pistols, and when they went up to bring Prior out of hiding, they found more ammunition with him. Only Gemma knew how to load them. Her late husband had apparently been in the military when he was younger. Pearl—and all the others—were bracing themselves for one final defense.

The plan was simple: Marken would push the island hard for home. Their navigator was dead, but all of them felt confident that the rising sun—due east—was as fine a bearing as any. Ten Tides was a massive continent. Surely they couldn't miss it. As they made preparations, Pearl found herself watching Prior. The coward had changed into a spare pair of pants that were too big for him. He kept tugging the waist up whenever he walked. Naomi would not speak to him. Nor would the others. Only Gemma had been kind enough to offer him a ration. He ate the jerky like a rat in the far corner of the room. Pearl watched him and wondered: *Do you know? Did you hear what I did to the warden? Do you know what I am?*

Maybe she'd made a mistake. Last night Marken had turned, ready to blast Prior with the same kind of magic he'd used on Levi, but instinct had forced Pearl to speak up. Her mind couldn't place Prior in the same category as Levi and Kell. Those two were clear-cut killers. They'd been determined to see her imprisoned—or worse, executed. Prior might be a brat, but he hadn't actively participated in the ambush. Now she worried her goodwill might echo back in all the wrong ways. After all, anyone who knew her secret was a threat, weren't they?

Upstairs, Marken was making preparations. Pearl maneuvered past him and went to the closet where Prior had been during the exchange. It smelled terrible inside. She tried to ignore the odor as she tested out closing the door behind her, leaving only the slightest crack. And then she raised her voice to a normal volume, "I can't believe they were hiding in here that whole time."

Marken spoke from the other room. The sound of his voice

was muffled, but she found she could make out the words if she strained. "What did you say?"

Her test felt inconclusive. The truth was that Prior might have heard her. It just depended on how loudly she'd issued her command when she told Kell to leap from the building. And she thought she remembered the door being completely closed? Instead of slightly cracked? That might have muted her words even more. Only Prior knew the truth of what he'd heard the night before. She pushed back out into the main room.

"Sorry. I was saying that I couldn't believe they were in here. While all of us were walking around and talking to each other. Helene tried to get this door open, remember? She said it was jammed."

"I'd bet someone was holding the handle," Marken replied. "Kell is military trained. Levi is too. My guess is that the three of them were already here when we first arrived. Waiting at the top of the tower for us. We posted Wally and Warner as sentries and then we ran back to the beach. It was clever, really. The decision to leave the two of them alone. Killing them would have only alerted us that they were nearby. So, they waited—and even I took the bait. I assumed that our guards being alive meant Kell was somewhere else. But no, he was here."

Pearl shook her head at the note of guilt in his voice. "We all made that assumption."

"Then the two of them waited for the right moment. When we first came up to this room, we had numbers. They would have had to go toe-to-toe with my magic. Kell must have had Levi hold the handle. Helene couldn't get it to budge, so she assumed it was locked. And we just . . . never checked it again.

The three of them waited until it was just the two of us, alone up here . . ."

He trailed off, deep in thought. She watched the emotions shift on his face. As if it was the first time he was remembering what the two of them had been speaking about before the attack. Each of them in possession of the other's secrets. Marken knew about the dragoness. She knew about his plan to escape back onto the mainland. *But you don't know my true secret,* she thought. *You didn't see what happened to the warden.*

When Marken finally looked up, their eyes met. "I know it was unreasonable," he said. "Expecting you to . . . to want to stay with me. I'm wanted for murder. Warden Kell? He's just the first in a long line of people who will pursue me. They'll send someone else. I'll be a fugitive until the Guild decides to clear my name. Until I can clear my name. It's not the kind of life that I could ever really invite someone else into. Maybe there's some other world where we'd have met in some other way . . ."

Pearl shook her head. She highly doubted there was any other world where their paths might have crossed. No, this felt like the only potential crossing for these particular stars. A girl smuggling a dragoness aboard a ship. A boy being escorted to his own execution. She could not imagine an alternative world where they met by chance over drinks or for coffee. Nothing that quaint felt real after all they'd been through together.

"Maybe," she said, entertaining his hope. "Maybe in some other life."

Marken looked satisfied that she was willing to dream of it, at least. He nodded once and settled into the waiting chair. Sunlight was starting to warm the room. Pearl headed for the stairs.

"I'll tell the others we're starting."

She nearly walked right into Gemma. The woman startled back, almost enough to fall down the stairs. Pearl grabbed hold of the woman's arm until she was certain she was steady. Gemma thanked her, took a breath to reset, and then nodded to say she was okay.

"Oh, Pearl. You scared the life right out of me. I was sent up here to ask when we'd be starting. The others are . . . eager to be home."

"Now," Pearl confirmed. "Let's go get ready."

The woman looked put out to have to go back down after just coming up. "Can I just stay up here? Catch my breath for a moment?"

"Of course," Pearl replied. "When Marken activates the island's engines, we'll want everyone upstairs anyways. Go on. I'll fetch the others."

She slid around the woman without a second thought.

28

Marken watched as Gemma traded places with Pearl in the upper room. He found it somewhat remarkable that the older woman had survived everything to this point. She moved fairly well for her age, but still. The fact that a stray bullet or spear thrust hadn't found her during any of the melees was quite a feat. Marken smiled warmly as the woman peered around the room for the first time. He'd never met any of his grandparents, but he imagined they might have looked like this. The silver braid, the laugh lines, the old-fashioned locket. She glanced back at the stairwell, then crossed the room to where he was seated.

"Marken," she said softly. "I wanted to show you my husband's picture."

Of course. The locket. He'd seen her fussing with it around camp. Always rubbing the golden circle between two fingers.

Truly, it was a wonder the metal hadn't worn away. Her offer to show him the picture after all this time was odd. He squinted as she worked the clasp.

"He wasn't a very handsome man."

Another strange thing to say. At first he didn't understand what he was seeing. Then he understood. He knew the man in the portrait. It was the windmaster. The same person she'd been seated near on the airship. The one who'd died at the beginning of their voyage. He frowned.

"But you told us . . . I thought your husband . . ."

"I have no husband," she clarified. "That sort of life never suited me. This is not a picture of the man that I married. It's a picture of my target. Look, we don't have much time, Marken. The others will be coming up soon. I boarded that ship under false pretenses. The woman who was supposed to have my ticket woke up rather sick that morning. The real Gemma never made it to the docking station. The Guild sent me in her place. You see, the high mage has no interest in you making it to that trial in Pasca. He can't intervene openly. That much should be obvious to you. It's the same reason that he did not openly help hide you when you were on the run. To intervene and have it be traced back to the Guild? That would cause outrage, but he did send me to make sure the *Grand Gesture* never reached its destination."

Marken stared at her, shocked into silence. So much had happened that he'd almost forgotten that the windmaster was poisoned. When no one approached him after the crash, he'd assumed that if there *was* an agent on board, they'd been one of the unlucky ones who died. Now she stood before him. An unexpected ally, here to see him through the rest of the journey.

"I'll keep quiet," Gemma was saying. "For now let's just get you home, okay?"

There were creaks along the stairs. The others were coming. Marken nodded fervently back, and watched how casually Gemma maneuvered to the far end of the room. She pretended she'd been looking out at the forest this entire time. Marken forced himself to take long, slow breaths. Pearl and the others rounded the corner a moment later. His mind was still racing.

The Guild had not abandoned him after all.

They'd sent someone to help him, and that someone was still alive. Still hidden from the others too. His escape felt all but secured now. He thought back through the events that had unfolded on the ship. Gemma had been seated near the man. In the same row as him. She must have somehow poisoned him.

God's body. The chaos you created with that one decision.

He suspected that she had not imagined all of *this* happening. No, it would have been far more reasonable to assume that once the windmaster was dead—and once the storm began pulling them dangerously out to sea—that the warden would dispel the null thread so that Marken could save them all. Gemma's goal—the Guild's goal—would have been achieved then. Marken could have commandeered the *Grand Gesture* and escaped onto the mainland once more.

So many revelations were branching out from that first one. He found he could not even look at the older woman without his heart rate picking up. The others were standing by the windows. Looking around the island. Pointing to their old camp or the western docks they hadn't seen before. Marken's entire body was humming, though, electric with the secret he'd just discovered. But then the secret began to spoil uncomfortably in his gut. Not unlike the poison that Gemma had used to kill the windmaster. It led to a realization.

Gemma hasn't helped me out here. Not even one time . . .

Oh.

Yes, she had derailed the ship. Irreversibly altering its course. The crash had happened. There had been so many moments when she might have helped him. Perhaps she'd wanted to keep herself hidden as some sort of last resort—but he felt as if he could see another truth buried there. The Guild would have been just as satisfied if he died out here. Not executed as an official traitor to the crown. No public examination of magic and all its effects on wider society. He would have been a dead wizard buried and forgotten in this desolate place. In truth, it would have meant expending less resources for them. No need to keep him hidden in their various safe houses. No reason to fight the legislation forming against him.

Gemma's decision to reveal herself now meant she was entering a new phase of this game. Now that he'd won—the warden dead—she wanted to link herself to him again. It could be what he'd first imagined: a promise of support. But he also felt it was a quiet reminder that the Guild would be watching his return to Ten Tides. Marken was so lost in thought that he didn't realize the others had spread out around the room. Ready to scout in all directions. Everyone waiting on him.

Pearl turned. "All good?"

He swallowed and nodded. "All good. Let's get home."

Beneath their feet, the world began to rumble.

29

Pearl felt the hairs on the back of her neck standing up. Below them the great engines were turning. The entire island seemed to shudder, and then it was moving. She could feel the way Marken slipped into the waiting flow of Heatherly's magical creation. Not for the first time, she wondered if she had enough strength to power the island.

She wouldn't dare attempt it—not in front of the others—but if she had to? Could she? Her silvertongue magic wasn't the same as what Marken could do. His relied on an astonishing amount of creativity. A necessary intuition. Her magic was far simpler and yet more feared. Magic woven into spoken commands. She'd learned, ever since she was little, to be cautious with her words.

Once, she'd told Andi Winnow to *go away*. The girl had been bullying one of Pearl's friends at school. She'd been surprised when the girl turned on her heel and left the room. Later she would hear the rest of the story from her parents. The poor girl had been found one town over. She'd apparently kept on walking. Out of the school. Across farms and dirt roads. The command Pearl had given her had taken a few days to wear off. They'd had to strap her down to keep her from leaving again. When the magic faded, Annie couldn't explain what had happened.

After that Pearl became far more cautious. She understood immediately that what she'd done was some form of magic. She also understood that it was tied in some way to the same pigs she'd been asked to start learning how to butcher. Marken had said that anchoring to animals was frowned upon, but even a younger Pearl had easily justified her choice. What difference was there really? Butchering a pig for someone's table versus draining one to perform a necessary spell? She was the butcher's daughter. It had been easy to morally accept that exchange.

But that didn't make her unnecessarily cruel. They were still *her* pigs, after all. She was their primary caretaker, even if they squirmed and fussed whenever one of their number had to die in that unnatural way. Pearl used the magic only as a last resort normally. There was the time with Aunt Hath. The woman was so stubborn. She wouldn't change her mind about the whole smuggling business. Pearl couldn't make her see reason, and so she'd been convincing in the only way she knew how. A magic-woven command. A simple one: "Let me work with you."

And she had.

Pearl's natural intuition to hide the gift from everyone had likely saved her life. She didn't understand the fullness of that until she started researching the subject. When she visited the public library, she would gather books on animal anatomy and veterinarian practices. Piling them on a table before retrieving one book each visit that covered magical theory instead. A lot of her learning was retroactive. Less about acquiring methodology, and more about learning the actual terms for what she'd already been doing. Her pigs were what wizards referred to as an anchor point. The living ecosystem to which a person bound their magic. Most wizards, she learned, did not do this until being officially commissioned by something called the Guild. She'd never heard of them before. That discovery had unnerved her. Did it mean that she'd broken a law? It wasn't until she found her actual branch of magic—silvertongues—that she realized precisely how much danger she'd been in the entire time. What a terrible thrill it had been to realize that what she could do was considered criminal. Outlawed by every single territory in Ten Tides. A power that only the most ambitious rulers ever dared to wield, and even then, it rarely lasted for longer than a year or two. Pearl had known after just one paragraph that she would have to hide what she was for the rest of her life.

Her magic might not be as complex as Marken's, but she'd patiently learned safeguards and strategies. Parents often taught their children that "please" was a magic word. In Pearl's case, that was actually true. Using that word acted as a shield against accidental castings. If she could begin her sentence with "please," it would keep any request from transforming into a magic-laced command. She'd also learned how to act subservient. Putting on a nervous demeanor that she didn't truly feel deep down. She never demanded anything, never spoke to anyone with real force. Through rigorous effort, she avoided repeating the mistake she'd made with Andi Winnow.

But there were times when she'd been forced to use her power. There had been the boy who'd discovered her in the middle of packing smuggled goods for shipment. Pearl had sent him away with a whispered word before her aunt could return and panic about it. Most instances were about safety, covering her own tracks. Dismissing the man who'd stumbled drunkenly after her as she walked home one night. Demanding quiet from a woman who recognized her at the market from a previous smuggling run. Always the magic was used for self-preservation.

On this journey, she'd been forced to use her magic more than ever.

Nine times by her count. First to calm herself at the beginning of the flight. That felt frivolous looking back. It had helped to steel her nerves, but she knew now she could steady herself without magic. Her second casting had failed. An attempt to command the dragoness. That had been a mistake. After all the dust had settled, she'd remembered her research. Dragons could not be manipulated by magic. Their bodies were vulnerable—as Marken had proven—but their minds were far too complex to be infiltrated in that way. Predictably, the dragoness had shaken off her command as if it were an annoying fly buzzing in her mind.

Pearl's third spell had been an accident. She'd forgotten her normal rules and she'd shouted for the crowd to be quiet in the aftermath of the dragoness's first attack. It had come out as a command. She felt certain the only reason no one noticed the magic was that her command had been forced to spread out amongst *all* of them. It hadn't resulted in the usual, whiplike obedience she'd summoned before. Instead, they'd all been forced to do her bidding by a much quieter voice.

Another unintentional spell the following day. Kell stepped in her path, and she'd commanded him to move aside. That might have been the most dangerous mistake. Casting something *on* a warden *in front of* a wizard. Thankfully, the two of them were so focused on their venom for each other that they never seemed to notice the third danger in their midst. The moment had passed. She'd remained undiscovered.

The fifth spell came during the mutiny. As Withers fled into the woods, she'd shouted for him to stop. If anyone had witnessed that, they would have known. They'd have seen the unnatural way her spoken command dug into him—like a hook yanking the inside of a fish's cheek. There had been too much chaos, though. The deckhands gutted the man and her secret had died with him. Her sixth spell had been used on Marken. She'd told him to stop before he could magically dig Aunt Hath's grave. There'd been a lot of flaring emotions between them. Once more, Marken hadn't commented on the way his entire body had gone rigid at her command. The final three commands had been for Warden Kell.

Let go of me.

Walk to the broken window.

Jump.

Pearl swallowed as she remembered that moment. She could not escape the truth: she'd used her magic to kill a man. That thought roiled inside her gut. She snuck a glance back at Marken. He was so lost in the island's magic that he didn't notice. Pearl wondered if they were the same now. Was her action any different from whatever mistake he'd made back in Ten Tides? Had she been acting out of self-defense? Did it really matter? She had no intention of letting some court back home decide her fate. Her eyes flicked left. She caught Prior watching her. He quickly looked back outside, making a pretense of scouting the forest in that direction.

Do you know? Did you hear us?

"We're gaining speed now," Marken announced. "Based on the maps, we're going to be fighting the tides on our return. I'd imagine the way home will take about twice as long as the journey out. If you can call that a journey. More like we got dragged by our collar out to sea. I'd say . . . two days of powering the island? Give me a heads-up if you see anything."

A boring hour passed. Their progress was obvious now. There was a great churning at the "front" of the island. Great swells, whitecapped and huge, were being shoved north and south. No one seemed much for chatting, and so the silence held until she heard the noise.

A scraping sound.

Pearl shook herself. She thought she was imagining it, but there it was again. Closer this time. She was stationed by the original shattered window. The same one she'd ordered Kell to leap from. Now she edged forward. Shards of glass crunched under her boots. She glanced down. Nothing. Not at first. When she edged a bit closer, precarious enough that one misstep would send her plummeting to her death, she finally saw movement. The dragoness was scaling the tower.

"Marken!" Her voice drew everyone's attention. "Marken, she's here!"

Pearl saw she was wearing a new stone skin that matched the very tower she was climbing. Smoke-black scales that didn't reflect the light. Her eyes that haunting blue color. When she saw Pearl, she let out a hiss and started climbing faster. "Marken!"

He'd detached from the chair already. His chest was heaving.

"A moment," he said. "I'm not—buy me time!"

Pearl turned and realized their plan was a bad one. She was one of the only ones without a pistol, and yet she'd been stationed in front of the most exposed area. Nor had Marken measured out how long he'd need between releasing the tower's magic and accessing his own. Gemma was the first one to rally to her side. It was a strange sight—the older woman holding a pistol—but she moved as close as she could to the window's edge, aimed, and fired. The blast was deafening. It was also followed by a roar. Pearl looked down in time to see two scales spinning away from the creature. She altered her climbing now, trying to weave back and forth with each extension of her reptilian limbs. "Pistols!" Pearl shouted. "Where are the other pistols?"

Warner and Naomi were already crossing the room. Ellis had a pistol too, but he stood across the room by the other broken window, frozen in place. She saw in that flickering moment that he was someone who'd seen too many friends die, and he had no plans to join them. Pearl focused on the other two instead. Warner's hands were shaking. Naomi looked more resolute, even if that didn't mean she was a good shot. Both of them edged up to the threshold before pointing their weapons down. The dragoness was halfway up. Before they could fire, though, there was a great shattering of glass. Their target vanished from sight.

"Heatherly's room," Pearl said, remembering the double-paned windows. "She's inside."

Marken staggered across the room. "I'm—I'm ready. Everyone, back up! To me!"

The group fell into a makeshift formation. Marken stood at the front, both palms aimed at the stairwell. Warner and Naomi flanked him with their pistols, and Gemma and Pearl were one step behind them. She glanced back to see Prior with his back pressed to the closet door. He looked like he wanted to go inside again and hide there for the rest of time. She thought she could hear rummaging in the room below. A door swinging on its hinges? They all waited in breathless silence as Marken moved a step closer to the stairwell. All of them startled when a shot rang out.

It wasn't Naomi or Warner. No, there was a trail of smoke curling up from Ellis's pistol. They turned to see that he'd missed his mark. The dragoness had executed a feint. She'd entered Heatherly's room, waited a few seconds, and then doubled back. Even going as far as spiraling *around* the tower and aiming for the only other weak point. Now she had him by the leg, her claws digging into his calf, and she was pulling him ever closer to the ledge.

Marken stepped forward—all confidence—and unleashed a blast of purple energy. The dragoness didn't even attempt to dodge the magic. Instead she lowered her shoulder *into* his spell. The blast struck her side. All of her scales shivered end to end with fractured light. Whatever damage the spell was designed to deliver simply *absorbed* into her. She hissed with satisfaction at Marken, taunting him, and then took Ellis screaming over the ledge with her.

Pearl and the others stared in disbelief.

The final crewmate of the *Grand Gesture* was gone.

30

There were debates about what to do next. Grim, depressing, terrible debates. Marken thought they should press on. His primary argument being that the dragoness was likely *feeding* at the moment and they'd be able to cover a fairly large amount of ocean while she did. It felt like the most terrible hypothesis he'd ever presented to a group of people, and sure enough Pearl had thrown him one of her more impressive scowls. He resisted pointing out that she hadn't even known the poor deckhand's name until yesterday.

Her counterargument, nonetheless, was a strong one. She explained that the dragoness wasn't *feeding* on them exactly. Her current hunt wasn't about sustenance. It was about fulfilling the promise she'd made on that first night. And if the goal was annihilation, Pearl believed that the creature would double back for another attack soon.

Marken and the others agreed to wait before activating the island's magic again. He went to set up a magical barrier around the upper room—and discovered something he had not noticed before. When he cast spells in the middle of a fight, his awareness of that other place was flickering and quick. Glimpse and gone. Now he saw what he'd missed about his precious valley.

No, no, no . . .

He'd successfully cut off the main fire that had broken out because of Kell's null thread. Draining the bordering rows had worked. He saw now that he'd been wrong about the secondary fire. He looked out in quiet devastation. The entire southern hillside was . . . gone. Years and years and years of magic. For the first time in his life, he saw the natural end point of his power. There was a very finite, very specific amount left. He started walking the rows like a ghost. Scorched pedals dusted beneath his outstretched fingers. There was only one section that remained untouched. He quietly counted what was left. He cursed the world. Counted again. It couldn't be the right number.

Thirty-eight flowers, he thought. *I have thirty-eight flowers left.*

He drained one.

Thirty-seven. I have thirty-seven flowers left.

When he returned to the tower, he cast his protective spell across the threshold of the room, covering both of the gaping windows with the casting. The magic he wielded felt heavier somehow. More substantial, perhaps, because it was more precious to him now. His mind raced ahead. He knew the flowers *could* grow back. They were flowers. They had their own little survival mechanisms. They'd work to pollinate the neighboring areas, but how long would it take for those scorched sections of the earth to allow the passage of a seed? To support the rooting of a bud? He was not a botanist. The truth was he had no idea if they could ever fully grow back.

And then there was the immediate future to consider.

If they survived the island, he needed enough magic to escape. Enough magic to avoid capture in the coming months. It was no longer as simple as accounting for the spells required to guide the island home or to defeat the dragoness. He also had to ration enough power for what came after. His eyes locked on Pearl across the room and he nearly blurted out the truth he'd just discovered. But the others were in the room. He saw the comfort his counterspells had brought. How the tension in their bodies was allowed to briefly relax. He couldn't bring himself to shatter that yet. Not to mention Gemma was there. If she knew he was nearly out of magic, what would she do? Would the Guild still have an interest in saving him? *Not good, not good, not good . . .*

Less than an hour passed.

They heard the same scraping sound as before. Claws against stone. Marken found himself ready for battle. He wanted an end to this. If the dragoness decided to cross the threshold, tried to worm her way past his defenses, she'd be caught in an invisible mesh net that he'd created. Designed to tighten the more movement it sensed. Any panic on her part would transform it into a death trap.

The survivors huddled at the back of the room. The pistols were all loaded again, but Gemma informed them this was the final round of bullets. They'd need to be wise about when to take their shots. More scraping. Closer and closer. All of them saw the dragoness at the same time. The smoke-black scales. Those glowing eyes peered in at them from the eastern window. She assessed the scene—their protective formation—and Marken waited for her to lunge into the room.

Come on, come on, come on!

Instead she reached out and scraped a lone claw against the edges of the barrier. There was a subtle pulse of magic. She hissed once and disappeared from sight. The others started to creep forward and Marken snapped at them. "Hey! She *just* pulled this gambit. No one move."

Sure enough, the creature appeared by the other opening. She tested his magic the same way. A single claw grazing the edges of his spell. Not enough force to actually spring the trap. Once more, she hissed and disappeared. Only this time he saw the flickering black of her tail going down the side of the tower. No one moved for a long time. Marken eventually detached from the others, tiptoeing forward, and spotted the dragoness below. She'd retreated but was no longer bothering to hide. Instead she lounged on the roof of the largest of the buildings. Her blackened scales drinking in the sunlight. He watched her curl up like some kind of massive cat—and realized what this meant.

"She's waiting," he whispered. The others came to look. There was no trick that he could see. No, this was more taunting. "She knows how the magic works. She knows my counter-spells will vanish when I try to activate the island."

"She's right there! Can't you just blast her?"

This genius idea came from Prior.

"Blast her?" Marken echoed. "Earlier, you watched her absorb one of my most powerful projectile spells from about twenty paces. How do you imagine that will improve from this distance, exactly? Besides, the skin she's wearing, it's the same substance as this tower. The same as the chair over there. The stone is some kind of magical conductor. It's clever, really. She's using the modified scales to absorb my spells across her entire body, and then allowing it to dissipate when it's no longer concentrated energy. Which means I can't 'blast' her, no."

Prior frowned. "Then . . . what's stopping her from just killing us?"

Not much, Marken almost said, before realizing the group was depressed enough.

"Physical attacks are still effective. I could always drop a building on top of her, but that would require her standing very, very still and not moving as I tore the foundations out of the ground." He let out a helpless sigh just imagining that attempt. "The pistols can still do damage. Spears too. But the real answer is that we needed her to attack us. The spell I've cast around us is what's called *threshold* magic. It forces her to cross into my domain, where she is subjected to my rules. Projectile magic works in the opposite way. My spell is crossing into *her* domain, so to speak. It's then subjected to *her* rules. That's kind of the whole principle of magical dueling. The most powerful wizards are the ones who can play by your rules and still beat you."

"And you can't do that?" Prior asked.

"Can you?" Marken threw back. Pearl didn't even shoot him a warning look either. Apparently she was equally annoyed by Prior's obnoxious questions. "She's a *dragoness*. Magic is literally pumping through her body like blood. It's not like I can just snap my fingers and defeat her. I was close earlier. In the forest. She'd taken on a form that was particularly vulnerable to one of my spells, but Helene got in the way. The dragoness has adapted since then. She's learned enough about us to know that she can just wait for my warding spells to vanish."

Pearl looked deep in thought. "Maybe we can . . . trick her into a different form? One that's easier for you to fight? Her water form or one of the others?"

"Maybe. Yeah, that might work."

Neither of them had an actual plan for how to do that. Not yet at least. The reality was that they were in the middle of a standoff. If he powered up the tower again, then the protective spells would vanish, the dragoness would notice, and she'd move to attack. They'd be facing the exact same scenario as before. A few pistols and spears situated around a relatively defensible room. Warner wondered aloud if they could lock themselves in a closet while Marken powered the island. Pearl was kind enough to point out that Marken would be vulnerable in that scenario. They came to a collective understanding that rinsing and repeating the experience they'd just been through was a terrible idea. They'd run out of bullets. Secretly, Marken knew he would also run out of magic.

More people would die.

Naomi was the one who finally offered a plausible suggestion. "If she wants to wait, why don't we wait?" the girl said. "We covered a lot of ground earlier today. It's possible we reached one of the shipping lanes. If a boat finds us, we're rescued. This is all over."

The others were so enthusiastic about that plan that Marken felt he couldn't really say much to counter it. They all agreed to bunker in the upper room. With great caution, the most important possessions were fetched from downstairs. This included wool blankets, extra knives, and the last of their rations, which were now alarmingly low. Enough for a meager meal tonight, but the final item in the crate was a wrapped flank that would require a campfire that they didn't have. Marken was too focused on his other problem to do much complaining. As the others shuffled around, organizing the room, Pearl sat next to him. Her voice was quiet.

Only for him.

"I'm surprised you didn't push back. About waiting."

He looked around, confirming Gemma was across the room. "It's my magic," he whispered. "Kell's null thread damaged my anchor point. I used to have thousands of lightflowers. A nearly infinite supply that would grow back each spring. Now I'm down to about sixty spells."

He wasn't sure why he was lying about the actual number. Maybe he was just too prideful to acknowledge the truth. Too afraid to quantify his own usefulness in that terrible, precise way.

"If we play the dragoness's game, and I have to keep recasting all these spells, I'm going to run out of magic. I'll have nothing left for when I get back to the mainland. You're right. I don't want to wait around for a ship, but what else can I do? If I power the island, she attacks. If I defend the group, we're stuck."

Pearl listened thoughtfully. He saw her start to say something, some thought on the tip of her tongue, before chewing on her own lip. After a long pause, she whispered.

"I think we have to destroy her."

He breathed that idea in. "I think you're right."

31

"So none of the chapters you read specified how to kill a dragoness?!"

Pearl rolled her eyes. "The book was focused on domesticating and sustaining the species. Not hunting them."

"Oh, great. Now you're going to tell me they're endangered or something. I'm already a wanted man. I don't need the Gaming Commission joining in on the hunt when I return."

She smiled, but his words had her thoughts drifting back to the beginning. When she'd watched a boy board their airship in chains. An escort of eight guards around him. A warden trailing him like a shadow. All they'd been through, and she still hadn't asked him. What had happened? What was he accused of doing and what was *his* version of the story? She wanted to know, but at the moment, she was too busy trying to bury her own guilt.

The answer to their group's dilemma was painfully simple. How could they power the island without losing Marken's protective magic? The answer was *her*. Pearl Trask. She'd nearly spoken it aloud to him: *I have magic too,* she almost said. *I can help you. I can be the one to get us home.*

Instinct told her that if she revealed the secret, they'd make it home. The dragoness might probe at their defenses, but with Marken's counterspells active, the group would be out of reach. Pearl would guide them home as he stood guard. When they reached the continent, she felt quite certain they'd have immediate help. Other ships would spot the landmass gliding toward their harbors. Authorities would be notified. Heatherly's missing island, returned after all these years? The Ten Tides government would be rerouting every crew they could to perform investigations. Marken could slip away before they made landfall. And the others would survive. No more dying.

But then what would happen to her?

The other five survivors would know her darkest secret. The sort of secret that could get a person executed. It was possible Prior already knew something. Or at least suspected something? She knew she could try to extract promises from them. Offer to save the day in exchange for their silence. That could work. For a while. Those promises would last for a day or a month or a year. Really, it didn't matter how long, because the truth was someone would eventually break. Too many drinks at a tavern. Eager to impress their friends with a story they'd never told anyone else. One of them would let slip that they'd once survived a harrowing journey because of a girl who could speak magic into existence. An actual silvertongue. On that day, the hunt for Pearl Trask would begin.

She knew she was being selfish by keeping silent, but there was a logical part of her mind that whispered back: *It's not your fault.* The world had made this decision for her. The fact that someone like her could be killed simply for existing? Not for abusing her powers, but for having them in the first place? No. She would not take the blame for having to hide that truth. Still, every time her eyes landed on the chair at the center of the room, she felt nauseous all over again.

It was easier to focus on the task at hand. Their common enemy. As the meridian sun burned outside, she and Marken talked through strategies. She offered up the rest of what she'd researched about their species. Hunting habits. Sleep cycles. Anything that might help. Final rations were being passed out by Naomi. Everyone chewed their portions grimly, like prisoners being offered last meals. Hours passed and she felt they'd gotten no closer to a sound plan.

Once more her eyes drifted to the chair.

It looked like an empty throne. A symbol of the power she should have had every right to claim. Marken could sit there. He had already. When he took his "rightful" place and powered the island's engines to life, everyone marveled at him. He was their rescuer, their hero. She found herself imagining it going that way for her. She wanted the others to understand—for someone to *finally* see—just how powerful she was. All she had to do was cross the room and claim that seat . . .

Don't tell them.

The warning came in a voice she recognized. An echo of her aunt's final words. Pearl remembered how tightly the woman had gripped her arm in that final moment. Thinking back, she'd assumed those three words were referring to the dragoness. Don't tell them. Don't reveal that we were the ones who brought her to this place. It had seemed like such sound advice—but now she wasn't sure if she'd fully understood the warning. Aunt Hath had known Pearl better than anyone. If there was a person in this world who could have learned of her secret gift, it would have been Hathaway Trask.

Her aunt would have heard the story of Andi Winnow. What if she'd also witnessed the moment with the boy at the docks? How easily Pearl had turned him away, shutting down his curiosity with no more than a word. And she'd certainly been there when Pearl had used her power to stop Withers before he could escape into the woods. That was when she'd reached up, grabbed Pearl by the arm, and offered that final, echoing piece of advice.

Don't tell them.

Pearl tore her eyes from the chair, from all that power. It was not easy, but she decided to make herself small instead. She listened intently as Marken walked through a branch of magical spells she knew nothing about. Nodded at all the right moments. A few of the others were napping under their makeshift blankets. No one had slept the night before, and Pearl suspected this moment likely felt as safe a harbor as any they'd be granted. Her own thoughts felt too haunted for sleep. She was picturing her aunt. Buried out on that beach. All the bodies they'd abandoned there . . .

"Wait."

A lightning strike. A whisper of a possibility.

"Wait, wait, wait," Pearl said. It wasn't until she'd repeated the word four times that Marken finally stopped speaking. "I have an idea. Do you—I mean, could you *force* her to transform? Could you activate the magic she normally uses when she shifts?"

He frowned thoughtfully. "Actually, yes. It would be—it's complicated, but yes. I can draw her back to previously used magic with a spell. The problem is that I'd have to actively hold her in that form with my magic. Do you see the problem? Even if I could get her back into her fire form, for example, I'd have to let go in order to reach for the *next* spell. By the time I release her, reach for the magic, and then unleash a second spell—she'd easily escape or transform. It's a good idea, but I don't think that—"

"You wouldn't need a second spell," Pearl said, confident now. "And I don't want you to shift her back into a previous skin. I have an idea for a new material."

Marken's eyes glittered when he heard that.

"Come on," Pearl said. "I'll explain."

Their first task was retrieval. Pearl didn't want to wake the entire group. She was worried, too, that the others might not . . . morally approve of their plan. And so she quietly shook Naomi by the shoulder. The girl blinked awake. Her only role in the plan was to stand by the window and watch the dragoness. If the creature moved, they needed Naomi to shout at the top of her lungs. The girl promised to do just that as Marken and Pearl began their descent. The wizard was practically buzzing with curiosity by the time they'd reached the bloody bottom floor. Pearl glanced around at the dried markings and figured it was as good a place as any to execute the plan.

"All right. First we need a body."

Marken raised an eyebrow. "A body?"

"A body," Pearl confirmed. "I know you don't want to waste

any more magic than you need to, but do you think it's worth one of your flowers to levitate a body back to us? That way we don't have to risk running out there and getting killed."

Marken frowned. "I suppose it depends on . . . what you want to do with the body."

"It's a part of the plan," she explained. "We'll need . . . flesh?"

She hated how grim that sounded, but Marken didn't even bat an eye. "Are we going to use magic on the body in some way? As a part of this plan of yours?"

Pearl nodded.

"Then no to levitation. The Law of Divided Intent. If you cast a spell on an object that causes a specific effect, then it is far likelier to reject an alternative manipulation later. It's already *accepted* one magical command and it doesn't want to take a new one. I think it would be safer to go grab one and bring it back ourselves." He shrugged then. "Well, as safe as it can be to run outside and grab a body with a deadly predator nearby."

Pearl had already counted on having to take this risk. As quietly as possible, she unbarred the door. There was the slightest groan—and then light trickled into where they stood. It almost looked like a normal day. If one could ignore the stomach-turning scent of the dead. The day's heat was starting to sour the corpses. Pearl tugged her shirt up over her nose. The warden's body was somewhere off to the right. Not in their field of vision. The larger pile of corpses they'd created after the recent ambush stood about fifty paces ahead, stacked against the side of the nearest building. Pearl had lost her orientation somewhat as they walked the tight circles to descend the tower, but she felt confident the dragoness was somewhere diagonally to their left? Beyond that first building that was blocking their view? She watched as Marken reached out with a hand, almost the same way someone would to see if it was raining. His magical barrier flashed visibly into the air. Pearl saw how it stretched across the face of the entryway, but the spell extended no farther than that. Which meant as soon as they left the tower, they'd be vulnerable.

"Levi's body is the closest," Marken noted.

Pearl had forgotten about him. She tiptoed to her right, adjusting her angle, and sure enough the guard's body was there. About half the distance they'd have to travel to get to the others.

"Do you think we can carry him?" she asked. "Helene or Agnes would lighter."

"Lighter, but twice as far. If we can get a good grip on Levi, I think the two of us could get him back here together. Are you — do we really need a body for this?"

Pearl nodded. "Trust me. We need a body."

"Right. Okay. Sure. Just . . . get a body. No problem."

Both of them edged closer to the dying grass that marked the barrier between the tower and the outside world. Marken's magic had faded back to an almost-invisible glimmer in the air. Pearl took a deep breath. The two of them locked eyes, counted down, and then shot forward. There was the faintest *pop* as they crossed the barrier into unprotected territory. She felt a rush of wind. The bright sunlight briefly dazzling her eyes so that she couldn't quite make out their surroundings. Her heart thrashed in her chest as she closed in on the corpse. She found herself listening in quiet terror for the sound of Naomi's warning call, but it didn't come.

She was nearly to the body when she felt it. Something caught the back of her heel. She let out a clipped curse before spinning into the dirt. Marken cursed too. Absolute fools. They'd tripped over each other. Both of them looked up, the dust stirring obviously all around them, and there was a throat-tightening panic mirrored on each face. They scrambled the rest of the distance on all fours. The scent of the body, when they reached it, was an absolute nightmare. Pearl had a strong stomach, but she saw Marken working hard not to retch. Even she was put to the test, though, as she dug her fingers down in the first attempt to get underneath the body.

There was something terrible about the juxtaposition between those bloated, wobbling arms and the ungiving stiffness of his skin. Marken recovered enough to get a decent grip. They silently signaled and then heaved him up into the air. That was when Naomi's voice rang out.

"Moving! She's moving!"

So were Pearl and Marken, though. Half stumbling and half running in a terribly uncoordinated effort, but they were *moving*. It was the longest twenty paces she'd ever covered. They managed to heave Levi's body over the threshold. Pearl heard that brief pop as they fell across after him. She whipped around in time to see the dragoness appear. The creature was freshly perched on the nearest building like a gargoyle, her head tilted as she studied them. Marken turned too, setting his feet as if ready for a fight. She didn't attack. Instead her eyes flicked from Pearl to Marken to the corpse with curiosity. Pearl answered the creature's unasked question by slamming the door shut and barring the entrance again.

"Don't want her to see what we're doing," she said.

"What *are* we doing?" Marken asked.

"The rest of us want to know too."

This came from Gemma. Pearl's chest was still heaving as she looked up and saw the others tentatively peeking around the corner. She'd been hoping to avoid explaining the particulars to all of them, but she saw now that wasn't possible. And really, what was one more grim truth? At least the blasphemous plan she had in mind would get them safely home. She gestured to Levi.

"We're going to kill the dragoness," she said. "With him."

32

No one liked the plan, but nor did they offer a better one. At least they'd picked the right body. Levi had disgraced himself, murdering half the other people who were currently piled up outside. He was easily the least upsetting corpse they could have chosen for their purposes. One by one, the others excused themselves and retreated back upstairs until it was just Marken and Pearl once again. When the sound of their footsteps faded, he turned to her.

"You don't have to do this. I know you're feeling . . . guilty. But it doesn't have to be you, Pearl. You don't need to be the one—"

"No one else will do it."

Marken fell quiet then. He could not take her place himself. He had his own role to play. Instead of trying to offer some half-hearted condolence, the two of them rolled up their sleeves and got to work. Normally he could cast minor spells to ease their task. Magic that might reduce the terrible scent around the room or a spell to sharpen the skinning knives Pearl was using. But with his lightflowers so scarce, he didn't dare use any magic unless it was strictly necessary.

Pearl didn't complain. He found himself marveling at how unflinchingly she faced such a gruesome task. With the others absent, he tried his best to play the part of assistant, but three separate times he had to stumble away and retch in a corner. When he returned, he'd mutter his apologies, but Pearl remained locked in. An hour passed. He pointed out the obvious.

"You're quite good at this. You could be a doctor."

"I butcher pigs" was her reply. She was using a rag to wipe away the layers of grime forming on her palms. Marken averted his eyes before he had to retch again. Pearl went on, "Back on our farm, that's my job. I'm the one who preps them for market. Eventually you get used to the way it all looks."

And a human body isn't so different, when you start taking it apart like this.

Pearl complained that the knife wasn't as sharp as she'd have liked, but that did not stop her from plunging on, making steady progress with great slabs piled to one side. Levi was still there in spirit but most certainly not in form. Marken noted movement by the stairs. Naomi was there, fulfilling a requested delivery: needle, thread, and as much leather as she could find. The girl left those items on the top step and looked as desperate as Marken to not make eye contact with what was unfolding on the tower's main floor. Pearl thanked her and kept working. Eventually Marken found one strategy for keeping himself from throwing up was to talk through the details.

"All right. How long are her claws?" he asked for what felt like the third time.

"Full grown, they'll be eight inches. She's nowhere near full grown, though."

"Right. So, at her current age . . ."

Pearl traded one knife for another. "Five inches? At most?"

"It's going to be close," Marken said. "Closer than I'd like it to be."

"I think it will work. As long as you can do your part, wizard."

He grinned at that, but he sensed she was egging him on in an effort to avoid her own fear. There was so much risk built into this plan. It *could* work, but it could also fail in such fractional, terrible ways. And nearly all those fractional differences would result in Pearl's death. He felt certain of that.

Night came. The others could be heard sorting out a scouting rotation. An effort to get some sleep for at least a few of them, but he suspected the scent of what they were doing below was starting to waft up to the upper reaches of the tower. *It's not easy to rest with the dead so close.* Sure enough, he heard their muted conversations for the next few hours. A restless sound. The dragoness never tested his summoned barriers. He could sense her—the magic flowing through her veins—just outside. Waiting with the sort of patience only true hunters possessed.

Pearl finally traded the knives for the needle and thread. From the leather, she had Marken cut strips of a matching length. He'd gotten used to the scent by now and could finally act as a more effective helper. Knotting the fabric with nimble fingers. Holding a strap tight so that Pearl could wind another around it. When it was done, they both stepped back to examine their work.

It was far from a masterpiece. A sort of misshapen breastplate. Five layers of necrotic flesh that were thicker than a clenched fist. Pearl had painstakingly knitted thread through all five layers of the skin armor, running it all along the edges, and now she tested her work. She lifted the entire slab into the air, holding the top between her pinched thumb and forefinger.

"Wow," Marken said admiringly. "It actually holds."

They'd punched holes in the upper corners. Through those they'd used the leather to attach straps that he hoped were long enough. Pearl gave the signal and Marken circled. His fingers grazed her shoulders as he pulled each strap around to her back and began the work of tying them together. It might have been romantic, like those scenes from stories where the person clasps a beautiful necklace around the neck of the woman they're falling in love with, except he was patiently attaching a piece of skin armor to her. Not to mention he had no idea what love felt like. He'd been an instrument of the empire since before he could remember. There had been no real room for romantic endeavors. He couldn't tell if he was merely infatuated with this girl because of their shared circumstances—or if this *was* what love felt like and he'd simply had no other experience with which to hold up a mirror and compare it. Either way, his hands trembled nervously and his breathing came in embarrassing heaves as he finished tying the knot.

"It works," Pearl said, as he circled back around. "It will be subjected to force, though, so I'd like to add straps for the lower section. If we can tie those around my waist, and then attach them along my back, I think it would hold no matter how hard she hits me."

He circled again. "I don't like how exposed your sides are . . ."

"We already talked about this," Pearl replied patiently. "She aims for vitals. The neck or the chest . . ."

"The face? What if she hits you in the face?"

"She's not going to hit me in the face. I'll make the target zone obvious."

She patted the breastplate for emphasis. He nodded. It was far from perfect, but to create this under pressure in just a few hours? It could actually work. He reached out.

"How's the weight feel?"

This time Pearl shivered at his touch. He pulled away, realizing that he'd basically set his hand against her ribs. Again, it might have been romantic if the thing between them was not a flesh-made piece of armor. "It's bulky," Pearl confirmed, her cheeks brightening slightly. "But I'm not going to be out there sprinting. The point isn't to escape."

"Right. Okay. Walk me through the plan one more time."

Pearl sighed. "I walk outside. I piss her off. She takes a swing at me."

"I cast my first spell. The boon."

"While I stand there and try to avoid dying."

"And then I cast the second spell."

"Transformation. Done. We win."

"Look." He would never forgive himself if he didn't try one more time to talk her out of this. "This is brave as hell. It's also not something you *need* to do. It's not your fault that the windmaster died or that the ship crashed or that she escaped. None of that's on you, Pearl."

She shook her head. "I'm doing it because it needs to be done."

For a moment they were silent. Weighing each other. Finding each other satisfactory in some odd, delirious way. He swallowed once. "Who knows, maybe we'll wake up in the morning and there will be boats surrounding the island."

And for the first time, he actually wished that would happen. Hoped for something that would potentially complicate his own escape. If it might save Pearl from this task.

She nodded. "Maybe. But if we wake up to an empty horizon, this is the plan."

There was nothing else to say. Pearl removed the skin armor. The two of them did their best to wash away the grime and the dirt. There was no way to totally rid themselves of the scent, but at least they wouldn't be bringing bits of flesh back upstairs with them. As they made the ascent, Marken reached out for her. More out of instinct than with some design on what might come next.

His hand grazed her elbow. Barely an invitation at all, but she took it, turning around in the dark of that stairwell. She stood one step above him, and given their difference in heights, this left them at eye level. It made for an easy kiss. A brief searching for each other's lips. He found he didn't know what to do. Maybe it would have been embarrassing, but Pearl guided his hands to her hips. Patiently moved her lips until he sensed how to kiss back in a way that was pleasant instead of jarring. The moment could not have lasted for more than ten seconds—but he felt as if his feet had briefly left the ground and the entire world had spun, rotating fast enough to transform those meager seconds into the passage of years. He felt it had taken too long for him to arrive at this feeling, and at the same time it had happened too quickly. This feeling of perfect and yet not enough.

As they pulled away, it felt like dispelled magic. The other senses returning. That terrible scent clogging the air. Instead of smiling coyly or laughing, both of them fell to hacking coughs. He set one hand on the small of her back, urging her on, and they ascended the seemingly endless spirals, as eager to remember that moment as they were to forget the rest.

33

They didn't kiss again. Not in the halfway room, where the bed looked like it belonged to a ghost. Not there on the landing, where the glass had shattered inward from the dragoness's feint. They didn't upstairs, where the others were shifting restlessly in some sort of almost-sleep. They didn't seek each other out in the cover of that darkness and fumble nervously beneath a blanket. They didn't find each other when morning light finally crept over the island to show them a horizon bereft of rescue ships. They didn't kiss before making the final descent to execute their mad plan. They didn't pause on the threshold as sometimes lovers do in the stories, armoring themselves in some final affection. They didn't kiss again.

Instead, Marken quietly helped Pearl into a breastplate made of necrotic skin. His fingers made quick work of the straps dangling at her upper back. Quick enough that she didn't shiver this time beneath his touch. When the harness was cinched, she checked her movements, testing the makeshift armor before putting a borrowed shirt on over top of it. She wasn't sure who it belonged to, but the larger size and dangling fabric allowed her to hide the armor completely before tucking what was left into her waistline. Marken circled once before giving his approval. She kept eyeing him for some trace of regret. Some hint that his kiss represented an ulterior motive. An attempt to seal their alliance, rather than what it had actually felt like: *His first kiss. How is that possible?*

She saw no trace of deception. The fumbling had been sincere. The stone-stiff movements and the hesitations and the hitch in his breath. All signs that this boy—this achingly beautiful creature—had never kissed someone. Pearl was his first kiss. She wasn't sure what to do with that knowledge. Even in her smaller village, with other prettier girls around, she'd managed that task a handful of times with a handful of people. Had Marken simply held himself apart all these years? Or was there some other reason? She wasn't planning on asking. No, as they pushed the door to the tower open with a graveyard groan, there was no more room for small questions.

There was only the task at hand.

"Here we go," Pearl said, more to herself than to him.

She started walking. There was a pistol tucked into the back of her pants. Only there in case of an emergency. She fought the urge to look up to the top floor of the tower, but she knew the others were there. Watching with morbid curiosity. She also knew the room behind her was now empty. Marken would be rushing to the halfway room. Once there, he'd navigate around the glass as quietly as possible before lowering himself down, out of sight, to position himself for what came next. In a way, this was the most terrifying moment. No magic to support her. No pistols trained on the target. It was just Pearl Trask and the creature she'd accidentally loosed on the island.

The dragoness lifted its head. Those blue-glowing eyes drank in their surroundings. Squinting at the door. Then up. Clearly searching for Marken. When she found no sign of him, her entire body unfurled. Pearl watched her perform the same morning stretch that cats often do, their backs arching and their arms reaching out to bring the muscles quickly back to life. In that moment, she also saw the glinting claws and wondered if they'd gotten the measurements right.

God's body, those look longer than five inches.

Too late to make adjustments. Pearl paused at what might have felt like the halfway point, but it had been exactly thirty-two paces from the entrance. Marken had asked her to count them off, because the distance represented the ideal range for the two spells he'd need to perform. Pearl took a deep breath, raised her hands in a gesture of peace, and called out to the dragoness.

"Can we speak?! I want to talk to you!"

The great, scaled head tilted at those words. Again, her eyes flicked around in search of what she viewed as the true threat. Pearl hoped that Marken was already lowering himself down from the window on the other side of the tower—but they'd both agreed that she needed to burn as much time as possible in case there was some unexpected delay. A parlay felt like the best way to do that. She stood there, thinking the dragoness might refuse. Perhaps she was too wild in this form to remember she had the ability to converse with them, too deep in her animal nature to consider negotiating. And then a thunderous slash of magic.

The dragoness transformed as she leapt down from the building, changing before her feet could hit the ground. All the light briefly fractured, and then she was approaching in a new form. Not the blackened stones, but also not the human form, either. She looked like the distant forest. Great vines roping together like dreadlocks, tossing from shoulder to shoulder as she came. Spores pulsing at her hips and along her shoulders. A collar of bark wrapping beneath her neck, neatly guarding her jugular. They were just fifteen paces apart, Pearl growing more and more nervous, when the dragoness paused. Another transformation. Fire this time. Bright and lashing. As frightening as it was entrancing. Transformation. She turned back into the softer sandstone that she'd used to sneak up on the deckhands along the beach that night. Another one. Her water form. Again. Finally, the human skin.

Pearl's gut began to churn. She could stomach carving up a corpse, but this was where her bravery faltered. Face-to-face with something that had evolved over the centuries as a killing machine. The flash of all those different forms had her nervous, too. Did the dragoness somehow know their plan? Or was she performing a territorial display? The same way certain birds executed bright dances or the way bears would stand on their hind legs to show their height to a rival. Maybe it was just her way of saying, *Behold me. Am I not powerful?*

Her stomach was also turning for another reason. She found it hard to look at the dragoness in her current form. She was not human. She might be wearing human shoulders and human hips and human everything, but in the light of day, it looked like an ill-fitting costume. The dragoness wore an expression of distaste, too, as if she did not like wearing this smaller, less-deserving vessel.

"Insensate," she said by way of greeting. "What could you say to me?"

Pearl resisted the terrible urge to glance over her right shoulder. *Are you there, Marken? Are you in position? How long do I need to keep her talking?* She knew the answer. As long as possible.

"Insensate," Pearl echoed, her voice trembling slightly. "I'm surprised you still think of us that way. You've witnessed us working together. Our group has been fighting back against you for days now. We've tried to help each other. We've looked out for one another. We're not insensate."

"Who has killed more of you? Me? Or your own kind?"

Pearl swallowed. She did not need to count up the corpses to know the answer. The initial crash had killed many. From that point, there had been far more murders than there had been victims of the creature's hunting. She considered pointing out that none of that would have happened if the dragoness had not been applying pressure to their camp—but the truth was it still might have happened. When pushed to the edge, their species had claws as sharp as any.

"You are just a hatchling." The dragoness spoke over her thoughts. "Small and new and stupid. If I let you live long enough, you would learn this truth. It would seem as natural to you as breathing. Your kind does not change. It knows no other way. Don't worry, hatchling, I will keep you from having to learn this lesson."

The threat shivered down Pearl's spine. She tried to respond with a confidence she did not feel, all while thinking: *Please be ready, Marken. Please be ready. Please.*

"Hatchling?! What does that make you? You were born just a few months ago. We—" Pearl caught herself. There was no telling how far her voice might carry. If the others could hear them, she didn't want to reveal the fact that she was responsible for this monster. "I can tell from your size. You're not old enough to know any more of the world than I do."

The dragoness lifted her chin. "I am ancient. I have lived a thousand lives. I have taken a thousand forms. I have hunted. I have been hunted. I have been a queen and I have been vermin beneath the heels of giants. You could not possibly grasp the story that I've carved across the worlds, little hatchling."

Pearl had no response to that. Nothing she'd read about their kind had hinted at a concept quite this complex. Sure, there were studies that believed the creatures understood deities and worship and power. But the idea that she believed in her own past lives? That she possessed some knowledge of her previous existences? It had the hairs on Pearl's arms standing on end. The creature's next words only made it worse.

"I am close to completing my task."

It was Pearl's turn to snort. "Well, that shows how much you know."

The dragoness had started to look impatient. Almost bored with the conversation. Now the creature tilted her head with that same curiosity as before. "Explain."

"You think you're almost done?" Pearl couldn't help laughing. "There are six of us left, but that's just on this island. If you really knew what you were talking about—if you'd lived all those other lives you claim to have lived—then you'd know there are *millions* of us back home. An empire that spans from coast to coast. Entire cities full of people. Kill the rest of us if you'd like, but out there?" She stabbed a finger in the direction of Ten Tides. "You don't stand a chance. You'll be the one they track and hunt and kill. I bet you wouldn't last a week on the mainland."

Enough time had to have passed. Marken *had* to be in position by now. Carefully, she adjusted her footing. She also tried to puff her chest out, hoping to ensure it looked like the most vulnerable strike zone. When she looked up, though, she didn't see the expected anger. Instead, she saw that she'd made a mistake. Just like she had in the first conversation. She'd lost herself in the rhythm of the conversation. Revealed something she hadn't intended to reveal. The dragoness's eyes were narrowed with deadly intrigue.

"There are more of you," she whispered. "Out there?"

Pearl saw the consequence of this revelation playing out. The dragoness finding her way to Ten Tides. Hunting as many people as she could. It was true that the actual government of Ten Tides had mechanisms in place to control wildlife. Hundreds of wizards at their disposal. A massive army with countless units that could be called into action. The cities, too, were layered with all manner of defenses. It wasn't as if the dragoness would usher some doom on their society—but how many more people would she kill before they captured her? A huntress as deadly as this one? Loosed on some farming village? Whispering through the streets of some coastal town? Pearl didn't want to risk allowing that thought to take root.

"It hardly matters," she said. "You can't even beat us."

A half snarl formed on the woman's lips. *Good. Get angry*

with me. Come a little closer. The dragoness stared at her like a predator considering whether or not its intended prey was poisonous. When she made no move to attack, Pearl worried they were on the verge of losing her. That they might miss out on their carefully plotted opportunity. She could not allow that.

"You know, I'm *purposed* too."

That word caught the dragoness's attention. Pearl needed more than her attention, though. She needed anger. Enough anger to draw out an attack. What could stoke the growing flames better than the creature's own words?

"It's my purpose to keep these people alive. Anyone who tries to take them from me?" Pearl spat on the ground between them. "I will feed them to the sun. I will give that enemy to the moon. The ground will dine upon them. The ocean—"

She moved too fast for Pearl's eyes to follow. Three lunging steps and a *blink* of a transformation happened mid-stride. Pearl watched as a human hand reared back, but it was a stone-sharp claw that came swinging down and across her chest. She cried out with a pure, animal terror as those claws made contact with the breastplate. She felt *sharpness*. Nails breaking her actual skin, but they weren't deep cuts. Just scrapes. She also heard a sort of nasty, flapping *thud*.

When she looked down, she saw their tailored creation had been torn shoulder to hip by a perfect strike. The creature's claws were snagged, though, in the thickest layers of flesh near the bottom strap of Pearl's right hip. For a terrifying moment, the two of them stared.

Face-to-face. Predator and prey.

Then she felt Marken's first spell. A strange solidification coursed through her upper body. The muscles in both arms rippled with a power she'd never felt before. She knew this was Marken's magical boon. He was somehow redirecting the strength of unused muscles up into her arms and chest. Pearl took all that added strength and she seized the dragoness's forearms with both hands. The creature jolted back instinctively, but Pearl didn't budge. With all that impossible strength, she kept the creature pinned in place. Her claws were still caught in the dead-skin armor.

"Now!" Pearl screamed. "Do it now, Marken!"

Magic whispered over Pearl's right shoulder. A colorless bolt struck the dragoness in the right collarbone. She reared back again, desperate now to flee, but Pearl held tight as the second spell *began*. She'd gotten the idea from that first encounter. The haunting image of the dragoness and the bleeding deckhand. Her claws had been attached at the base of his skull. Actively touching blood and muscle and skin. All of it had been alive and working as it should be. She'd managed to pull all that *humanity* into her own form to summon a skin that bore a resemblance to them.

Now the magic forced her to wear something she could not survive.

The new substance raced up from her claws to her elbow. Pearl saw how the blackened scales transformed from something shimmering and vibrant into something rotten and lifeless. The effect rippled higher. Claiming a shoulder. Blooming across her chest. Rising up her neck. Pearl heard a rattling gasp as the creature's throat began to die, as crucial organs began to fail. She was close enough to see the dawning fear. The realization of what would come next. Desperate, the dragoness struck again and, this time, brought the claws of her free hand raking across Pearl's forearms. Pearl cried out in true pain. Blood rushed out from twin wounds, but still, she held on.

It ends here.

Their plan worked with haunting perfection. The creature had transformed before. Sand and water and stone. But this new skin was not something she could survive. There was a bleating, pitiful sort of sound. A throaty cry for mercy. Pearl almost reached out the way a mother would to a child. *I'm sorry,* she wanted to say. *You can't exist. You're too dangerous. Like me.*

The necrotic flesh had nearly finished its dark work. Like a disease that wanted to reach every corner of its new continent. The scales had vanished. Replaced by that bloodless, fleshy exterior. On and on it went until Pearl knew it was finished. All this was finally over. She ripped away from the creature's grasp and looked up in time to see the glowing blue eyes gutter out. Faded to a colorless white. For a terrible moment, the creature still stood. Towering and fearsome. A full-sized dragon that looked as if it had clawed its way out of a nearby grave and had come to drag her down into the waiting underworld. It took one lifeless step—and then it collapsed. Pearl stepped back in time to avoid being crushed. Marken came running from the side of the tower.

"Pearl! We did it! Oh, your arm . . ."

His words sounded far away. The world was quiet too. She slumped down beside the huntress's body. A true marvel. Built to hunt. More powerful than almost any other creature that was native to Ten Tides. The kind of animal that could change an entire ecosystem if it traveled too far north or ranged too far south. Really, one of the last true dangers left.

Pearl set her hand on the fleshy snout.

One day, they'll try to kill me, too.

With that pleasant thought echoing through her mind, she passed out.

34

Marken gasped as he let go of the spell powering the island.

Hours had passed. Pearl, according to the others, was still asleep. He'd fallen into a habit of asking how she was doing every fifteen minutes or so. One of the others would smile, descend to check on her, and report that she was still resting. No one minded such a small duty after so large a victory. When the dragoness had fallen, Marken burned one of his lightflowers to patch up Pearl's wounds. Gemma and Naomi had come out of the tower to help. Together they'd ferried her to the halfway room, and that was where she'd been sleeping ever since. Now Marken needed that same rest. They'd made steady progress, covering mile after mile, but night had fallen. It wouldn't exactly be safe for them to continue plunging through moonlit waters. It was possible they'd run into a ship. It was also possible they'd sail a little too close to Ten Tides. He didn't want to reach the mainland until Pearl was awake and they'd had a chance to speak. When he asked to rest, the others had no issue with it. There wasn't the same urgency as before. All their hunters were dead.

Levi and the warden and the dragoness. All gone. Really, the only danger left for Marken Burke was on the horizon. He eyed that deeper dark, knowing Ten Tides was out there *somewhere*. His best guess was that he'd need a few more hours of powering the island in the morning—in the proper light of day—for the survivors to catch their first glimpse of the coastline. No one else seemed to have noticed the fact that he was guiding them *fractionally* north with each passing hour. Using the chair's levers, he'd been aiming them away from all the major cities. Landing in the middle section of the continent would come with all sorts of complications. He thought about Gemma—a living symbol of the Guild's watchful eye on his return. And then there was Kell's lifeless body pointing to the truth that another warden would soon be assigned to his case.

Unless he found a way to make that all . . . go away. He had a few ideas on that subject.

For now he descended to check on Pearl—and was pleasantly surprised to find her awake. He also spied the others outside through the shattered windows. Night had come, but dueling lights framed the survivors. There was a fire on their right. Flickering tongues of amber. A reminder, as on that first night, that they were alive. And then on their left, the stars. Faint, but ever watchful. He took a seat on the edge of the bed, enjoying how peaceful the others looked, before glancing at Pearl.

"She lives."

He received one of her quieter smiles. "It worked," she said. "The poor creature."

"Oh, God's body, we're not going to go feeling *sorry* for the dragoness. She literally tried to *eviscerate* you a few hours ago. Did you forget that part when you passed out?"

"No, I didn't forget that part. You're right. It was her or us—and it wasn't going to be us."

"My sentiments exactly."

For a moment they watched the others. Gemma kept fussing with the fire, adjusting the angles of sticks, as if there were some perfect way to achieve the highest flame. Naomi had unwrapped the last pork flank and she was arguing with Warner about whether or not they could use some of the seasonings they'd found in one of the abandoned houses. Their voices drifted in and out of his hearing. Marken thought a decade was a long time for pepper flakes to remain fresh. He was about to make a comment on that when Pearl's voice cut back through the room.

"What was it?"

He frowned. "What was what?"

"Your crime. What were you accused of doing?"

So, they'd finally arrived at this part. He'd almost allowed himself to think it would never happen. He'd referenced it a few times. Almost to probe at her and see if she cared enough to ask or know the truth. When she never asked, he'd started to believe that it might never happen. That she simply didn't care. Kell's big speech by the graveyard had been heard by the others—but Pearl and her aunt had been sneaking off into the forest at the time. Pursuing their own secrets, which had kept his story a secret to her. She'd finally come back for the truth.

"Does it matter? After all this?"

He couldn't help feeling defensive. He thought it was fair of her to ask, but he also secretly wished she wouldn't care. That she might see him for who he'd been on this journey, and ignore whatever else he'd been before they'd met. Pearl didn't flinch away, though. Of course not. She hadn't flinched back from anything since her aunt's passing. She was too bold to be denied now.

"It matters to me," she said. "If . . . one day . . . who knows. I just want to know."

He swallowed. There was some promise beneath her words. Some hint of a future? He could not stop himself from craving it. However small and impossible it sounded. God's body, he wanted it. He wanted all of it. And so he quietly arranged his thoughts—and then he began. His version of the story. With all its minor modifications. Best to start with a question.

"What do you know about West Lily?"

"I know the story," Pearl replied. "The people all died."

"Yes. The people all died. The warden—and the Ten Tides government—blamed me for that. When they refer to the 'Butcher of West Lily,' they're referring to me." He saw the way that slashed across her expression and rushed to explain. "But that's because the real butcher is dead. The Ten Tides government *needs* a living person to blame. It looks a lot better in court when you can point a finger at a person instead of at a casket. A public case benefits their cause. Makes it easier to pass restrictive legislation on the Guild, and on wizards like me."

She was watching him with narrowed eyes. "There has to be more to it than that."

"There is," he said. "I'm not . . . innocent. Not completely. I know you're smart enough to know that they wouldn't just arrest me for no reason. I was in the area near West Lily on a routine assignment. When I arrived, I learned that another wizard was also on site. A mage by the name of Silas Lynch. He's one of the old guard. Been around since before I was born."

At this point Marken's jaw quivered. He forced himself to compartmentalize. The way he had his entire life. Setting certain truths into certain boxes, or else he risked revealing more of himself than he ever had before.

"Lynch and I have a complicated history. We do not see eye to eye on how to conduct our business. When I arrived, it came to my attention that he had been using less-than-savory practices in the area. Essentially tormenting some of the local populace. I brought this up to him. There was a disagreement on how to proceed—and I made a mistake."

Pearl frowned. "What mistake?"

"Protocol is that you take any disagreement between two wizards back to the Guild. We have methods for relatively quick communication. Disagreements get brought before a board, and when that ruling body issues an order, the involved wizards are immediately subject to their decision. This protocol was put into place because wizards, on the whole, are disagreeable people. We all have our own methods. Preferences on how to approach the same issue. When Lynch told me to leave, I should have issued an official complaint to the board of records. Then, if they had responded in my favor, I could have asked Lynch to leave the area. Maybe I could have even forced the Guild into reviewing his membership status . . ."

He could not help the biting tone that slipped out at the end. The Guild never really got rid of skilled mages. Not unless they committed egregious acts that could be proven beyond a shadow of a doubt—and even then, the truly talented ones would have their judgments delayed until they were forgotten about and could be returned to some other region. It was only when the Ten Tides public and government rallied against someone that they ever took action.

"I didn't follow protocol," Marken said in a tired voice. "I pushed back on Lynch. He pushed back on me. We threatened each other—and then we were dueling each other. Even then, damage might have been avoided, but Lynch was going for my throat and I was going for his. He's very gifted, but I was being serious when I told Helene that I am one of the most skilled wizards in the world. I won the duel, and I did so by forcing him to burn through his entire anchor."

This was the part where he had to be careful to frame things a certain way. He did not know how much Pearl knew about wizards and magic. Earlier she'd surprised him by referencing the *Razorback* Experiment. An experiment that was obscure enough that he would have guessed no one else aboard the original ship would have known about it with the exceptions of the windmaster, the warden, and maybe the captain. Unsure of the extent of Pearl's knowledge, he'd need to craft the next lie with great care.

"An anchorless wizard backed into a corner is a dangerous thing," he finally said. "When I moved to finish Lynch off, he did what wizards do when their anchor is destroyed and they think they're about to die. Animal instinct tells them to reach for a *new* source. Our magic, it's a trade, death for life. Something must be killed in order to create—"

Pearl interrupted him. "Did you have to kill him?"

Marken frowned. "Well, yeah, I told you he was going for my throat the whole time. And remember, all of this happens faster than you can even *think*. It's like the fight you saw between me and the dragoness in the forest. Act and react, act and react. It's not like—"

"But you said you'd cut him off from his anchor. Was he still a threat?"

He hesitated before answering. "There's no proven research that says *exactly* what happens at that point. Anecdotally, we have instances in our history where wizards, cut off from their original anchor, are left as empty husks. Incapable of magic. There are also a few instances, historically, where that is precisely when a wizard is *most* dangerous. I was unwilling to risk Lynch's survival."

The answer wasn't strictly true. Pearl considered his words before firing another question at him. "When he reached for a new source, wouldn't he have reached for you? And by extension, *your* anchor point? You were the closest living thing to him."

Well, that complicated things. It was the first time he'd ever been annoyed that someone had done proper research. Why the hell did she know so much about this? He might have been able to explain it away. Dismissed what felt like the worst part of what he'd actually done in the destruction of West Lily. Now, though, he could not avoid saying it out loud. No, he could only try to soften the truth with a lie. That was the best he could manage when someone knew this much about his craft.

"Yes," he said. "Lynch reached for me first. And by extension, my anchor point. This is another facet of magic that's nearly impossible to assess. It hasn't even happened enough times to know with any exactness . . ."

"Marken," Pearl said, shaking her head. "Please."

Right. He'd started sounding dodgy even to himself. "The answer is yes. He reached for my magic. The Guild teaches us to shield ourselves if there's no risk to the surrounding populace. The correct protocol, if there are civilians nearby, is to funnel your opponent's reach into your own anchor point. His final spell would have drawn on that energy. It's impossible to say what would have happened. If he would have drained a few flowers—or my entire crop. I think it's likely that he would have done significant damage. Final spells are often powerful, because they're fueled by one desperate reach for magic. I . . . made my second mistake at that point. Instinct took over. I shielded him from my anchor point and that forced him to reach for the next closest source."

Pearl nodded. "The people of West Lily."

Before she could form some final conclusion about him, he tried to offer his own summary of the events. "I told you, I'm not innocent. I didn't back off when I was clearly in disagreement with another wizard. I didn't back off when the fighting started, either. And when I had the chance to save people, I made the wrong decision in a split-second moment. I'm talking about this." He snapped his fingers. "It happens *that* fast, Pearl. Trust me, I feel terrible about what happened to that town. I have nightmares about those people. I know I'm not innocent, but surely you can see the difference between what I did and the accusations against me? I'm not some butcher who set out to murder hundreds of people. That was Lynch."

Pearl seemed to be weighing the entire story. A part of him—a very immature part—wanted to shove up to his feet and leave the room. Who was *she* to judge him? Who was *she* to have any say on his story and his life and his truth? It was *one* mistake. One bloody mistake and they wanted to act like the rest of what he'd done for the world no longer mattered. They could all rot in hell for all he cared. He did not push up to his feet, though. He said none of those thoughts aloud, because deep down, he *did* care what she thought. Instead of offering judgment, Pearl spoke a command.

"Tell me the truth."

Marken felt something inside him unlock. All his carefully tended rooms with their sturdy doors—opening now for some strange reason. Tears ran down his face. He did not reach up to wipe them away, because he was too focused on obeying the words Pearl had spoken.

"Silas Lynch. The truth is that I *hated* that man. My parents died when I was young. An accident with a wagon. I was just five years old when we buried them." He felt the pain of having that truth out in the air between them. He hadn't spoken to anyone about them in so long. So long. "The Guild found me because when I was told my parents were dead, I nearly set the entire city block on fire. They took me in and started training me. I was one of the youngest students they ever took on. Lynch, he used to be one of the professors. I told you he was the old guard, and he took that mantle seriously. As cruel a human being as I've ever met. Tried to humiliate me in front of the others, even though I was already small and young and alone. When I stood up to him, he dug in and isolated me further. The better I performed, the worse it got. At one point, it was me versus the rest of the class. They'd find me in the hallway. Assigned to hunt me down and harass me by Lynch. None of them dared to be my friend, because they knew they'd just be targeted next. When the headmaster found out, he called us both into his office. Lynch didn't even deny it. He claimed that he saw potential in me, and he said the best way to bring that out was to push me to the limits."

Marken was sobbing now. His entire body shaking. Why was he telling her so much? Why couldn't he stop? "But the way he pushed . . . They would steal my clothes whenever I took a bath. Put things in my food so that I'd be sick for days—and then Lynch would give me detention for missing class, just so he could rap my knuckles three time a minute with that iron ruler of his." Marken was physically shaking. His sadness was turning slowly to anger. It was the same path he'd taken in life. Allowing his brokenness to become a sort of twisted strength. "I avoided him for a long time. Even as I rose through the ranks, I'd make sure we were never stationed near each other. And then one day I found myself heading to West Lily. I knew . . . the area was rural. Not many witnesses. I also had been told that Silas Lynch was there. Instead of avoiding him, I went there *looking* for him. I'd built it up in my head that it was time to face him. Speak my mind. I was strong enough now to stand up to any bully.

"He'd been assigned to fix the nearby dam, but several of the workers had drowned because he wasn't willing to expend more magic than was strictly necessary. I was . . . angry. I knew he was doing to them what he'd done to me. Wielding his power to harass people who couldn't do anything about it. And so I confronted him. I told him to stop or that I would intervene. He challenged me. God's body, I wanted him to challenge me. I *knew* I should walk away, but I couldn't. I'd been waiting for that fight for my entire life. You were right, too. I could have spared him. Once he was cut off from his anchor point, I could have marched him home like the *nothing* he was. But I was just so . . . mad. I kept going because I wanted him *gone*. And then when he reached for my magic, I made a selfish choice. I couldn't stand the idea of that man being the one who took my magic from me. It was a terrible thing to do, but I wanted him to leave me alone. Just . . . leave me alone . . ."

He was no longer crying, but his face felt swollen and tired. He couldn't believe he'd actually told her all of that. Embarrassed, he tried to recover. "Pearl. You must think I'm some kind of—"

"I think you're tired," she interrupted. "And I think you've been alone for far too long, Marken."

The words struck an unexpected chord. He felt the tears come again. Sudden streaks of heat on both cheeks. How long had he been holding all this in? How long had it been pressing down on his shoulders? Long enough that he'd gotten used to the weight. Long enough that he'd been made stronger by it—but it also had made him colder. Incapable of the very connection he'd somehow built with Pearl. Now she reached out and pulled him close enough to hug. He buried himself in her shoulder for a time. Eventually, though, she pulled back to study him.

"I'm so sorry. I really am, Marken."

In the quiet that followed, he allowed himself to be led downstairs. He took a long moment at the entrance to the tower to wipe his face and dry his eyes. It was one thing for

Pearl to have seen this side of him, but he didn't want the others to know. When Pearl saw him trying to gather himself, she nodded once and started walking to the fire ahead of him. It gave him a moment to himself. He was about to follow, but something kept nagging at the back of his mind.

Why did I do that? Why did I tell her all of that?!

It was unlike him. He was not an honest creature. Not about those subjects. He tried to trace back in the conversation and found his memory of it was faint but not completely gone. She'd said something, hadn't she? Right before he started spilling his guts. He'd been carefully navigating through his own version of the story. Quietly guiding her to a specific image of who he was—and then she'd said something? His heart beat fast as he pictured it in his mind. The words were . . . muted for some reason. As if they'd sunk too deeply into his mind and could no longer be accessed. He focused, instead, on the shape of those four words on her lips. What they'd done to him as they tongued through the air. The way he'd suddenly revealed so much. It almost felt like . . .

"Magic."

35

Morning seemed to come earlier than expected—and Pearl realized it was because they'd traveled the day before. Crossing the sprawling ocean into a longitude where the sun *would* greet them sooner. A bittersweet reminder that she'd soon be forced to part ways with Marken Burke.

He was quietly snoring under his blanket. His hair had slowly been growing back in the entire time. A dark brown that verged on black. She imagined he looked handsome with it long and styled. Maybe they'd shaved his head when he'd first been captured? She'd never thought to ask. The truth was she was still trying to reckon with what she *did* know about him.

Last night, she'd finally put him to the question because she wanted clarity. Either he'd done something so terrible that she could comfortably part ways with him, or he'd done something small enough that she could overlook it entirely. Instead, she found that his story kept her feet firmly in a gray between. It felt like the sort of moral dilemma that she imagined professors at fancy universities would put their poor students through as some sort of exercise on human ethics.

Was Marken guilty? How much of the guilt belonged to him? And guilty of *what*, exactly? She could not dismiss the actual consequences of his actions. Three hundred people were dead. Another person had technically been the one to kill them, but Marken had done nothing to stop it. By her count, there were four separate moments when he could have made a different choice. He could have avoid seeking out Lynch in the first place. He could have backed away when he sensed the duel coming on. He could have stopped short of killing him, once the man's anchor was destroyed. And he could have sacrificed his magic—or some part of his magic—to ensure the safety of the people of West Lily. Four chances. Pearl felt that was more than a split-second mistake. He'd intentionally taken those actions and West Lily suffered the consequences.

At the same time, she understood his motivation. This man, Silas Lynch, had clearly terrorized Marken. Pearl suspected that he'd never shared that entire story with anyone. Her command had all but ripped the secret out of him. She still felt slightly guilty about that, but it had offered her an explanation of the Marken she'd come to know. The abrasive personality. The way he hid beneath one-liners and snark. Even the fumbling intimacy of the night before. All of those felt like natural extensions of a person who—in their most formative years—had been tormented by their peers and hunted by the very professor who should have protected them. He'd stepped out of that hateful realm and into the real world. Commissioned by the government as a powerful tool, even though he'd been only twelve years old. Even then, true connection would have been difficult. How do you make friends with a god? How do you fall in love with a person who came when there were problems and left when they'd been solved? She felt sympathy for how alone he must have felt, but there was a gap between sympathy and action. Just because she felt for him didn't mean she was destined to be his solution. A small part of her *craved* to be. She felt attraction to him. On several levels. But a more logical voice whispered the two of them might never see each other again.

As soon as they landed, Marken would be on the run. Even if he had a plan to escape, Pearl could not go with him. She needed to return home. Check on the pigs and the farm. Make contact with the man who'd hired them to smuggle the dragoness. Would she have minded company? Not at all. She'd even imagined introducing Marken to her parents. Showing him around their little town. But *when* would that happen? After he'd escaped from the *next* warden? And if he did seek her out, wouldn't he just be bringing more unwanted attention to her doorstep? There were so many variables at play that she had a hard time imagining the kiss they'd shared in that haunted tower could ever become anything more than what it was: a stolen moment from some other life.

Pearl took one final look at him before rising. The others were awake. There was enough light now to check for ships. Everyone was eager for home. Prior went up the tower first. Pearl, Naomi, and Warner all followed him. Gemma excused herself from another ascent, complaining about an ache in her back. Before Pearl could even reach the top of the stairs, Prior let out a crow of excitement. "A ship! There's a ship!"

She felt it a little unfair that the coward received the honor of announcing their welcome ship. Their survival had nothing to do with him. But as the rest of the group reached the upper room, they found the truth written there on the horizon: an airship. They had no way to signal them, but any captain worth a dime could see that the island wasn't supposed to be here. The airship drifted along its course for an uncomfortable stretch before finally banking right. A slow turn that brought it hooking back in their direction. There was a collective cheer from the group. When they were certain the ship was aimed for the island, they marked its bearings, coordinated that with the landmarks below, and began a final descent of that cursed tower. Marken was awake. He and Gemma looked to have been chatting idly. He offered Pearl a smile, but she saw how tentative it was. As if he wasn't sure where they stood after last night's revelations.

Pearl smiled back. "There's a ship. We're heading to the beach. Rescue is on the way."

Everyone started gathering their things. Whatever small treasures they felt were actually worth taking back to Ten Tides. The airship's approach was taking them vaguely in the direction of the original beach. Near the crash. There was some small discussion about that. Would the *Grand Gesture* still be there? Or would it have washed away with the tides as they drove the island? Warner pointed out that the island actually extended *out* into the water. The "shallows" they'd landed in *were* part of the island. They'd simply been submerged. For the first time, they realized how much worse the crash might have been. A hundred more paces out to sea, the edge of the island would have ended sharply. From shallows to open ocean. She imagined their ship plunging into the deeps and it was the same feeling she'd had when they'd inspected the maintenance room down in the basement of the tower. A creeping shiver over what might have been.

As the others began through the woods, Marken lingered behind. Pearl met his gaze.

"Have you decided what you're going to do?" she asked.

"I was about to ask you the same question."

She'd come to a decision. Even if she didn't like the choice she was making. "Marken, I like you. I really do. But I have to go home. My parents can't run the farm without me. My aunt—I have to tell them about her death. Arrange a funeral. And then there's . . . her side of the business."

"About that," he said. "I found some crates. When I was casting that first barrier around our camp, I surveyed the surrounding woods. It was curious. They contained some very strange-looking harnesses. The kind you might use to subdue a very large creature. Potentially damning evidence, if you ask me . . ."

Pearl stared back at him. She understood the implication but couldn't tell if he was trying to get a reaction out of her or if he was being serious. Marken eventually smiled.

"I destroyed them, though. Once I figured out what they were."

Pearl nodded. God's body, why was he making all of this so hard? For someone who was an enemy of the state, he was about as loyal a person as she'd ever met. As soon as the two of them had formed their unspoken alliance, he'd been in step with her the entire time. Unflinchingly so.

"Thank you. For taking care of that. But I—I have to go

home. I'm going back to put everything in order. It will take a long time. I'll have to keep my head down for a while. I don't want anyone digging into what happened here and blaming any of it on me, you know?"

He sighed. "I wouldn't worry much about that. They'll be too busy blaming me."

She hadn't thought that far ahead, but of course, he was right. Maybe the other survivors would offer testimony in support of Marken. All the people who'd fomented the actual rebellion—Helene and Agnes and the rest—were dead. Kell and his guards were gone as well. But the truth was that it wouldn't matter what they said. Eventually the attention of the investigators would turn to the escaped wizard who was already accused of murder before the crash took place.

"Now what?" Pearl asked. "Board the ship? Slip back into Ten Tides?"

He shook his head. "I'm not boarding any ship."

Her eyes flicked from him to the tower and back again.

"You're taking the island."

He nodded. "Bargaining chip. I will trade it to the Guild for my freedom. It's one of the single most valuable properties in the world. I know exactly how important a third island market could be to them. I'd daresay that it's enough to buy my name back. I don't know what will happen . . ." He gestured vaguely. "With my magic. I'm hopeful the flowers will grow back. It might take some time. When they do, I want my name cleared so that I can go back to my life. And maybe then . . ."

Her heart beat a little faster as she imagined the end of that sentence. *Maybe then I can come find you. Maybe then I could see you again.* She answered with all her heart.

DEVIOUS PREY

"Maybe then," she said. "Genetta."

He frowned. "Genetta?"

"That's the name of our town. You'll have to squint to find it on the map."

"I've always had good eyesight. Perks of being a wizard," he said, a smile bleeding onto his face. "Goodbye, Pearl Trask. If 'maybe then' is all we get, then I hope you know . . . how much . . ."

She smiled at his awkwardness. "I like you too, Marken."

He nodded, clearly grateful she'd said it for him. It was almost enough for her to fall for him all over again. She stood on the tips of her toes and kissed him on the forehead. They hugged one final time. A whispered goodbye—and then she was walking through the forest. Every step carrying her away from some alternative future and back to the world she'd lived in for the last five years. A drunken father. An inactive mother. Only now she went back without her aunt to guide her.

It was the most difficult trek she'd ever made.

The beach quietly emerged through the gaps in the trees. The other survivors were all there. No one remarked on Marken's absence. There must have been some discussion. Some understanding that he was unlikely to join them. It was down to five now.

Gemma, Naomi, Warner, Prior, and Pearl.

Warner made a joke about being late for his meeting that had all of them smiling wryly. The sound of the ship's engines grew louder and louder as it approached. Prior stood when it got close enough that they could read the lettering on the side.

"Hey. I know that ship! That's my father's ship!"

He walked to the edge of the surf, waving his arms in

excitement. The letters on the side of the boat glittered in the light: *Thunderhead*. She shook her head at the name. It felt like a typical masculine choice. Something dark and broody. It certainly fit Prior's persona. Pearl did not love that their final bridge home required assistance from anyone connected to Prior, but beggars could not be choosers. She also felt bad they were abandoning Marken. The truth, though, was that she wanted home. She missed warm baths and the quiet comforts of their village. The sound of her pigs underfoot. Even her father's snoring in the barn. Anything but what they'd lived through these past . . . days? Could it really only have been a handful of days? She felt as if she'd been here for years.

"You're looking tired, dear."

This came from Gemma. The others were on their feet. Waving and hollering at the ship. It was close enough that they could see the faces of the crew. Someone who looked related to Prior was calling down from near the prow. Barely intelligible with all the engine noise. Pearl realized she was tired. Too tired to stand and cheer, but not so tired that she couldn't rise when the time came and board the ship that was here to rescue them. She turned to say that and saw Gemma fishing through a pocket.

"Here," the woman said. "Saved some for when we finally had something to celebrate."

A half-wrapped chocolate. A great slab of it. Kind of like the ones they sold in the public markets. The biggest ones were the size of a melon, completely solid all the way through. The cheaper chocolates were like little bird eggs. Just small enough to pop right in your mouth and devour as you walked around to look at all the other goods. Pearl nearly reached out and took it. Chocolate sounded so lovely right now—but her mind stumbled over a strange sense of repetition. As if she'd lived this moment before. There was something in the sound of the distant engines and the sight of the paper-faded wings of the ship and . . . the chocolate.

Lightning struck. Illuminating a detail she'd forgotten. When she'd first observed the windmaster, he'd already been slouching in his chair. If he'd been poisoned, it almost certainly had already happened at that point. Most likely the slumping had come as he started to feel the effect of what had been done to him. Pearl remembered the one detail she'd not thought about in all this time. The man had melted crumbs of chocolate on his collar. When she'd checked him, though, he hadn't had anything like that on his person. His pockets had been empty. She might not have inspected his bag thoroughly, but now she felt confident, the chocolate had not been his.

Gemma wagged the slab a little. "Dear? Have a bite."

She realized she hadn't responded to the offer. Hopefully she'd just come off as dazed.

"Sorry," she said. "I'm not much of a sweet tooth. Thanks, Gemma. I'm actually going to go use the bathroom one more time. Before we board the ship."

Gemma nodded sagely, muttering she might need to do the same. Pearl retreated quickly from the beach and back to the tree line. She slipped behind the largest tree she could find, and then did her best to glance back without being obvious. Naomi had backtracked to where Gemma was sitting. They were all gathering their bags one final time. Pearl watched, eager to see if Gemma would offer the chocolate to the other girl, since it had been saved for the sake of "celebration." As she watched, though, the older woman stood. She smoothed her dress and tucked the wrapped treat back into her shawl. A hundred different questions bloomed in Pearl's mind.

What is going on?! Why would she offer it to me? And why would she have it in the first place? But the question that won out over all the others was the most time sensitive: *What do I do now?!*

The *Thunderhead* had adjusted the angle of its approach. Pearl's heart was thrashing in her chest. She pretended to be finishing her business, and then she crossed back out onto the beach. The entire time, she kept a ready command on her tongue, just in case. Naomi glanced back at her with a smile. Was that the same smile as before? Or was Pearl imagining that subtle hitch in her features? Warner looked nervous, but he'd been a ball of nerves the entire journey. As they stood there, the ship touched down out in the water. There was a great lurching and then it settled. A proper gangplank was already being lowered. A walkway that extended from the ship's main deck all the way down to the beach. Prior, who hadn't helped once in camp, now moved as if he'd been born to a family of deckhands. They watched him attach counterweights at the base of the ramp—and then the person she'd seen before came roaring down to greet him.

"God's body! He lives! Knew you'd survive! Told every man on this crew, Prior Swiftson is a *survivor*." The man's eyes flicked to the rest of them. "Come on, then! Welcome aboard the *Thunderhead*. I'm Bell Swiftson. Prior's my nephew. You all look like you could use a meal or three."

Warner did not need to be invited twice. He scrambled past the captain and up the ramp. Gemma and Naomi had started forward too. Pearl watched as Prior hugged his uncle. Was it her imagination, or did he whisper something to the man? They pulled away and clapped shoulders. Prior glanced back, eyes briefly flicking to her and the others, and then he started walking up the ramp, calling out to a few of the sailors. Pearl hadn't moved yet. She didn't know what to do. If she acted strangely now, then it would only confirm suspicions. Had Prior said something? Why would Gemma want to harm her? Or was Pearl imagining all of it?

It was hard to sort through her thoughts as Prior's uncle continued on in that booming voice of his. ". . . word sent back home! A dozen ships already coming. You lot don't have to deal with anything else. What you need is a hot meal and a ride home. We'll have the engines burning twice as hot, have you lot touching down before noon tea. How does that sound?"

Again, Pearl could not help feeling as if the man was now watching *her* specifically as he spoke. Gemma had reached the end of the ramp. Bell held out a hand to pull her up. Naomi was right behind her. There was only way to find out and not completely blow her cover. Pearl hesitated for a moment, and then called out to the girl.

"Hey! Naomi! Can you help me with this bag?"

She slid the carrier bag off her shoulder. Awkwardly, she made a pretense of crossing the beach and holding the thing out to the other girl, even though there was nothing in there that she could possibly want. Naomi frowned too. Pearl saw the effort it took to turn away from their rescue and set foot back on the beach that had haunted them for the past few days, but she felt enormous affection when the girl braved those two steps and met her in the middle. Pearl handed her the bag and asked the only question she could think to ask.

"Do you know what I am?"

Naomi's eyes flicked up. Widened. The truth was written there. She didn't even have to say it out loud. Instead, Pearl held the bag tight and they continued to stare at each other.

"Who told you?"

Naomi stared back for a moment. "Prior. He told us about the warden. How you . . ."

Pearl released the bag, pretending to smile at the girl as she thanked her for her help. And then she nodded to the ramp. "Come on. We don't want to miss our flight."

She nudged Naomi into walking slightly ahead of her. It looked strange, the girl walking with both bags while Pearl came empty-handed behind her. Prior, she saw, was loudly talking and playing up his return to a crew that clearly knew him, but she also saw the way his eyes kept darting back over to check the unfolding scene. His uncle, too, had not stopped staring at her, even though Naomi was the one who'd been dating his nephew. Not her. Pearl reached the ramp and stopped.

"Captain Swiftson," she commanded. "Leave this place. Take these people home. Do not allow any of your crew to disembark until they're back on Ten Tides. Never return to this place."

She heard the terrible squealing sounds. Smelled the mud of home. And then her mind was fully back on the beach. For a moment, it looked like Prior's uncle would ignore her instructions. He walked down the ramp and onto the beach, forcing Pearl to step to one side. She was readying another command when she realized he was picking up the counterweights. Heaving them up, he turned without even glancing her way and followed Naomi up the ramp. The scene was earning attention. Some of the crewmates were watching. Prior looked confused by what was happening. He pushed through the gathering crowd and went to face his uncle. Gemma was watching. Eyeing the entire scene with an intensity that Pearl had never seen from the woman. Pearl had so many questions, but they hardly mattered now.

The captain barked orders to pull the ramp. His crew, like any proper crew, immediately fell into line with his command. *Not so different from my power, is it, Captain?* Gemma was protesting. Complaining that they couldn't leave Pearl behind. Prior was making noise about it too. It was too late. She watched with grim satisfaction as the captain, pulled along by the weight of her silver-laced command, started shouting back at them. He'd lock them up if they didn't keep quiet. The ramp vanished back into the belly of the ship. The great sails adjusted and the engines kicked on. In less than thirty seconds, she found herself watching as the ship meant to rescue her sailed away.

Pearl stood on that beach long enough to make sure her command was obeyed. A great sense of loss went with that parting ship. A realization that her old life was dead. The old Pearl? Dead with it. They knew her secret. Prior had overheard her command to the warden and he'd pieced it all together. Then that poor fool had told the others. Now any chance of going home, back to the life she'd always known, was cutting through the waiting blue.

36

Marken watched the rescue ship knife through the distant clouds. It was surprising how quickly they'd loaded everyone up and left. No searching the beach or recovery efforts. No debate about whether or not there was anyone else to rescue. He supposed it made sense that they'd get the survivors home and leave the official investigation to the Ten Tides government. Answers on that front came sooner than expected. As the first airship grew smaller, several other brushstrokes along the horizon were growing more distinct. Quietly closing in on the island.

"Time to go," he said to no one. "Catch me if you can."

He sat down in the now-familiar chair. His mind fractured and he was looking out over his valley. The scorched earth and the barren rows. He was down to roughly thirty flowers, which meant he could power up this island thirty times. His hope was to strike a deal with the Guild long before he exhausted that supply. Ideally, they'd send a wizard to make contact and discuss terms while he still had enough magic to defend himself as needed. Marken tallied the remaining flowers before kneeling down and running his fingers through the blackened soil.

It wasn't over.

Spring would come again. A whisper of hope. Maybe the next bloom would offer a bigger return than what he saw now. Wasn't that what spring had always been? A restoration. A new start? If it didn't work, he'd already decided to visit the valley himself. Reaching it would be the hardest part—he'd need to wait until the peak of summer to even try—but if he could get there, maybe there were methods for tending to the soil. Strategies for tilling or digging or aerating the soil. He would do whatever was necessary to restore his magic to its former glory. It was either that or get a normal job. He almost laughed at that. What about his life had ever been normal? How could that ever suit him? No, he'd make this work. He had to make it work.

"Marken?"

He glanced up. Pearl stood there, framed by his remaining lightflowers, a vision. He blinked a few times, surprised to see her in that hallowed place—and then his vision of the tower returned to him. She stood at the top of the landing by the stairs. Framed not by flowers but by all the broken glass of the very window that Heatherly had been pushed through. Marken's heart divided as easily as his mind in that moment. There was the one side that beat faster to think that maybe she'd stayed. She'd come back because she'd chosen him. And then there was the other side that thrashed like a wild animal, warning him to cast a spell before *she* could. Before her voice, woven through with magic, could whisper across the space that separated him and take control.

Do you know that I know?!

"Pearl," he blurted out. "You're not on the ship."

"It wasn't safe for me," she replied. "The ship belonged to Prior's father. His uncle was the commander. The two of us witnessed what he did up here, Marken. His cowardice. I don't think he wants that story going back to the mainland."

Marken cracked a smile. "That's a very pretty lie."

Pearl stared back at him. As always, she was trying to read him. He decided it was best to cut to the chase. "They knew, didn't they? That you're a silvertongue?"

He saw the way her throat tightened. The ridges of her shoulders adjusting and her feet sliding naturally into a defensive position. There was no doubt in his mind that she had a command ready on her lips. *Whose magic would be faster? Yours or mine?* He did not reach for a spell, though.

"You knew?" Pearl asked.

"I figured it out, yes. 'Tell me the truth.' It was interesting. When I went back to that memory, I couldn't actually hear the words you used. It was like . . . they were inaccessible. As if they'd dug somewhere deeper than memory. I'd imagine for most people, they don't have any recollection of being commanded by you, do they? It seems the only way you'd be discovered is if someone else witnessed the exchange."

Pearl nodded. "Like Prior. He must have heard me."

"And that's what happened to the warden? You commanded him to jump?"

"Yes. I would have done it sooner, before he wrapped you in the null thread, but Levi—"

"Had a hand clamped over your mouth," Marken said, remembering. "That was unlucky. And then afterward . . . you tried to wake me up. Levi was upstairs. You could have used your magic, but you waited for me to blast him. Clever. Two soldiers falling to their deaths would have raised suspicions. Allowing me to take care of one of them was an elegant solution."

"It wasn't clever enough," Pearl said. "If it was, I'd be on that ship. Heading home."

Marken couldn't help being curious. Pearl had asked him so many questions, and it only felt right now to return the favor. "What's your anchor point?"

"That's a rather personal question to ask a wizard." She offered a half smile as she spoke his own words back to him. Then she answered, "The pigs. Back on my family's farm."

He snorted at that. "Fascinating. I'm assuming that happened early on. You bound yourself to them by accident. It's certainly better than horses. No wonder you looked so sick when we were talking about that on the beach. Brushing up so close to your truth. It also explains why you knew so bloody much about magic. I mean, what rural farm girl knows about the *Razorback* Experiment? I must have been a fool not to have seen it sooner."

Pearl shrugged. "You were distracted."

It was true. He'd been distracted by her. Now he arrived at the question that might have mattered most to him. Not a question of magic or power, but a question of the heart.

"And was that by design? Was it your way of . . . keeping my eyes elsewhere?"

Pearl's features softened. "Marken. God's body, you poor thing. No. I wasn't flirting with you in an attempt to stay hidden. I just . . . like you. It's really that simple."

He drank that in like a fine wine. Sat in the weighty truth of it until it dripped down into his bones and felt real. He knew she wasn't lying. She really did like him. The moments of affection had not been a cover. They'd been *real*. All of that led to one final question.

"Well, now what?"

A repeat of her question for him earlier in the day. Both of them had agreed to separate. He had his plan and she had hers. They'd agreed that maybe one day—if all the pieces fell into the right places—maybe then they'd see each other again. So much had changed in the span of an hour. Pearl looked out over the horizon. She saw the same ships he'd seen. They'd transformed from blips into bobbing apples. Bigger and closer with each passing minute.

"Now? I guess it depends," Pearl said.

"On what?"

"Is that invitation still on the table? Can I . . . join you?"

She gestured to the tower. To the island. Marken's heart beat wildly. He knew this would complicate his own plan. In a way, Pearl Trask was more dangerous to the Ten Tides government than he was. Trading the island to clear his own name? That would have been a straightforward process. Maybe the Guild would have hemmed and hawed and tried to barter, but in the end, he felt confident that he would have gotten his life back. But if Prior and the others had marked Pearl for what she really was, if word got out that one of the survivors was a silvertongue, then a simple trade wouldn't be possible. The more likely scenario was that they'd have to forge some unknown path forward. Carve a new world into existence.

"You could just command me," he said. "Say the word, and I'd have to take you."

Pearl shook her head. "If I wanted to do it that way, I would have already."

He could not help smiling at that. A part of him wondered how that might have gone. It was the part of him that had been so competitive at school. The part that loved a proper duel. Would he have gotten his spell off first? Or would Pearl's command have stopped him before he could form the magic in the air? She'd used her magic on him once and even now he marveled at how much power had been in that one command. A truth he'd kept buried his entire life had come rolling off his tongue like honey. That kind of power would breed fear in just about anyone else in the world.

But he was Marken Burke.

"You're not afraid of me?" Pearl asked, as if she could hear his thoughts.

He shrugged. "Not really. Are you afraid of me?"

The two of them stared for a moment. It was like before. A brief weighing and measuring, and then the odd realization that they found the other one satisfactory. He liked her. She liked him. He was powerful. So was she. There was an unexpected balance there. They didn't need to fear each other as long as they were together. Maybe it was Ten Tides that should be afraid. Maybe there was a continent out there on the horizon that should be trembling at what might come to its shores. Marken smiled to himself, then pushed to his feet. He gestured to the chair.

"Do you want to drive?"

He saw how her chin lifted proudly in response. It was as if her entire body had been waiting for that invitation. Without hesitation, she strode across the room and took her place. He couldn't tell if the seat had transformed her into a queen or if her sitting there had transformed an ordinary chair into a throne. Either way, it felt like a magic that flowed both ways.

Pearl set her hands on the controls. He knew she'd been watching him drive. She knew what to do. He felt, too, the way her magic fell into rhythm with the tower's waiting mechanisms. She was a natural at this. After she found her mental footing, Pearl unleashed a command.

"Begin."

The island's engines thundered to life. Marken felt the humming power released by that single word. Once more, he marveled at the hidden strength of Pearl Trask. He took his place by the windows and watched as she began to turn the island. Without needing to be told, she wheeled them north. He saw the way the approaching ships slowly vanished to his left. Once they started moving, the island would pull speeds that their pursuers could not keep up with. He knew there were logistical complications to sort out. Pearl would have to find some way to send money to her family's farm. If the pigs were her anchor point, she'd need to make sure the herd was well tended and looked after. His flowers required the same care and attention. And then, of course, there was the question of where they'd go and what they'd do, but for now, it was enough to stand there in the presence of another dangerous creature, her claws finally out and glinting in the light of day, and to know that she was not hunting him. He was not hunting her. No, the world was their prey now.

Marken Burke smiled at that thought. Pearl Trask smiled back.

The island rumbled on into that waiting blue.

ACKNOWLEDGMENTS

Devious Prey is a great example of how this industry teaches us to be patient. My first attempt to get published in the adult market space was a manuscript about a group of people who boarded an airship, crashed on a desolate island, and found themselves hunted by a dragoness. Sounds familiar, doesn't it?! I had already sold into the young adult and middle-grade markets. That book, I thought, was going to get my work into a new category and really solidify my career for the next decade. Except that didn't happen. The original version, entitled *The Possible Meridian*, never found a home. And do you want to know a secret I won't admit anywhere else?! All those editors were right! The original version was way too complex. I tried to put everything and the kitchen sink in that book—and as a result, nothing really seemed to shine. It was just a pile of stuff. Cool stuff, but a pile nonetheless.

Nearly a decade later, I revisited the concept. I stripped the story down to its core. I kept the concepts that felt most vital, and the result was *Devious Prey*. I have to start by thanking Kristin Nelson. I have an agent who was brave enough to tell me the first time around that she didn't think the concept was ready. Turned out she was right. But she's also an agent who is kind enough to let me know when something *is* ready, as she did with this version. Thank you, Kristin, for being someone who I can rely on for an honest opinion at every phase of my career.

Another big thank-you to my editor, Kate Prosswimmer, as well as to Justin Chanda. I know that technically this book was a curveball. Thank you for allowing me to trust my gut and swing into writing a completely different book than what we'd initially planned. The constant support I've felt from the team at Margaret K. McElderry has been everything an artist could dream of—and it shows up in both the big and small moments. That was a big one for me. Thank you.

I'm grateful to my publicist, Tara Shanahan, for always working behind the scenes. All the thanks in the world as well to Andrenae Jones, Stephanie Evans, Karen Wojtyla, Jen Strada, Greg Stadnyk, Tatyana Rosalia, Alissa Rashid, and everyone else at Simon & Schuster. Publishing sometimes *feels* like crash-landing on an island and trying not to be eaten by a rogue dragoness, and there's no crew I'd rather be stranded with than you all.

I am nothing without my family. Thank you to my wife, Katie, for being my co-survivor in raising three kids together. Most days those little dragonesses *do* seem to devour us, but hey, at least we're getting eaten together? All my love to Henry, Thomas, and Scottie. Every story I write is for you. Thank you to my parents and in-laws as well. When you watch our kids, I get more time to write—but I think my favorite part of that is that they're forming these deep, rich relationships with you at the same time. I'm so glad they have four unique teachers to learn things I could not teach them on my own. Thank you.

Finally, a specific thank-you to Keith Dupuis. This book was dedicated to you because I can't count how many times, over the course of a manuscript, that I hear something you've said bouncing around in my head. I'll make these minor adjustments each time, following the lead of your voice, and it has saved me hundreds of times. Thank you for all that you taught me over the years.